A FANTASY NOVEL

Tales of the Deer Witch

MICHELE LEIGH

authorHOUSE®

AuthorHouse™
1663 Liberty Drive
Bloomington, IN 47403
www.authorhouse.com
Phone: 1-800-839-8640

Published by AuthorHouse   12/28/2012

ISBN: 978-1-4772-9030-9 (sc)
ISBN: 978-1-4772-9029-3 (hc)
ISBN: 978-1-4772-8995-2 (e)

Library of Congress Control Number: 2012921425

www.deerwitch.com
storyteller@deerwitch.com

Cernunnos is the one who guards the portals of the Underworld and ushers those seeking transformation into the mysteries . . .

DAY I:

Cernunnos
Island

As we descend toward the tiny island I feel my stomach flip again. Small planes are a killer for someone with my sensitivity to motion sickness, and this is the second plane we've been on today. The first was a long commercial flight to Athens, where we transferred to this "puddle jumper," a tiny plane with a bubble top that conjured up images of Snoopy and the Red Baron. In the spirit of adventure I had climbed into the back seat and convinced myself that we would only be up here for fifteen minutes as I thought we were headed for one of the islands off the coast. But it's been over an hour, and my vomit threat level has gone from maybe to definitely-gonna-happen.

Jack taps the window. "Get this shot, Babe!"

I glare at him, fumbling for my cell phone. How could my husband of fifteen years not realize how close I am to throwing up? I select the camera option, aim down at the thicket of palm trees below, and wonder, not for the first time today, where the hell we are going.

Jack planned this spring getaway as a surprise to celebrate my fortieth birthday, and at first I welcomed the opportunity to sit back and enjoy the ride. But right now my inner control freak is running out of patience, and I'm praying that this island beneath us is our final destination. I don't care if it's overrun by wild monkeys; I just want to stop moving and be still. It occurs to me to wonder how long we have been traveling, and I quickly add up the hours in my head, guesstimating that we are almost twelve hours from New York City.

Just then the pilot does a loop-de-loop around the crescent-shaped island to give me a better photo opportunity. The island reminds me of a macaroon cookie, with the ends dipped in chocolate and rolled in slivered almonds, the kind you can only get at a *good* Jersey diner. Two beaches, sparkling under the sun where they meet the darker water, give way to higher ground mounded with dense foliage. But the idea of macaroons is all my stomach needs to clench and unclench again like a giant fist. *Oh crap,* I beg the powers-that-be, *please don't let me throw up all over this shiny new plane.*

Meanwhile, Jack is sitting upfront with the pilot hanging on to the guy's every word like a little kid. Desperate in the backseat, I am now sweating and burping my way through that deep breathing exercise I read about in *Yoga Journal.* Nothing seems to be working. I pop another mint. Peppermint is supposed to calm the stomach.

Nope, not working.

I try chanting quietly to myself, *Sa-Ta-Na-Ma. Sa-Ta-Na-Ma.*

Still not working. I am officially beginning to panic when I spot a small terry cloth towel on the floor and clutch it to my face just in time to surrender my lunch. Jack and the thrill-seeking pilot don't even seem to notice. Between the loud buzzing of propellers and the preparation for our descent, they are both oblivious to my ordeal in the back seat. With a sideways glance at their heads clad in giant headsets I squish the towel into a tight, compact ball and look around the small compartment, wondering what to do with this fistful of puke.

I press my forehead against the cool glass window and watch the blue-green water come closer and meet us with a splash and then a slow rolling motion I could do without. Moments later we're gliding into a parallel-parking situation at the dock of the private island. The pilot kills the engine and unlatches the bubble top in a series of swift, purposeful movements. The silence of the propellers and first gush of fresh air are positively glorious.

I can't get out fast enough. On my first hasty attempt the seatbelt snaps me back into place, and I fumble with the buckle, cursing under my breath. Finally I am climbing out of the plane, my legs a bit shaky. It feels amazing to plant my feet on the ground, and I have to resist the urge to drop to my knees and kiss the dock. Instead I breathe in the salty air and take in my new surroundings.

The landing dock is deserted. Actually the whole island seems deserted. Part of me is expecting a reggae band or a concierge with a tray of cocktails complete with tiny paper umbrellas. I realize that I'm still clutching the balled-up soiled towel, so I plunge it deep into a trashcan and turn toward Jack, who has slid his sunglasses to the top of his head and is extending his arms wide, tilting his head back, and pointing his face up toward the sun.

"Welcome to Cernunnos Island!" he bellows in his loud, confident voice. As he turns to look at me his eyes are green and bright, confirming his excitement. We both have these hazel eyes that turn different colors based on our mood. Mine are large with flecks of amber and green. People always say that they go with my chestnut hair, but Jack says when I'm tired or angry they get really dark. The greener they are the happier I am; even I have noticed that. Sometimes I feel like I'm wearing two big mood rings on my face.

Taking another deep breath I try to focus on what Jack is saying as he starts spouting out facts like a seasoned tour guide.

"Isn't there anyone here to greet us?" I interrupt him.

"It's all part of the mystique." He smiles one of his devilish smiles where he lowers his chin and flashes his eyes over his perfectly sculpted, almost aristocratic, nose. "This island is named after a magical creature from ancient mythology." He pauses for effect, and I give him a head bob to continue. "This island is part of the Dodecanese cluster, a loose grouping of more than a 150 islands in the Aegean Sea between Crete and Turkey."

It's like a travelogue script he has memorized. He's cute the way he draws out each sentence like an authoritative voice-over and then ends it all with a little hand flourish.

Supposedly celebrities and royalty frequent this isolated island, he goes on to tell me in his real-Jack voice. Bookings are often taken years in advance, and Jack has hinted that he had to pull all kinds of strings to get us this reservation. But one of Jack's gifts is his ability to negotiate, and he's known for working add-ons into client contracts. Season tickets to the New York City Ballet and box seats at Yankee Stadium are a couple of favorites of mine. Leave it to Jack to find this place completely off the grid.

The pilot unloads our bags and hands me a folded note with *Welcome Gwen* written on the outside.

I've always hated my name, Gwen, short for Guinevere like the legendary King Arthur's queen. I don't know what the hell my parents were thinking when they named me. The truth is, I'm not even sure *who* is to blame for the over-the-top name, my adopted or my biological mother.

Unfolding the note, I read aloud, "Your bungalow is built on a hillside. Follow the rose petals sprinkled along the sandy path to find your way."

Rose petals? Seriously?

We wave good-bye to the pilot, watching the propellers spin to life as he starts up the engine with a loud roar. The small plane speeds through waves and then lifts into the sky and disappears into the clouds. As the buzz of propellers fades into the distance, I become more aware of birds chirping wildly in the bushes that begin a few yards beyond the dock. But that's the only sound: the birds, along with seawater lapping up against the shore.

Jack scoops up the heavy stuff while I carefully lift two of the smallest bags, cursing my back and all its limitations. After the car accident I suffered a punctured lung, a broken collarbone, and several cracked ribs, not to mention a head injury that left me dead for nine minutes. But the lingering symptoms of the physical injuries are nothing compared to the physiological damage. Just the other day while meeting a new client, I shook his hand and became overwhelmed by a powerful vision, this man at the dinner table with a pregnant wife and three small boys running around the overcrowded apartment. I could feel his certainty that his wife was having the baby girl they both desired but didn't have the heart to tell him it was going to be another wild boy. These moments of *unexplained knowing* still happen from time to time.

I shake it off and try to focus on the progress I've made since the accident. Six months ago I couldn't even bend over to tie my shoes, so I should be thankful I'm standing upright now, able to carry a few bags. *Progress not perfection*, I tell myself in the singsong voice of my perky physical therapist.

We head down the sandy path, which is indeed sprinkled with fresh pink rose petals. Surrounded as we are here by thick walls of overgrown plants and colorful flowers, my nose fills with a mixture of overwhelming scents I can't quite identify. My nausea and bad back fade from my mind as we wind our way through the unique vegetation of the island. Butterflies dance around the plants, landing every now and then on an especially unique flower. A fuchsia-hued blossom sways under the weight of three huge orange and blue butterflies that look like nothing I've ever seen, while a blue champagne-fluted cluster of blooms open to welcome a cloud of the more familiar monarch-like variety. I'm struck by the thought that I certainly have never seen flowers like this in my mother-in-law's extensive garden.

The flora becomes denser the further we travel, and as we turn each corner we frequently need to push back branches of flowers dangling over the walkway. The air is hot but not humid, and there is a constant breeze blowing through the leaves of the palm trees towering above us.

Turning one blind corner, we're startled by two female deer appearing on the path, their shiny brown coats glistening in the sunlight like expensive chocolate. *An unusual color for deer,* I think, as their leaf-shaped ears flip up and they examine us with curious doe eyes.

"What the . . . ?" Jack stops short.

Deer on a tropical island? And these two look like something out of a fairy tale, with almost human intelligence showing in their expressions. We all stand there gawking at each other for a long moment. Then one of them backs up before crooking a foreleg and almost kneeling to pick up a rose petal on the grass in front of her. She chews it delicately; then suddenly both does are leaping away in a zigzag pattern, disappearing into the underbrush.

The path has unexpectedly opened to a small clearing, and we find ourselves standing in front of an old-fashioned bungalow with white shutters. The word *Gwen* is spelled out in rose petals near the wooden steps.

"This must be it." Jack turns to me and winks.

Yikes, where did he find this place? I remember discussing a budget for this little excursion and immediately regretted agreeing to a price range instead of a hard number. This trip was going to cost a fortune, and I was not looking forward to next month's Visa bill.

We climb the steps to our new home for the next ten days and cross a spacious deck, stepping into a grand living room decorated in sandy beige tones. Dropping the bags with a thump I run my hands through the long champagne-colored drapes, something I would never have dreamed of doing in my parents' house. The house I grew up in never really felt like a home. It was a place filled with things to be looked at but never touched. I'd always felt like a bull in a china shop, too big and clumsy for the delicate dining room chairs with the stiletto legs. Kicking off my shoes, I sink my feet into the thick cream-colored carpet.

"Champagne?" Jack points to an ice bucket and two elaborate goblets.

One might expect crystal flutes to go with this décor, but these medieval goblets look like antiques. I nod. Still a little nauseous, I reason that the bubbles might help settle my stomach. Besides, I could use a drink after all that traveling. Next to the bottle is a big bowl of fruit overflowing with plump raspberries and deep red strawberries. I continue padding through the luxurious carpet in my bare feet while Jack works the cork off the champagne, and I drop a strawberry into each goblet. He fills the giant glasses, and we clink them and sample the sweet, pink champagne. I'm happy to find that the bubbles actually do help settle my stomach. Taking another long sip, I feel myself easing right into vacation mode.

"Marilyn used to drink pink champagne." I giggle, wondering if she ever stayed here. I'd always been fascinated with Marilyn Monroe. Her love of glamour and troubled childhood made me feel somehow connected to her. When Jack and I were first married he surprised me with coveted tickets to the auction of the star's personal belongings at Christie's Auction House. We agreed to max out our credit cards and decided to bid on a pair of rhinestone earrings, the ones she wore to the premiere of *Some Like it Hot*. I remember sharing the handle of the bidding paddle with Jack and waving it high in the air before things quickly got scary. The auctioneer banged his gavel on the podium when an anonymous caller outbid everyone with an outrageous offer *ten* times more than the experts anticipated. In fact all the auction items sold for much more than projected, and I imagine many hopeful bidders walked away empty-handed that night.

"Check this out!' Jack points his goblet at some extensive built-in shelving that runs the entire perimeter of the spacious living room. The shelves are jam-packed with an assortment of old books, and I squint up at their spines trying to make out some of the titles but quickly give up. *How would I get any of them down, anyway?* I look around for a television before remembering another thing Jack told me about this island: no TV. No telephone and no Internet. I instinctively pull my cell phone from my back pocket and find the LCD panel dull, with no green bars. *This is going to be interesting.* At first I welcomed the idea of ten days with no outside distractions, but here I am on day one with a strong desire to check my e-mail.

Wandering through the living room and into the open kitchen, Jack pulls open the large European refrigerator, the kind with the freezer on the bottom. The top part is jammed with fresh fruit, platters of grilled vegetables, cold salads, and all kinds of cheese. My stomach makes a small noise, and although I am not quite ready to eat, I see that everything looks delicious. I open the door on a large pantry to find it overflowing with packages and tins of assorted nuts, chips, crackers, and a variety of other snacks.

We continue our tour of the bungalow down a long hallway at the end of which I'm forced to hand my goblet to Jack because I need both hands to open the French doors to the bedroom. At first I think someone has left on a sound machine, but I quickly realize that the rushing sound is from waves crashing on the shore. It's coming from the open terrace facing the sea, because the sliding glass doors have been left open. Long, lacy curtains dance into the room on a sudden warm breeze. Completely delighted, I rush through the room to step out onto the stone balcony, gaze out at the vast ocean only a few hundred yards away, and think, *To hell with the Visa bill.*

"Damn, look at all these pillows." Jack tosses a satin neck roll at me. Too eager to see the breathtaking view, I've neglected to take in our fabulous room with its giant four-poster bed atop an elevated platform. Mini staircases on either side emphasize the bed's height, offering access through surrounding layers of sheer netting with small, shiny beads sewn along its edges. Through the gauzy drapery I can see how the massive bed is piled high with an assortment of silken pillows, and there's Jack standing on one of the stair steps, about to toss another of the pillows at me.

"Admit you love this place or I'll fire!" He's grinning. His eyes are bright with the recognition that he's nailed the perfect gift. I give him a huge, appreciative smile and imagine that my eyes are bright green right about now.

The last room on the "tour" is the bathroom. Like a blue and green marble grotto, it's twice the size of our master bath back home, Jack points out the oversized tub before disappearing under an archway. I follow him. Here a passageway leads to a door, and beyond that to an outdoor shower with a circular stall surrounded by tall bamboo plants and large floppy white flowers.

"This is exactly where we should start our vacation." Jack nods, stripping off his T-shirt.

Suddenly I can't wait to get out of these sweaty clothes. I quickly unwrap the sweater I've had tied around my waist all this time and find that my lower back is drenched in sweat from the extra material and the change in temperature. Jack heads back to the living room to refill our empty goblets while I peel off my clothes and step into the round stall. The multiple showerheads sputter to life and spray needles of hot water in every direction. It takes me a while to figure out the faucet system, but after some tinkering I am happy with the hot-cold water ratio and let out an extended sigh.

A moment later, I freeze. I'm afraid to move. It's as if, even though the shower is completely secluded, I know that someone or something is watching me.

That's what I get for drinking on a nervous stomach, I think, shaking myself out of immobility. Standing on my tiptoes and peeking over the tops of bamboo stalks, I stare fixedly into the surrounding bushes. The sides of the bungalow are dense with the same type of thick foliage that adorned the path, and I scan these bushes looking for movement. After a few minutes I give up, shut my eyes against the stream of water, and let it run down my neck and shoulders. The heat releases the tight muscles and everything slowly begins to unclench. Reaching for the coconut-scented soap, I work it into a thick lather while my mind drifts until I find myself thinking of work.

Owning and operating a busy project management shop in Manhattan, some might say that Jack and I work hard and play hard, but actually it's been quite some time since we've played at all. When we aren't working, we're talking about work or thinking about it.

Just as I'm getting into obsessing about whether we can afford to take the time to be here, Jack joins me in the shower. He takes the coconut soap from my hand and turns me around, lathering my back with slow methodical strokes. Between his hands and the jets I forget all about work. I feel his strong wet arms tighten around me as I turn into him, and he lifts me, pressing my back against the slick bamboo wall. Then I'm winding my legs around his waist and thinking, *Happy Birthday to me,* as the water continues to pound down around us.

Sometime later with the glow of vacation sex on our pruned skin we step from the shower and dry ourselves with big fluffy towels. I wrap a towel around my wet hair and accept one of the robes Jack found hanging in the closet, a chocolate-brown luxurious terry wrap with white trim around the neck and wrists. I pull it tightly around me. It feels like a mixture of thin velvet and silk. Jack has swaddled himself in the other, larger version, and we lounge around the suite in our fancy robes for a while until I feel the need to unpack. I connect my cell phone to portable speakers and select a playlist of Stevie Ray Vaughan. Soon moaning strands of guitar fill the empty room, and then Stevie begins to sing.

Flipping open the lid of my suitcase, I inspect the numerous long logs of rolled-up clothes. Somewhere I've read that this technique keeps clothes from wrinkling, and I'm pleased with the results as I unroll the many bathing suits, cover-ups, and sun dresses I managed to jam into my suitcase. Even though the vacation was a surprise, Jack gave me clues about what to bring.

"You'll need bathing suits by day and pretty dresses for dinner," he would text me during the workweek to get me excited about the trip.

I carefully unroll my favorite new purchase: a long, lavender cocktail dress with layers of sheer material and a billowing skirt, the kind that'll float out around me if I spin in a circle. I pull at all the loose threads where I cut the labels, which I always do when I buy new clothes, telling myself it's because labels and tags always itch me. This is only partly true; mostly it's that I don't need to see a size every time I pull something over my head. Especially when some designer insists on using the word *Grande* to describe a curvy girl like myself.

Forever self-conscious about my body, I am always trying to lose another ten pounds. But for now, holding the dress against my body and looking into the mirror, I resolve to focus on the things I like about my reflection.

Well, I like the way the straps can be adjusted to hike up the "girls."

"We're forty years old now," I say aloud to my tits in the mirror. "At forty, you double-Ds can use all the support you can get." But to myself, I wonder as I often do if my big boobs were passed down from my biological mother. Could be. I've been told very little about where I came from, but I do know that the woman I call "Mother" is barely a B.

Adopted at six months, I was the only child of a well-to-do professional couple living in upstate New York. My parents were perfectly happy leading the lives of DINKs (double-income-no-kids) until they finally succumbed to the pressure of a society that insists that every married couple should have a child. Though I've never asked, I can imagine that my workaholic parents probably paid someone plenty for a healthy baby girl.

My father was a lawyer, and my mother ran her own interior design business. They both commuted to Manhattan where they worked long hours, including nights and weekends. Probably I got my work ethic from watching them suit up and head out to work or hearing them talking, during one of the rare dinners we had together, about what the latest development was in a case of my father or how Mother's crazy new client wanted to pretend that he or she knew anything about color. As for me, I spent most of my time with a nanny, Valentina, who sang to me in Portuguese. She often would read to me, though I learned later that she didn't actually know how to read but simply made up stories to go along with the pictures. I felt more connected to Valentina than to either of my parents.

Successful though he was, my father seemed almost disillusioned by how his life turned out. He tended to look confused or discontent somehow in our family photos. Those albums offered arrays of awkward shots of me, with my mother toasting her martini glass high in the air and my father squinting into the lens as if to say, "What am I doing here?" I could never be sure exactly what my father had expected out of life, but this clearly was not it. The thing I remembered most about my father was a plaque he displayed in his home office:

Spending money we haven't earned
To buy things we don't need
To impress people we don't like

I didn't really understand the plaque until much later in life when I came to see that it summed up my father pretty well.

My mother, and most of the women she was friendly with in Westchester County, all had the same Stepford Wife look–straight blond hair and French-manicured nails. All of them were so thin

12

you could see their pelvic bones poking through the material of their expensive clothes. Their daughters were generally cast in the same mold. With my dark frizzy hair, chipped nail polish, and generous emerging curves that I tried to camouflage with layers of dark bulky clothes, I knew I didn't fit in.

Valentina was the only person who knew how to handle my long, unruly hair. I remember sitting perfectly still while she dipped the comb in a glass of water and methodically untangled all the knots. Once my hair was tangle-free she would smooth it into a long, thick braid and add two spit curls on either side of my face. Whenever Valentina styled my hair I would sleep like a mummy and try to keep it neat like that for days.

It was Valentina who bought me my very first bra and took me out for ice cream the day I got my first period, acting like this was something to celebrate, this becoming a woman. She explained how the female reproductive system worked in her broken English while I thought about how much the hot fudge was helping my cramps.

Whenever I felt cheated by my real mother giving me away or my adopted mother being so cold and unapproachable, I always felt lucky to have Valentina. What she didn't get around to teaching me I learned from books or movies.

Spending most of my childhood alone, I would read, watch movies, and listen to music, anything to escape the stilted uncomfortable atmosphere in our house. I found that I would rather explore imaginary worlds than deal with the monotony of the real world. Don't get me wrong; I knew the difference between fantasy and reality—I just preferred fantasy. Sometimes I would stand on the cocktail table, clutch an upside-down soup ladle, and belt out all the words to *Judy Garland, Live at Carnegie Hall*. I had the whole two-and-a-half-hour concert memorized right down to the throat clearings and the tiny sob near the end of "Somewhere over the Rainbow." My mother made me take piano lessons for several years, but I lacked the discipline to ever be any good, although I can still pluck out "You are my Sunshine" in a pinch.

When I was a child I longed for a pet, more precisely a cat. I'd imagine a big fluffy cat that lovingly followed me around, jumping on my lap or curling up beside me in bed. I begged for a kitten, but my mother would never allow something so hairy in the house. And Dad wanted to know where it was going to poop.

"It's a giant rodent," Mother insisted, scrunching her nose in disgust.

I remember trying to catch a stray cat, hoping to sneak it into the house to hide in my bedroom. I rigged a box with string over a bowl of milk and sat outside waiting like that for hours. After several failed attempts, I dragged my bulky cat trap home, bouncing it against the sidewalk in defeat.

Sometimes I conjured up stories about what my biological parents might be like. Maybe my father was a ruggedly handsome officer who had been enjoying a weekend pass from the Marine Corps. I could see him in his dress whites with a shiny brimmed hat just like the movie poster for *An Officer and a Gentleman*. Across a crowded cabaret, he would spot my mother on stage in a sequined dress singing a bluesy ballad. Draped across a piano, she'd have a long cigarette holder in one hand and an old-fashioned boxy microphone in the other. Their eyes would meet, and there would be instant fiery attraction. He would wait for her backstage, and they would have one night of passion before he shipped out the next morning. The whole thing played out like an old black-and-white movie in my head.

When I turned eighteen I officially began the search for my biological parents. As with most adopted children, there was a part of me that desperately needed to understand where I came from. The good, the bad, and the ugly; I just wanted to know. This need starting creeping up in my early teens, but I didn't have the guts to act on it until I was eighteen—or the money for that matter. But right around my eighteenth birthday my great aunt Nora died at the ripe old age of ninety-one and left me a chunk of money along with one directive: *Do something that needs to be done.* That's what she actually wrote in her will.

I took it as a sign that it was time to find my true mother and demand to know just why she discarded me like an unwanted sweater. But because I thought I needed to cushion the blow, I told my folks that I needed to know more about my medical history.

"In case I ever want to have kids one day," I explained. My mother listened while regarding me frostily, her thin arms crossed against her chest. And I remember how my father squinted at me like I was fine print.

I recruited a private detective, a guy who appealed to me frankly because he reminded me of *Magnum PI.* But the whole experience left me deflated when, after an exhaustive search, Magnum called me to his office for a debriefing.

He fingered the thin folder on his desk, unable to meet my eyes. "Every so often a case comes along that frustrates you at every turn," he said. Taking his glasses off, he placed them on top of the manila folder and gently explained how all leads pointed to a group of Rumanians traveling through Europe in the late sixties. Well, more correctly, they were *gypsies*, he said. One family among them in particular had several girls ranging in age from twelve to sixteen.

Here he eyed me somewhat awkwardly. "You know how those are peak child-bearing years in gypsy tradition." I didn't know, but I waited while he drifted off, not wanting to go into details, I figured. Anyway, it seems that gypsies don't typically leave a paper trail such as birth certificates, school records, or tax forms. They keep to themselves, living outside conventional society, and most private investigators say chasing a gypsy is like trying to chase a ghost.

"So at this juncture . . ." Magnum leaned on his arms and peered at me across the desk. It took all my restraint not to grab my case folder from under his elbows.

"We would need additional funds to continue the search, but quite frankly I believe we are on a wild goose chase here." He finally handed over the folder with a heavy sigh.

I read and reread every word of the final report, but nothing ever rang true. I thought I would have an "ah-ha" moment, but I felt no connection to the gypsies I read about and was no closer to understanding my background than when I originally hired this guy. Had he made the whole thing up, unable to come up with anything else? Maybe I'd been unrealistic, expecting an 8x10 glossy on both parents with a complete bio and current address. But I certainly hadn't hired him to hear a story about a rambling clan of vagabonds.

"Maybe I can try to find them on my own," I murmured, knowing that Aunt Nora's money was all but gone.

"The trail is completely wiped clean," he said and then suggested that my father, being a lawyer and all, might have had something to do with that.

But whenever I asked my father about my biological parents, he would wave me away with an irritated shrug. "Why would you want to find someone who doesn't want to be found?" he'd asked the last time I brought it up. After that, I knew I'd never speak to him about it again.

I turn from the mirror and dig deeper into the suitcase, pulling out a beaded bag and shell-jewelry dyed lavender to match the dress. *I probably over-packed*, I think, pulling out more evening bags, a bunch of lacy shawls, and a big floppy hat. Since I couldn't decide exactly what to bring I had pretty much brought everything.

Jack pads into the bedroom still wearing the robe and announces that he is getting hungry, so we decide to dress for dinner and head over to the restaurant. He pulls on a light blue shirt with a muted tropical theme, and I wear a green sundress with gold sandals, the ones I decided would match everything. My hair is still damp from the shower sex, so I comb it into a side ponytail and add a pair of earrings that jingle like wind chimes whenever I move my head.

"Oh good, like a cat wearing a bell around your neck," Jack teases. "I'll know where you are at all times."

We step outside just as the sun is about to set. We probably have another hour of daylight and can't figure out if we should bring our sunglasses or not, finally deciding against it. The sky is turning amazing shades of pink and purple, and the night is warm but breezy as we set out in search of the restaurant. My beaded bag swings in a leisurely pattern from my wrist as we walk hand in hand down the sandy path, which appears likely to circle the island with little offshoot paths leading this way and that. We make a few wrong turns, feeling like mice in a maze, and finally following our noses to the beach.

One lone table sits near the water's edge. The table and its two chairs are surrounded by tall tiki torches stuck deep into the sand. Waves gently rolling in toward land and then ebbing out provide the only sound on the empty beach. Clumps of sand get caught in my sandals, so I quickly slide them off and carry them. As we get closer, I can make out the folded card on the table with a handwritten *Gwen* in flamboyant script.

"Where the hell are all the other guests?" I wonder aloud.

"Maybe there's a later seating."

Jack wanders over to the main house, and I follow close behind, still carrying my sandals and shaking off the excess sand. We figure that the large white structure with the wraparound porch serves as the restaurant, but the doors are locked so we peer through the windows. Even though the place has the feel of a haunted house, everything is polished and clean, free from any dust or cobwebs. Tables are set with fresh linen, fancy silverware, and elaborate flower arrangements. It reminds me of the time we arrived early for a friend's wedding and got to enter the ballroom before everyone else, when everything seemed frozen in eternal perfection.

That's when I have my first official vision of the day. I've been so preoccupied with the stress of traveling that I haven't focused on the low buzzing that seems to be my constant companion these days. Usually I can manage to block out the walkie-talkie in my head that's turned down but never completely off. Most of its static anyway, but every now and then it crackles to life abruptly after long periods of dead air, a kind of telepathic transmission of images. The visions are triggered by touch and are usually accompanied by a wave of emotion. I'm still struggling to understand my newfound sensitivity, but I've learned intense feelings like fear, anger, jealousy, or sadness "broadcast" the loudest. And so it happens that when I touch the metal door handle of the restaurant for one more wiggle, I am struck by a wavy image of a dining room devoid of people on board the *Titanic*. It's like an underwater camera depicting tables elegantly set up for a dinner about to be served at the bottom of the sea.

I pull my hand away as if the handle is hot, and Jack snaps his head in my direction.

"What is it?"

I shake off the sensation. "Nothing. I mean, it's just . . . I had one of those visions." Rolling my eyes as if poking fun at myself and pausing because I'm not sure how much I want to share, I shrug. "Like we were touring a sunken ship."

I feel almost apologetic since the accident, offering these descriptions. The visions are always similar to a dream in the sense that it's hard to remember the details once they're over, and right now I can't decide what made me think it was the *Titanic*. Jack seems to be evaluating my words, but then he turns to look again into the empty dining room.

After a minute, he says, "I figured a private island would be the perfect place to escape this newfound talent of yours." Turning toward me and lowering his voice needlessly, he adds, "Anyway, I thought it only happened when you touched someone directly."

"Yeah, at first. But lately it's been happening with metal objects." We both look down at the shiny doorknob.

"But I thought you said the metal held lingering energy. So that would mean someone had to touch that doorknob recently, right?" He looks around doubtfully.

"Look, I don't know the exact expiration date of the energy on the knob; I'm just telling you what I saw." Annoyed now and wishing I had kept the image to myself, I stomp through the sand back to the table and am not yet seated when a peel of laughter cuts through the silence almost like a siren. We both notice that it seems to be coming from right around the corner.

"Guess we're not alone." Jack moves down the porch and motions for me to follow.

On the other side of the restaurant we find an outdoor bar under a white canvas canopy. Several mahogany barstools with cushioned seats are not yet occupied. The laughter is coming from the only patron seated here, a woman perched on the edge of her stool leaning toward the bartender, a dark-haired fellow in a crisp white shirt and black vest. His customer flips over an empty shot glass with a delicate hand clad in a lace glove and places it on the bar in front of her. She is wearing a dress of eggplant satin with a plunging back and a long strand of black pearls that gleam against her alabaster skin. Her skin is so white that I can't imagine what she's doing in this sunny paradise. *Definitely the kind of woman who has to wear a big hat to the beach*, I decide.

The woman turns slowly toward us on her stool. She has a kewpie-doll face with bright red lips and a colorful scarf tied artfully around her head. Its long material is knotted under her left ear, and she wears gold hoop earrings and large round sunglasses. I feel underdressed with my casual sundress and curse myself for not breaking out one of my fancy outfits for our first dinner.

"You must be Gwen and Jack," the bartender calls out, welcoming us with a smile. My earrings jingle softly in response.

The bartender wears a nametag that says *Roscoe*, and sunglasses cover his eyes. Jack walks over and reaches across the bar to shake his hand while I smile politely at the woman, who looks like she just stepped out of an old Hollywood magazine.

"Where are you two from?" I can sense her looking me up and down behind her dark Jackie-O lenses.

Again my earrings jingle under her scrutiny and I make a point of trying to keep my head still.

"New York." I shift uncomfortably from one foot to the other, self-conscious under her gaze. "Where is everyone?" I direct my question at Roscoe.

"There was a big wedding originally scheduled this week, the heiress to the Jazeera dynasty." He runs a rag inside a wine glass and holds it up to the light. "Apparently the bride got cold feet and called the whole thing off."

The woman kicks back another shot and slams the glass down on the bar. "Dirty bastard was probably only after her money."

Roscoe dutifully fills another glass with a golden liquid, and I try to read the label on the bottle. *Some kind of tequila.* The lady is accumulating shot glasses in a U-shaped formation on the bar in front of her, and I assume she's trying to complete the circle.

Roscoe points toward the trees with the bottle. "All the bungalows were originally booked for the wedding guests. But with the last-minute cancellation the island is pretty much deserted this week."

"We've got the whole place to ourselves!" The woman sings out to no one in particular.

"So staff got cut way down."

"Doesn't the staff live here on the island?" Jack wonders aloud.

"Na." Roscoe shrugs. "We come back and forth by water taxi. Do most of our work behind the scenes." He pulls a wine list from under the bar and hands it to Jack. "Your table has been set with the welcome buffet. All you need to do is select a wine."

We settle on a bottle of pinot noir. But all the while I am anxious to get back to the table and touch the back of Jack's shirt and signal that we should sit. After the plane rides, vomiting, champagne, and sex, I am ready to eat.

We make our way around the porch and cross the beach to our table, where Jack pulls out my chair for me. Several large silver platters covered with shiny domes greet us, and as we lift each one we "ooohhh" and "aaahhh" our way through scalloped potatoes, creamed spinach, and antipasto with cheese, olives, and roasted vegetables. A wedge of baked brie sprinkled with caramelized almonds sits on a platter ringed by thinly sliced apples, and there is a heaping bowl of spinach salad sprinkled with gorgonzola cheese.

Meanwhile, Roscoe appears silently beside Jack, expertly uncorks the wine, and allows us to sample it before pouring. Then he places a small gold bell on the table for us to ring it if we needed anything, after which he disappears into the shadows gathering around the restaurant. As the sun slips into the water, darkness falls over the beach and we consume our food, both of us realizing the extent of our long-denied hunger.

Finally full, I cradle my wine glass and lean back in the chair, gazing out at the ocean. As my eyes adjust to the darkness I detect movement in the water like stones being skimmed or lily pads quickly bubbling across the surface.

"What the hell is that?"

"What? Where?" Jack twists around in his chair.

"Over there, swimming toward us." I point.

"I don't see anything."

Sitting forward in my chair I peer into the blackness, tempted to ring the bell for Roscoe. Cutting through the water in a swift approach are several brown shapes.

"Right there. Like a bunch of animals of some kind. Maybe dogs?"

"You see a pack of dogs swimming toward us? Okay. You are officially cut off." Jack reaches for my wine glass.

"No, seriously, right there. Don't you see their heads in the water?"

"Those aren't dogs. They look like . . . like . . . deer."

"Deer can't swim."

Jack laughs. "Of course they can. Where did you hear that?"

I snatch my glass back and then look again at the water. "Oh shit, they *are* deer!"

We watch as the animals approach the shoreline and, one by one, gracefully step onto the beach. They shake the seawater from their fur and move around the beach, their long legs taking purposeful strides as if acclimating themselves to walking on land again. Jack and I are struck by the beauty of their coats, still wet and glistening in the light cast by the tiki torches. Most are brown, but two are almond-colored, one is auburn, and one is black as ink. As the deer pass by close to the table their faces flash in the candlelight with round expressive eyes and small heads, but each face is slightly different.

There are twelve in all. The two largest males stand protectively around the black doe in the center. Each male in the herd has a set of tall, spiked antlers that arc up toward the dark sky.

Growing up in Westchester, I remember running from window to window with my camera whenever a deer wandered onto our property. Now a city dweller, I have almost forgotten how regal and graceful deer could be. These animals looked so healthy, maybe from swimming in the salt water. I'm unable to take my eyes off them, and apparently neither can Jack. Without looking, I fumble for my cell phone in my beaded bag, familiar enough with it to switch to camera mode with only a sideways glance. Then I zoom in on the trio in the center and snap a picture.

Jack raises his glass. "Here's to a lifestyle as carefree as theirs."

Holding my glass high in the air like the drunk lady at the bar, I add, "To swimming from island to island."

"And sleeping on the beach!" Jack chimes in, and we're about to go on with this when one small doe suddenly begins to approach us with slow delicate steps.

Remembering the deer we'd seen on our arrival, I pluck a few loose rose petals from the vase on our table and offer them to her. She comes closer and, after some sniffing, takes two or three from my hand. Her long tongue tickles the center of my palm, and I pull my hand away, letting the remaining petals fall to the ground. I feel a pull in the center of my stomach, something imperative that I know I should respond to. It's as if the deer is trying to tell me something, something of the utmost importance.

Man, I have had too much wine.

I absent-mindedly snap another picture, not focusing on anything in particular but just aiming into the group of deer. Suddenly I feel very tired and need to lie down, the adrenaline-fueled day finally taking its toll. Jack agrees that it's time to go, and we push back from the table and slowly walk back down the sandy path.

To our surprise the deer start walking down the path alongside us. Some are walking in front and some behind, while others leap in and out of the bushes in some animal version of hopscotch.

"This feels like a fucked-up Disney movie," I mumble. Still, I'm feeling strangely at ease in the company of the deer. As we climb the steps to the bungalow, they quickly scatter and disappear into the surrounding bushes.

Inside, Jack kicks off his shoes, unbuttons his shirt, and shuffles off toward the bedroom. "Well, I think that's a wrap for the first day of vacation."

"What time do we have to get up tomorrow?" I push back the curtains and peek out the windows looking for signs of the deer, but the surrounding bushes are still.

"We don't have to be anywhere until one thirty, baby!" He crumples his shirt and shoots it toward the open suitcase like a basketball player taking a shot from the foul line. He misses, and the shirt falls to the floor. I remind myself that we should unpack fully tomorrow and hang things up where they belong.

All that I remember when I wake up is having been in the bathroom washing my face and then falling into this big bed surrounded by large fluffy pillows and soft sheets that smell like vanilla. Completely exhausted, I had drifted easily off to sleep.

And now I've heard this thud from the living room.

I'm sitting up, reaching out to shake my husband awake. "Jack, did you hear that?"

He draws in a long snore and then lets it out like a sigh. He's fast asleep, his breathing regular and slow. Through the netting I can make out the shadow of the open suitcase. My sundress is draped across the lid, and Jack's crumpled shirt is still in a heap on the floor.

I lie back down.

Another noise from the living room. This time it's a clunk, louder than before. Still no sign of movement from the lump beside me. I start to think that it's yet another weird animal that's managed to make its way inside when we were too tipsy to notice.

On my way down the long hallway I lift a piece of decorative driftwood from the wall. It's part of a sort of sculpture suggesting a ship; convincing if you like modern art. But it's heavy and comes off easily, and I somehow felt better just having it.

Peering into the living room, I let my eyes adjust to the darkness. For a brief second, I feel as if I am still in some dream and haven't risen from bed at all. Then I manage to make out the shape of a man sitting comfortably on the couch, and terrified, I freeze as my mind races through possible options. *Scream! Run! Throw the wood at him—!*

The figure calmly finishes rolling a cigarette and pops it between his lips. Patting each pocket, he pulls out a lighter but has to flick it several times before getting a flame. He lights the hand-rolled cigarette and inhales deeply. The amber ash glows in the dark room, illuminating his angular face and sharp features, which are surrounded by dark red curls that hang down past his shoulders. His eyes are sapphire blue. They almost glow in the dark room.

The man is wearing ripped jeans and a black concert T-shirt so worn and faded that I can't make out any of the words. As I stare at him, he lifts his dirty bare feet and props them on the cocktail table, crossing his ankles casually. With a wide smile he offers me a drag, but I wave an arm, refusing. Just then the sweet, undeniable smell of marijuana hits me.

Opening my mouth to say something, he beats me to it.

"Hey, I'm Jonah!" The young stranger wipes his left hand on his jeans and offers it to me with a wide confident grin.

I step back. *Maybe this is a hallucination; maybe there was something in the food or wine they gave us at dinner.*

Nevertheless, I keep looking at him, at his outstretched hand. There's a small round tattoo on the inside of his wrist. He sees me looking at it and smiles again before taking another hit off the joint. He has a mellow vibe about him, but there is a hyper energy percolating just beneath the surface and something oddly familiar about him.

Pressing my back firmly against the wall, I decide to challenge him. "How did you get in here?"

"Front door." He gestures casually.

"You have a key?"

"I have many keys." His eyes widen as he continues smoking and stretches back to flick his ash out the open window. His eyes are mesmerizing.

"What do you want?" I cross my arms over my chest, trying to look unafraid, in charge.

"To see if there was anything you need." Those glowing blue eyes are fixed on mine.

"I . . . think I have everything I need." I tighten my stance.

"You *think*?" His eyebrows fly up.

"What?"

"You said you *think* you have everything you need. Don't you *know?*" He takes another long drag. "I'm just messing with you," he says then, chuckling and sinking back into the cushions. Still, those eyes don't stop watching my face. They don't appear to blink, and they draw me in, making it impossible for me to look away.

Then the man is shrugging, glancing down, almost normal. "I heard there was someone in this bungalow I should meet; that's all." Not sure what to say to this, I stay quiet, relaxing my grip on the driftwood.

He smiles again, a completely disarming smile, and rises. Turning, he heads toward the door, clicking his tongue on the roof of his mouth as he goes. To my surprise, two white cats I've never seen before jump up in response. It seems that they've been curled up on the overstuffed couch . . . *but how is it I haven't even noticed them until now?*

They are big and long-haired, white as snow except for beige markings on their tails and around their heads. They stand stretching and yawning, taking their time before hopping down from the couch. Then they slink toward Jonah, who is exiting my living room, their bushy tails waving from side to side like two cobras rising from a basket. Both cats rub their face against Jonah's leg, purring musically until the door closes with a quiet click.

I wake with a start, and it takes me a few seconds to realize where I am. Jack is still sound asleep, one arm thrown over me almost as if, in his sleep, he's been trying to protect me.

Climbing out of the big bed, I tiptoe down the long hallway and peer into the living room. Everything seems to be in order—no pillows disturbed, no long white cat hairs clinging to the velvet couch. Even the driftwood sculpture on the wall seems to be intact. *The whole thing must have been a dream.*

Still, just the faintest smell of marijuana hangs in the air.

DAY II:

Odd Shade of Blue

Jack snaps open the curtains as I grudgingly open my eyes and squint into the bright sunlight. Groaning, I pull the blanket up over my head, not ready to get up, but Jack is being pretty insistent. Apparently we've overslept and need to hurry for our afternoon appointment.

"It's almost one o'clock, babe."

What? I've never slept this late back home, even on a rare day off. On a workday the alarm clock is perpetually set for five thirty a.m. But here I am waking in the afternoon, and I become aware of having slept like I was in a coma but still can't find the energy to move from the luxurious bed.

"We're booked for a couple's massage," Jack confesses, tugging on the bottom of the blanket.

I finally give up on the tug-of-war, release the blanket, and climb out of bed. I've always enjoyed massages and since the accident have been scheduling them pretty regularly. Although the doctor-prescribed massages usually consist of the deep-tissue variety that make you grip the edge of the table, cursing under your breath and trying not to cry out, I'm hoping for a nice relaxing experience in an exclusive spa with lots of pampering.

"What kind?" I'm peeling off my shorty pajamas and heading toward the shower.

"No idea," Jack says. "Hurry up."

Fully awake now, I suddenly stop at the shower door, glance in the mirror, and realize that my heart is beating absurdly hard. "Jack, I had the strangest dream."

"Tell me later," he says.

I turn the water on, trying to keep myself from bringing back an image that floated through my sleep last night: a man sitting on our sofa, smoking a joint; a guy I've never seen before, with eyes like bright-blue glass.

"Creepy," I say out loud, shaking my head before ducking it into the pulsing streams of warm water. That helps, and I let the fragrant soap take over my senses as I slowly work it into a lather over my arms and legs.

A little later, I'm poking through piles of clothes trying to find something comfortable to wear. Finally settling on a pair of Capri pants and a soft cotton V-neck top, I hurriedly pull them on as Jack enters the bedroom. He's got wet hair and he's put the chocolate-brown robe on after his shower.

"Is that what you're wearing?"

He cranes his neck forward and looks down at himself. "No good?"

"You can't walk around in a bathrobe." Pulling clothes from his suitcase, I wave them in his direction.

"Why not? You heard the bartender. We pretty much have the island to ourselves."

"You know who walks around in their bathrobe?" He stares at me blankly, so I answer my own question. "Homeless people and mental patients."

"What about Hugh Hefner?" He raises his eyebrows hopefully, but I shake my head.

We find our way to the spa without the help of rose petals. Instead, we use an old-fashioned method. We follow a sign. It's carved into an old tree that points "this way" to the spa and directs us down a thin trail branching off from the main path. Jack un-tucks his shirt from his shorts, still pissed that I made him get dressed for our spa session.

A short walk through the Zen garden leads us to a rope bridge with knotted wooden planks and intricately carved handrails. The lightweight bridge seems to be the only way across the high rocks, and I stop dead in my tracks, a wave of panic coming over me. Since the accident, I've become one of those people afraid to do things others take in stride, like this rope bridge. A year ago I would have danced across the thing, stopping to pose for a picture in the middle.

Sensing my hesitation, Jack grabs the rail and shakes the bridge to check its sturdiness. He nods and then crosses it, looking back and extending his hand. I reach for it, close my eyes, and squeal my way across the bridge in a dozen small steps that make the bridge bounce up and down way more than necessary.

Safe on the other side I wipe the sweat beads from my forehead. "Why would they put something so stressful on the way to a spa?"

"Most people might not consider a rope bridge particularly stressful," Jack reasons, but after I shoot him a warning look he switches gears. "Maybe it holds some symbolic meaning. You know, the whole seven pillars of healing."

But I am still bugged as we continue through the garden and head toward the mushroom-capped tiki hut situated behind several rows of small, sinewy trees. The overgrown branches have created a trellis like the roof of a covered bridge. The ceiling of greenery is sprinkled with vibrant flowers, and the colored petals of burnt orange, sunflower yellow, and fuchsia sprinkle down, some getting caught in my hair. My tall husband needs to duck his head under the archway as we approach the smoked-glass door with a large lotus flower etched into the glass.

Part of me expects the front door to glide open like the automatic doors at a grocery store. When nothing happens, we knock and wait. Then we slide the doors open, remembering what Roscoe said about limited staff this week.

Two massage tables are situated side by side beneath an oversized chandelier. The antique light fixture is made of twisted metal vines and fixed with dozens of white candles casting a soft glow over the entire room. Taking a deep breath, I feel my senses fill with fresh lavender and the smell of vanilla candle wax. A soft mixture of drums and chanting emanates from strategically mounted speakers, and I feel my irritation melt away like a cube of ice dropped into hot chocolate. Jack points to the familiar rose petals spelling out *Gwen* on one of the tables, and we quickly undress and slide under the crisp, pale-yellow sheets.

Awkwardly trying to pull the blankets over my back, I whisper to Jack, "I wonder if we'll have to share a masseuse."

"Oh, yeah, one hand for each of us."

I settle into the table on my stomach and get comfortable the way I usually do: by taking care to adjust my big boobs against undue crushing. Rolling my shoulders back and inching my hands down my sides, I try to flatten out. The once-punctured lung, now healed, still makes it difficult to take a deep breath. The doctors say it should only be noticeable in cold weather, and I have not been looking forward to winter in the city this year.

Next to me, Jack has already drifted into a comfortable near-stupor. Meanwhile, I'm trying to slow my breathing and concentrate on blocking out that familiar low buzzing that seeps in whenever I am quiet or still. I doubt I'll pick up residual energy from the massage table unless I touch the metal parts, which I'm being careful not to do.

After a few labored breaths, I hear the whoosh of sliding glass doors, and even though my face is squished into the donut ring I can't resist opening my eyes to take a peek. Two sets of tan bare feet come into view. They're decorated with toe rings, their nails painted a dark red, almost black. The feet are small and delicate, and something immediately makes me think of twins or sisters.

Watching the feet dance around the room, I hear quiet whispers as they disappear near the back of the table. *Oh, good, we're starting with the legs. I love when they do that.* The bottom of the sheet is lifted, and I sigh when warm oil is drizzled over my calves and the bottoms of my feet. I anticipate the hands and the random visions that sometimes come from a stranger's touch. But there's only the smell of rose oil as the masseuse begins rubbing small circles up my legs. Relieved, my whole body relaxes, and even though I just woke up I easily drift off to sleep again.

I dream of the sand dunes and a woman playing an acoustic guitar. The instrument is dyed an odd shade of blue and adorned with mother-of-pearl stones. Her shiny black hair drifts over the guitar as she plucks out unusual melodies, and she sways slightly to the music, her eyes closed. There is something melancholy in the way she plays, almost as if she is trying to comfort herself.

Now flowers emerge from beneath the sand, a variety of blooms of every shade. I select a white lotus, plucking it and sticking it firmly behind my left ear. I want to tell the woman that this flower is exactly the same as the one etched into the glass at the spa, but instead I hum quietly as she continues to strum her guitar. Draped in a long white dress that sharply contrasts her dark skin, she wears a gold band around her head, and a similar band encircles each of her upper arms. She opens her eyes suddenly and then lowers the long spidery lashes (way too long to be real) brushing them against her high cheekbones.

"It's Sebastian!" She looks past me and motions with her sharp chin, extending her swanlike neck.

Twisting around I watch the man named Sebastian saunter toward us wearing faded jeans, a leather jacket, and lots of jewelry. His dirty-blond hair hangs down his back in a messy ponytail, and his feline eyes boast just a hint of guy-liner.

"Hello, darlings!" He kisses the woman on both cheeks and calls her Ruby.

"Join us," Ruby encourages.

Sebastian squats down to pull a bottle of wine from the sand, extracts the cork with his teeth, and then takes a long swallow. Rings adorn his fingers, and long silver chains hang from his neck. A thick strand of blond hair dangles across his lovely face, but he doesn't seem to notice, or care.

"This weekend I have eaten my body mass in food, drunk my liquid levels in wine, and thoroughly enjoyed myself." He grunts, his words accompanied by wild hand gestures and facial expressions.

After a moment, during which Ruby only smiles at him indulgently, Sebastian lifts the guitar from her lap and strums a series of chord progressions, repeating the pattern several times. She watches him intently and then takes the guitar and repeats the chords back in perfect succession. The two hum a haunting melody, harmonizing with the guitar and each other. While they're passing the instrument back and forth, I spot a familiar circular tattoo on the inside of their left wrists. These tattoos are similar but not exactly the same. I want to reach out and grab their arms to examine the tattoos more closely, but I'm aware that this would be awkward, even unappreciated. I grow anxious, almost suspicious. I'm sure I've seen a tattoo very much like these before.

But where?

I take the wine bottle from Sebastian and after taking a sip bring it close to my face to inspect it. Something is floating in the deep red liquid. Frowning, I discover a rose petal in my mouth, which I take out and examine between my fingers.

When Sebastian sees this he throws his head back and gives out a loud bark of a laugh. "Don't you enjoy rose petals?"

"Not to eat." I wipe my tongue with my thumb and forefinger.

"Why not? The pink ones are the sweetest."

I furrow my eyebrows, unconvinced. "Go ahead," he says.

I pop the rose petal back in my mouth, and it slides down my throat. "It *is* sweet; you're right."

"You should taste the flowers in PoG." He has the hint of an accent, but I can't quite place it.

"Where's PoG?" I repeat the unknown place, rhyming it with "log" as he did, and peer into the bottle again, searching for more petals.

"Not far from here." Sebastian's voice echoes like the announcer's at Yankee Stadium.

Jack is shaking me awake for the second time today. I open my eyes and try to figure out why I'm looking at the floor. Then I remember the warm massage oil and realize that the toe-ringed therapists have left.

"Did you enjoy your massage, sleepyhead?" He's leaning against the table, sliding his shorts back on.

"She was doing amazing things to my calves, and that's the last thing I remember." I take my time rolling off the table and then stand, rubbing my eyes.

"You slept through the whole massage." Jack runs his fingers through his rumpled hair, smoothing it back into place.

"How would you know?" My body is slick with oil, and it even feels as if the oil was combed through my hair.

"You were talking in your sleep."

Uh-oh. "Did I say anything interesting?" I'm trying to remember the strange dream. It was long and detailed, bizarre, but I can't identify in what way. Maybe I had been picking up a vision from the massage therapist after all.

Jack says, "Most of it was unintelligible," and I let myself relax. He's consulting a tiny notebook while I unsuccessfully try to peer over his shoulder. I am unable to see anything, because he keeps covering the pages with his hand and holding it close to his chest like a prized hand of poker. Apparently it contains the details of our schedule, because after some examination he concludes.

"Looks like the rest of the day is free time. What do you feel like doing?"

"Let's hit the beach." I'm feeling lazy and thinking that this might be the only time I get to weigh in on the itinerary. Lying in the sun with this oil in my hair should work like a deep conditioner, an old trick I learned from Valentina.

After a quick stop at the bungalow where we eat a light lunch and change into our bathing suits, we head back down the sandy path. As we travel through the bushes of vivid flowers, the sun moves behind a cloud and Jack shoulders the folded umbrella while I struggle with the overstuffed beach bag.

"Look!" He's pointing at two bright red parrots perched high in a palm tree. All around us, the trees are alive with chatter as if there's a bird convention going on, and every now and then a purple-winged dragonfly zips by as if to add its two cents.

Supposedly we are alone on the path, but I've suddenly become overwhelmed by an odd sense of presence. A bird nearly half my height steps between two dense bushes. Its swollen bulb of a body sits almost awkwardly on two long, skinny legs straight as sticks. This bird is not necessarily beautiful, but with its sword-like beak it does command attention.

The scene reminds me of an experience I once had when meeting a client in a federal building in Washington, DC. In a sudden burst of frenzy, the Secret Service had unexpectedly appeared to clear the hallway for the president. With my back pressed against the wall and my hands clasped in front of me as instructed, all I got to see of Mr. President was a flash of one white shirtsleeve peeking out from his grey suit jacket, but there had definitely been a marked energy shift in that hallway.

I'm trying frantically to dig through my beach bag for the cell phone to get a picture of this bird.

Jack turns and whispers, "Great blue heron."

Turns out the heron, just like the vanishing president, has appeared only for the instant required to cross our path. I'm not quick enough to get a good picture before he disappears into the bushes on the other side. When I hit the preview button on my cell phone I see that I managed to trip the multi-option feature, snapping several frames in a row. I must have selected some kooky effect, because the pictures show nothing but smudges of blue fuzz. The bird I intended to capture for all time might as well have been a special-effects technician's idea of a bluish-winged alien.

Trying to catch up with Jack, who is walking a few steps ahead, I show him the screen. "Hey, doesn't this look like a fairy?"

"Could be one of those creatures mentioned in the brochure."

"What creatures?"

He recites, the corners of his mouth turned up in an impish grin, "The powerful winged creatures that still haunt the island, unnamed blue species that are both elusive and unique to this locale."

I'm sure he's messing with me, so I toss the phone back into my bag, pull out my big floppy hat, plant it on my head, and look around for landmarks. *Aren't there supposed to be other bungalows around here?* Maybe they are all set back pretty far from the main path. I squint, peering through the underbrush and trees, but all there is, is more of the same.

Still, I'm getting used to moving around this horn-shaped island. I tell myself that I could get from our bungalow to the restaurant alone if I had to, and I could probably find my way back to the spa, although I wouldn't relish the idea of crossing that rope bridge again.

Jack has put on his movie-star sunglasses, and I notice the vacation-beard stubble springing up on his cheeks. He's one of those baby-faced men who don't need to shave every day. It actually takes him about forty-eight hours to achieve what most men would consider a five-o'clock shadow.

The truth is that my husband is aging nicely, just like a fine wine or a stone on the riverbank that grows smoother each year. *That is Jack.* The only real signs of age are the scattered gray hairs that are popping up near his temples and mingling with his sparse beard. Trying to be funny, he explains each grey hair: "Unreasonable client, tax bill, midtown traffic, disgruntled employee . . ."

But he isn't always being funny. As we get older it seems that work (in fact, life in general) has been stressing him out more and more. We often joke about selling the business and retiring to some remote island. It has occurred to me that in selecting this exotic little vacation, Jack may have been subconsciously laying the groundwork for just such a move.

He often tells the cautionary tale of the man who worked all his life at a job he despised. He dreamt endlessly of retirement, but exactly one week after he retired, he dropped dead of a brain embolism.

"Was dead before he hit the ground!" Jack would get really worked up during the rant. "Postponing all the things he really wanted to do and just doing what everyone expected of him. I see guys like that on the subway all the time, the ones with dead eyes just creeping along in their big metal coffin."

I would nod and think of my father, who always seemed to be wondering, *Is this all there is?*

And then there was that night of fantastical scheming, when the two of us drank way too much wine and talked about faking Jack's death and living off the insurance money. The plan included changing identities, buying a small faraway island, and saying good-bye to our families. Not a particularly off-putting concept for me, although neither of us wanted to think of leaving Jack's tribe. The next day we woke up and went to work with our hangovers. We smiled sheepishly at each other that morning, but we never talked about it again.

Arriving at the beach, Jack points to a patch of sand near the water and says, "How's this?"

We spread the blanket, and he spikes the umbrella into the sand, adjusting it a few times before becoming satisfied with the position. I glance up and down the empty beach and spot the white restaurant in the distance. The tiki torches from last night are gone, but for a moment I think I see movement from the bar. I peek over the top of my sunglasses and stare into the distance for a few seconds before finally deciding that it's just a linen napkin flapping in the breeze.

Lying back onto the blanket and using Jack's rolled-up shirt as a pillow, I try to escape into my paperback, annoyed to find that the book was written from the perspective of a teenage girl. *Don't we have enough of those books?* There's really only so much I can relate to a high school girl considering I've just turned forty.

Christ, *forty*.

When I was nineteen I started classes at New York University, and that's when I met Jack Michaels. Typically late for class, I was rushing up a big flight of stairs in the main commons. Jack was leaning over the railing, people-watching, he told me later. He smiled down at me with eyes that were both sexy and a little sad. I felt a jolt of familiarity, as if we had met before. Reaching the top of the stairs I joined the other students waiting for the next class, making sure to stand directly across from him as I leaned against the wall.

"Hey," I said kind of quietly, which sounded lame. I wasn't sure he'd heard me, because he didn't respond, but still I couldn't take my eyes off him. He was tall, over six feet, which meant that I would need to stand on my tiptoes to kiss him. He had a good head of wavy dark brown hair and hazel eyes that crinkled in the corners when he smiled. I noticed that their color was similar to mine but that the emerald rugby shirt he was wearing made his seem much more green.

The sense of "*There* you are!" came over me. Although I had never seen him before and didn't even realize that I was looking for him, *there he was*.

I repeated the "Hey," which was bold for me, and next we were having an easy conversation. Within days, I was uncharacteristically cutting class to hang out with the cute boy in the rugby shirt. I quickly learned that he had a big personality with charisma that could capture the attention of an entire room. After he easily convinced a waitress to give us a corner booth, we talked for hours about everything: books, movies, music art and politics. He listened to me intently, asking questions and entertaining my opinions no matter how out of left field they seemed. Qualities that my parents found strange or quirky Jack thought were imaginative and creative. If for nothing else, I would have loved him for that. I could totally be myself around him and didn't feel the need to escape so much anymore.

I lie back on the blanket now and observe my husband from behind my own sunglasses. He is paging through a magazine, unaware of my gaze. Early on in our relationship, he had explained that he was the oldest of four boys in a close-knit Irish Catholic family, one that expected great things from him. The Michaels were not well off, living in a narrow row house in New Jersey with neighbors so close you could hear them sneeze. But I was fascinated by the constant hustle and bustle of this warm and friendly house that he'd lived in all his life. Compared to the mausoleum that I'd grown up in, it seemed that there was always something exciting or wonderful happening there.

In time I would learn I was welcome in that house whenever I came (which was as much as I could). No sooner would I ring the doorbell than Jack's dad, Dan Michaels, would swing open the door, pull me into a tango pose, and dance me into the living room. Family, friends, and neighbors were always crowded into the house telling stories and laughing while his mother milled around the living room with platters of homemade kielbasa and folded linen napkins. Cory, his mother, always wore a pretty, flowery apron and would stop to kiss me hello and hand me a cocktail. One of Jack's brothers, Colin, would be fixing a pitcher of martinis while his other brother Ted loudly elbowed his way behind the bar.

"The gin is supposed to clear the ice, snapper-head!" he'd insisted, pushing his brother out of the way and adding more liquor to the mixture.

Being an only child, it took me a while to get used to the good-natured teasing that went on between these siblings.

Toward the end of family evenings together we'd all stand around the piano while Jack's dad belted out his rendition of "Danny Boy."

"Ah, singin' about himself again, is he, boys?" Cory would laugh, coming in with a platter of her famous cream puffs made with hand-whipped cream. Mama Michaels wouldn't have dreamed of serving whipped cream from a can. I'd often find her in the kitchen with her trusty whisk and stainless steel bowl fresh out of the freezer. "An old trick." She'd wink while standing at the counter in her heels throwing quick tireless strokes to whip the sugar and cream until it became peaked and frothy. In Cory's eyes, her family, which, I was delighted to realize, included me, was well worth the extra effort.

I'd never seen a family like this before, one whose members actually enjoyed one another's company. It was foreign to me, a kind of closeness and comfort I'd never even suspected could exist this way.

At exactly seven o'clock each night a tiny spotlight clicked on automatically to illuminate a large canvas oil painting hanging over the fireplace. In it, dressed in their Sunday best, Dan and Cory were seated in wing-back chairs, their expressions proud but sweetly reflective, as if they understood the great good fortune life had bestowed upon them. Standing around them were their four boys in age order: Jack, Ted, Colin, and Sean.

I knew, though, that the family unit had been forever altered when Jack's youngest brother, Sean, drowned during a family vacation. "He was only eight," Jack had told me with a look on his face that had made me desperately want to comfort him, *though I knew no one could*. "I was sixteen. The oldest. I should have been able to protect my little brother."

Later I would find out that Jack had taken Sean's death so hard that he'd had to see a therapist for several years.

"That's when our Jack's eyes turned sad." His mother told me one night her cheeks flushed from wine.

Very often I would find myself staring into the cherry wood cabinet filled with mementos of little Sean. I would examine and reexamine the framed candid photos, the small handprint dipped in blue paint, and the lock of dirty blond hair. One of my favorite snapshots had been taken at the Jersey shore the summer before he died. In it, Sean was laughing. He was standing at the edge of the waves with zinc on his nose and freckles on his cheeks. All the Michaels boys had similar features, and it was eerie to see a mini version of Jack frozen in time, a little boy who would never grow up.

In my family, when someone died it became taboo to ever speak of them. In Jack's house they loved evoking memories and images of Sean, how he adored jokes and couldn't wait to share a funny story. But there was a reverence they showed as well, a sad, thoughtful expression when something particularly dear about him was mentioned. Whenever Sean's name was spoken in the presence of Jack's mother, she made the sign of the cross and twice touched her chest with her fist.

Jack's family was far more religious than mine. My parents never went to church and didn't follow any particular religion. A statue of Buddha might suddenly grace our fireplace mantel but generally came from some home décor catalogue and were intended to work with Mother's newest color scheme.

What Jack learned from his brother's death was this: Life is short. And you'd better enjoy each moment, because you never knew when someone you loved was going to be snatched away.

The night I became Gwen Michaels was warm, an autumn evening that we celebrated on board the *Skyline Princess* floating along the Hudson River. Jack and I had dated all through college, and after graduation we both secured jobs in Manhattan. At twenty-five, and after more than five years together, we figured that it was time to make it official. More than a hundred of our favorite people mingled around the three-tiered boat as a band supplied the soundtrack for the ever-changing backdrop of New York City. The George Washington Bridge and the Statue of Liberty seemed to float by as guests raised their champagne glasses in a toast to the bride and groom.

I remember sipping the golden liquid and then, as I brought the glass away from my lips, suddenly being aware of an inky darkness like a shadow spiraling up through the drink. It made me draw back, and for a moment I felt faint. A few feet away, I saw Cory looking at me, concern showing in her eyes. She leaned in and mouthed something like, "Are you all right?" The moment had passed, though, and I was able to smile back at her. I had dared to glance at my glass again, finding that it held only lovely, clear champagne after all.

But I knew that something had happened. Something had informed me that all was not well. And almost instinctively I understood that it had to do with my new mother-in-law.

Later, on the third and highest deck, Jack and I swayed to the first dance surrounded by guests and feeling like we were on a moving mountaintop. He scooped me up and spun me around the dance floor under a black sky studded with hundreds of stars. My bell-shaped dress swung from side to side as my veil caught the wind and lifted straight up into the air like a giant tulle funnel. I was afraid my shoes might fly off and flexed my feet to prevent that from happening. At the end of the song, in perfect time to the final strand of music, Jack kissed me as he lowered me into a deep dip. Cameras flashed, and this was the photo we included in our thank-you cards.

That night Jack carried me over the threshold of our hotel room and we collapsed on the sofa of the honeymoon suite. I kicked off my shoes and dug exactly sixty-four bobby pins out of my hair. After sharing a joint in the oversized tub, we made love on the heart-shaped bed and consumed a box of Mike-and-Ike candy. My hero, Jack, had ventured out to find a vending machine, because it was too late for room service and we were starving. Turns out to be true what they say about never getting a chance to eat at your own wedding.

Snuggled in the warmth of my new husband's chest, I joined him in making plans for the rest of our lives. We'd vowed to work hard and build up our client base so we could open our own shop. The plan was to become independently wealthy so we could be free, travel the world, and live life with arms wide open.

I figured we would follow in my parents' footsteps and become DINKs. To hell with a society that says that every married couple should have a child. I had no desire to procreate my own unknown gene pool. Unable to find my biological parents, I had no idea what

I would be passing on to a child, physically or psychologically. Who knew what kind of nut job my mother really was, or my father for that matter (an officer and a lounge singer, my ass). I didn't want to take any chances, and Jack understood that. We always told ourselves that if we ever became overwhelmed with the desire to become parents we would adopt. There were plenty of unwanted children in the world; I should know, because I was one of them.

"I'm gonna get my pilot's license," Jack vowed, adding with conviction, "by the time I'm forty."

"And I'm going to write a novel. Maybe a murder mystery." I snuggled closer, feeling safer and certainly more beloved than I had ever been. I had forgotten all about the dark liquid that had spiraled up in my champagne.

As a wedding gift, Jack's whole family chipped in to buy us a ten-day honeymoon to Italy, so the next morning we boarded a plane to Rome. Soon after arriving we were taking a long, scenic train ride through southern Italy. Arriving in Sorrento late at night, we checked into a hotel built into the side of a cliff and holed up in our suite for days. We lived on champagne and room service and split our time between the bed and the massive stone balcony hanging over the Tyrrhenian Sea.

On the third day we decided to venture out and hopped a ferry to the Isle of Capri. After docking we watched everyone on the crowded boat immediately turn right and follow the same path worn deep through the grass. Jack grinned mischievously and pulled me to the left so we could explore the island on our own. We stepped through long grass and trekked over gravelly paths, moving in the opposite direction from the others. I looked back and watched them following one another down the path like little lambs.

We later learned that, had we followed the others, we would have ended up in the middle of town. Shops, restaurants, and open markets there teemed with tourists, or so we heard later. Instead we struck out on our own and soon encountered a mountain with steep steps cut into its side. This stone staircase that seemingly led to nowhere offered the kind of challenge we both loved, and we decided to take it on. Climbing, we soon saw that, though it twisted around the mountain, it seemed to keep going up. There was no side path we could take off the steps, no place to rest unless we sat down on the unforgiving stone.

Drenched in sweat, we reached the top and were relieved and delighted to find two things: a breathtaking view of the ocean and a new, descending path that led to a white sandy beach far below.

Like two kids, we sped down the incline and, after skipping through sand, stripped down and dove into the thick, salty water. We stayed in the ocean all afternoon while our sweaty clothes dried in the sun on the empty beach. Meanwhile, I suppose our fellow travelers were on the other side of the mountain cramming together in shops overpaying for souvenirs and trinkets featuring the word *Capri*.

It was as if we knew this adventure symbolized our future, the way we would live our lives. The road less traveled, as it were.

We returned from our honeymoon on a Friday night and went back to work on Monday morning. A few months later, as I was taking a moment to water my woefully neglected spider plant, the phone rang in our downtown apartment. It was evening, a Thursday, and Jack had only just come in. I heard him call that he would get it in the bedroom where he had gone with his laptop and a glass of scotch.

A moment later I heard a crash and knew what had happened.

I knew.

I closed my eyes, not wanting to see the picture in my mind of the dark color that had spiraled up in my wedding champagne or Jack's mother's gentle expression of concern that evening as she leaned toward me.

A chill passed through me. *How had I known that the shadow was a sign that death was coming to Cory Michaels?*

In the bedroom, Jack stood leaning against the nightstand, the phone still in his hand. His glass lay shattered on the floor, its contents beading and pooling around his shoes.

Cory had died of a massive heart attack. She was found on the kitchen floor while a tray of croissants sat cooling on the counter alongside a glass of wine with her signature pink lipstick marks pressed into the rim.

A three-day Irish Catholic wake for Cory Michaels was followed by a high mass. I watched as people lined up on the steps outside the church in the cold rain, waiting to pay their respects. Coming from a nonreligious background and from parents who kept to themselves so well that they had few close friends, this was something of a revelation to me. I'd seen silent tributes like this made by crowds only in documentaries on the Kennedy family. Truth be told, Jack's family did remind me of the Kennedys in some ways, especially in how both families maintained their composure in the face of tragedy. Jack's brothers greeted each guest by name, accepting their words of condolence and steering them away from Dan, who sat and stared at the coffin with wide, unblinking eyes.

Thirteen days later, Dan passed away in his sleep. I'd read how that happened sometimes with couples who had been together for many years, and Jack's parents had known each other since they were little kids. I watched my husband struggle with the loss of his parents and wondered if Jack would love me as Dan loved Cory. *And what if I died first? Would he soon follow like Dan?*

The Michaels' row house, full of memories, was emptied and sold, and everything was divided up. For some reason I really wanted the picture of Sean from that Jersey shore outing, and nobody fought me on it. We also inherited Jack's Dad's piano. And in time I added "Danny Boy" to my finger-plucking piano repertoire.

With all these thoughts still crowding my mind, I poke through my beach bag and pull out a bottle of sunscreen, trying to distract myself. I squirt a glob into my hand and run it over my arms and legs. Jack, though, waves it away.

"You'll be sorry."

"I want to get some color on this trip. You know, an Irish tan."

"Oh right, I believe they call that sunburn." Tossing the bottle back into the bag, I pull out my cell and switch to camera mode.

"Show me those pearly whites!"

I snap a picture of him and then squirm across the towel, handing him the camera because his arms are longer. We tilt our heads together as he extends his arm to take the shot. Before tossing the cell phone back into the bag I instinctively switch to the e-mail icon. The error message appears, telling me there is no signal. *Old habits die hard, I guess.*

"Did we bring any snacks?" Jack sits up, apparently still hungry even after the sandwich at the bungalow. Come to think of it, I am getting hungry too. Eating and napping seem to be our top two priorities around here, a nice change of pace from back home where meetings and e-mails usually take precedence over food and sleep.

I pull out the bag of red pistachio nuts that I snagged from the stocked pantry, and Jack claps his hands in delight. We prop ourselves up on our elbows and crack open the salty nuts, washing them down with small cans of cranberry juice.

I use a half shell to jimmy open a particularly stubborn nut and use it to motion toward the empty restaurant. "So where do you think the pale lady is today?"

"Probably sleeping it off."

"It *is* very easy to sleep here." I give up on the stubborn nut and reach for an easier candidate. "But I've been having the craziest dreams."

"You've always had crazy dreams, Gwen." Jack picks up the stubborn nut and pops it right open.

"I probably loosened that for you, you know. So, what did *you* dream about last night?"

"You know I don't remember my dreams."

"Sure you do. Try."

He thinks, mocks me by putting a finger to his chin, and then gives up. "Nope. Sorry." After a beat, he looks toward the water. "Hey, let's go for a swim."

"We're supposed to wait an hour after eating."

"Pistachio nuts are not *eating*. Besides, that's an old wives' tale."

Dropping our sunglasses on the blanket we dust our hands to get rid of the salt, but the red dye from the nuts still stains the tips of our fingers. We head toward the waves running on the hot sand until we reach the water's edge.

Once our feet are wet, the sandy bottom dips dramatically, and we feel the strong undertow pull us out until before we know it we are waist-high in the ocean. The water is aqua blue and crystal clear, and I can see my brightly colored toenails gripping the ocean floor as tiny yellow fish swim curiously around my legs. The water is not cold at all; *it actually feels like we're in a giant bathtub.*

Jack dives into a wave and starts swimming, and I follow, struggling to keep up. It doesn't take long for us to venture out pretty far and, looking back at the shore, I am slightly alarmed by how small our blanket looks on the sand. We stop and tread water for a few minutes, trying to catch our breath.

As if a sudden wave has crashed around us, *which it hasn't*, we find ourselves surrounded by a swirl of foam and bubbles with shadowy figures in their midst.

"What the hell?" Jack spins around.

"It's the deer from last night!" I gape in amazement as they churn in a circle once around us and then speed past. The antlers of the males spray water as they cut through the waves and remind me of car tires hydroplaning on a wet highway. They're gone as quickly as they appeared, and the water around us becomes still and calm.

Jack motions toward the shore and starts backstroking toward it, his legs bending and pushing like a frog. This is the swim stroke he thinks moves you the fastest. I follow his lead, turning on my back and staring up at the sky as I force my arms and legs to keep moving. But I'm still thinking about the deer and wondering how they appeared so quickly and where they've vanished to, because they are nowhere in sight now.

The current has become even stronger now, and it is twice as hard to make any progress in this direction. The clouds float above us in strange shapes, and the sky begins to change colors in the late afternoon light. I try to swim faster, and although I can't see Jack I know he is near. *He would never leave me.* But my heart is beating hard as I struggle to reach the shore; everything feels fantastic and unreal, and I can't really believe I am here.

Back at the bungalow we take long showers and raid the refrigerator. I'm feeling glamorous in my long midnight-blue stain nightgown as we carry loaded plates back to the bedroom and listen to Ziggy Marley deep into the night. Soon I easily drift off to sleep.

I dream of the sand dunes again, but this time the sun is just about to set, that moment between absolute beauty and sudden darkness. The dream is so real I can feel the beach beneath me and curl my toes into the warmth of the sand.

A large male deer stands at the water's edge, his silhouette tall and majestic in the soft light. His antlers spiral up from his head in a great arc, and I count six long prongs on each horn that claw upward toward the darkening sky.

The buck stares at me with familiar eyes, and his large ears twitch as if listening to music. Small white spots surround his wet nose, and his strong muscular body is covered with fur that gives off the scent of toasted almonds. The white ring encircling his neck looks like the ermine trim of a king's robe. In fact, everything about the deer screams royalty. *He might as well have a crown poised between his giant antlers.* As I picture the crown, I notice the corners of the deer's mouth turn slightly upward as if he can see the crown too.

Wait a minute. Can this creature hear my thoughts?

Stepping closer to the mysterious animal I reach out to touch his silky coat. Again I'm struck by how he smells of almonds and honey as he bows his head encouragingly toward my outreached hand. At the moment I make contact he gently knocks into me, and with a quick flip and a lift I find myself straddling this regal deer the way I would a horse. With a surge of excitement I grab onto his long antlers, and then he is breaking into a sprint down the beach. My knuckles turn white from clutching his antlers so tightly, and I clamp my legs together in an effort to stay astride. The blue material of my nightgown is flapping around me; I can feel his soft fur tickling my bare legs.

My feet flop in rhythm against the sides of the blond deer as he gallops straight into the water, and the wind lifts my hair and whips curls wildly around my face. The deer dives powerfully into the waves, the water splashing all around us as I laugh and shriek with delight while bouncing wildly on his back. Suddenly what seems like a trap door snaps open beneath us and we are dropping below the surface. Instinctively, I clamp my mouth shut, puff out my cheeks, and hold my breath.

Underwater I squint into the swirling sand that fogs my vision and slowly make out the shape of a black doe moving gracefully toward us, her blue eyes flashing with excitement. Her pointed face is fixed in concentration, and her tapered ears are pinned back close to her head. She swims by casually, flicking her front hooves, and then two shapely human hands emerge from the tips of her forelegs. Two quick pony kicks later, painted toenails precede two delicate feet that unfold from the hooves of her back legs. Swathed in the white material of her long dress are sloping, feminine thighs, softly rounded knees, and contoured calves.

My eyes grow wide as they take in the next metamorphosis, and the doe's ears grow and reach down her back, evolving into long strands of thick black hair. High cheekbones sculpt themselves into delicate position under her elaborately made-up eyes. Her contoured lips are full and red now, offering a playful smile as she passes me in a splash of bubbles. It's Ruby, I know. It's the woman from my dream.

At the same time, I am so distracted by Ruby's transformation that I don't immediately notice what is happening just beneath me. When

I do look down, I realize that I'm clutching fistfuls of blond hair and straddling Sebastian! His eyes flash with amusement as I open my mouth in surprise.

Waking in the dark bungalow, I sit straight up in bed with a loud gasp like Uma Thurman receiving a shot of adrenaline in *Pulp Fiction*.

DAY III

The Grotto

"You okay?" Jack murmurs, his voice thick with sleep.

"Weird dream," I gasp, only half-convinced that I'm not still in it. Then I settle back down on the pillow and try to catch my breath while Jack falls asleep almost immediately. Obviously he's getting used to being woken up by my dreams, especially lately. His breathing returns to sleep mode, even and slow, while I wonder why I dreamed of Ruby and Sebastian again.

And more importantly, why were they morphing out of the shapes of deer?

Almost afraid to go back to sleep I toss around in bed for a few hours and, just as light creeps into the bedroom, I fall into a dreamless slumber.

Later as Jack and I share the coconut soap in the outdoor shower I try to stifle a yawn while he tells me about today's agenda. Again we managed to sleep late, and it's already after noon; *so much for watching the sunrise at any point during this vacation*. Jack tells me that he's arranged for a boat so we can explore the outskirts of the island, and I immediately start to plan my outfit.

"Boating is an essential skill," Jack's father used to say, pointing his finger and emphasizing every word. "Like the ability to swim."

When we first started dating, Jack signed me up for a boating class so I could obtain my boat license and feel comfortable at the helm. Jack and his family spent many vacations, before and after Sean's death, on the water. His little brother's drowning didn't dampen the Michaels family's love of the water; it just seemed to deepen their respect of its tremendous power.

I hear Jack banging around in the kitchen as I yank on my figure-flattering swimsuit, black of course. The suit feels like a spandex glove as I first squat into it and then shimmy and yank the unforgiving material up my torso. Squeezing my arms through the armholes without dislocating a shoulder proves to be a challenge. Once the power suit is in place I add a long black cover-up made of mesh, like a fishermen's net, with holes so small you can barely make out the suit of armor underneath. The long sleeves are slit up the side, draping down gracefully, so now I have black wings whenever I extend my arms.

Checking my reflection in the mirror, I decide that the suit is worth the struggle. "What day is this?" I call to Jack as I lace up my espadrilles, the smell of eggs drifting down the long hallway now.

"Day three," he answers in an official-sounding voice.

In the kitchen, he is standing at the cooktop monitoring two pans. Although we have much in common, Jack prefers scrambled eggs to my sunny-side-up. He is adding marjoram and vanilla to the scrambled pan, and I find myself silently thanking Cory for passing down her cooking skills to her boys. With only sons she had no daughters on whom to bestow her heirloom recipes. Cory had tried to teach me some of her favorite dishes; however, I proved to be an unworthy student. Jack is a much better cook than I'll ever be, and his perfect egg-making skills are just the tip of the iceberg. Taking four slices of bread from the fresh loaf on the counter, I pop them into the toaster.

We carry our food out to the deck and the familiar sounds of the ocean and the birds greet us and serve as accompaniment to our homemade brunch. Gentle breeze rustles through the trees above as I watch Jack eat with one hand and flip through the pages of his tiny notebook with the other.

Damn that notebook.

I keep forgetting to sneak a peek at the pages that I'm now convinced contain all the details of our itinerary. Part of me desperately wants to know what's coming next, but the other part doesn't want to spoil the surprise. Besides, I am getting used to the laid-back atmosphere of this island and not having to worry about every little detail of the day. And I especially like the complete isolation of the island and the fact that we have very little interaction with other people. By this point back home, I would have already mingled with dozens of people on the busy sidewalks, in the subway, at the gym, and especially at the office. And lately, these interactions with other people always carry the possibility of some unwanted vision inserting itself, usually accompanied by a powerful wave of second-hand emotions.

Since arriving on Cernunnos Island, though, I've only had to encounter the bartender and one other guest. I don't let myself think about the massage therapists, since to me they were no more than two pairs of feet. Then again, there have been those colorful people from my dreams, Jonah, Ruby, and Sebastian. But I've finally decided that these creatures and their haunting blue eyes are just that, fabrications of my vivid dreams. Perhaps I've been absorbing the energy of the island and conjuring up characters from local folklore. After all, since the accident, I've been much more tuned into that sort of thing.

Absentmindedly I stroke the scar over my collarbone and watch Jack flip through the pages of his notebook. Then I rise and walk toward him, sit on his lap, and wrap my black-winged arms around his neck. He readjusts my weight to accommodate his bad knee, calls me Stevie Nicks, and inquires about my tambourine.

"Hey!" Teasing me about my clothes is nothing new—Jack has always done that—but I still take a jab at his chest with mock surprise.

We're heading out of the bungalow and are only a few paces down the sandy path when Jack squints up at the sun. "Damn, I forgot my sunglasses. I'm gonna run back."

"Okay. I'll check on the boat." Actually I'm anxious about getting such a late start and burning through the daylight.

My espadrilles make soft padding sounds on the slatted boards of the pier as I pass several small boats and a two-seater kayak. Eyeing the long canoe-shaped-tube, I silently hope it's not the boat Jack had in mind for today's outing.

At the end of the pier is a small shack constructed of bamboo with a *Gone Boating* sign tacked to the side. From this angle it looks like the hut is empty, but I can't be sure. I am taking a step forward and peeking over the railing when the familiar sensation of dread starts bubbling up in the pit of my stomach. The hut is suspended over the water by tall thin stilts that remind me of the long skinny legs of the great blue heron, and I get a bit queasy. It's the same freaked-out feeling I get when walking over subway grates in New York City.

I take a deep breath and try to screw up the courage to march over to the hut. With one hand on the structure for balance, I slowly follow the curve around to the empty counter.

Empty except for two large white cats that look like albino lion cubs sprawled on either side of the counter. They're poised like bookends, complete twins of one another, mirror images. At first I mistake them for statues. But then one of them lets out a loud meow (bordering on a roar) and the other cat squints an amber eye at me before settling back down on its paws.

I slowly inch forward, approaching the cats cautiously. The closer I get the more sure I am. Yes, I've seen these animals before. These are the same creatures that were sleeping on my couch the other night. *But wait. Hadn't I chalked that up to a dream? But I'm not sleeping now. Am I?* Just when the internal debate starts heating up, the guy I remember as Jonah pops up from behind the counter, his unmistakable red curls bobbing once and then settling past his shoulders.

"*Shit!*" I spit out in surprise. Blinking, I search his face for some kind of recognition. But there is none. Opening and closing my mouth like a beached fish, I look around for Jack. Or anyone. But of course, I am alone. Just like the last time Jonah appeared to me.

I stick my fingernails into the palm of my hand, the equivalent of a pinch to see if I'm dreaming.

"Hola! So what can I do for you?" He leans forward casually, folding his arms across the counter, and I get another glimpse of that wrist tattoo.

"Have . . . we . . . ah, *met?*" He is wearing a nametag crookedly pinned to his T-shirt that reads *Jonah*, spelled just like it sounds.

"Don't think so." He shakes his floppy red curls from side to side. He appears to be wearing the same clothes, but he's added a bandana around his forehead, and sunglasses peek from the top of his black concert tee.

I keep looking back for Jack when one of the cats jumps down, skips over to me, and drops at my feet. As he stares up at me I take note of the fact that one of its eyes is amber, the other blue.

"Beautiful, huh?"

I can feel Jonah watching me but can't bring myself to meet his gaze.

"I've never seen a cat like this before." *Except in my dreams*, I add silently.

He smiles. "They're indigenous to this area, and they love the water. Some call this species *swimming cats*." He whispers the last two words the same way some people whisper the word *sex* or *drugs*.

"Does he have a name?"

"That there is Monty." He motions with his chin to the cat at my feet. "He's the oldest known male of his breed."

The feline stares up at me with an expansive face filled with expression. He doesn't look old; in fact, his face is open and curious like a small toddler, though his whiskers are long and wiry, indicating his age. I want to take a picture so I'll have something to show Jack in case these apparitions disappear the way I expect them to, so I fumble in my pineapple-shaped bag for my cell phone. Monty puffs out his chest as if posing for the photo and then turns and runs for the railing, diving into the water and landing with a loud splash. Next he's paddling around in a circle, showing off, and I expect that at any minute he'll be spouting water like a whale. Amazed, I inch toward the railing, my desire to get a better look dueling with my unrelenting fear of heights. Landing at a compromise, I stop a few feet from the edge, point the lens over the railing, and snap blindly at the water below.

Jonah chuckles to himself and says, "And this here is Cleo."

Cleo looks directly at me like a Sphinx statue that's come to life. Then she languidly stretches out her long legs, crossing them gracefully in front of her and daring me to ask about *her* age.

"Wow, her eyes are different colors too!"

Okay, that's one detail missing from my dreams. I don't remember the David Bowie eye color of the cats. But I do remember the intensity of Jonah's stare. Reluctantly I raise my eyes to meet his.

Yup, just as hypnotic as the other night. *Or is this the other night, and have I just dreamed all the other, intervening stuff?*

No, that can't be. We're outside here, and the sun is very bright. And Jonah's eyes, reflecting the sunlight, seem to emit a signal like the blue lights on an airway strip. I am suddenly certain that his eyes could be seen from great distances.

Quickly looking away, I try to figure out what to say next. I go for a casual tone, considering something like, "Hey, dude, were you in my bungalow the other night?"

But that doesn't seem like the way to go. Figuring that it might be a good idea to get the word "husband" into the conversation whenever encountering a strange man on an isolated island I say, "Um. My *husband* booked a boat for us today."

If he noticed it, he did a good job of ignoring it. "Awesome. It's such an amazing day for a boat ride. Michaels, right?"

"That's right." I look back again. This would be a perfect time for Jack to make his entrance. *How long did it take to retrieve a pair of sunglasses?*

Jonah drops his red curls back and closes his eyes, smiling and nodding as if consulting the birds. Then he says, "Take this one." He tosses me a key attached to a gold, circular keychain. "She's dying to get out and have some fun."

She? Missing the throw I watch the key clamor to the ground and bend carefully to retrieve it. The metal of the keychain is smooth and cool to the touch, and when I scoop it up a name comes to me, clear and concise: *Ruby.*

With the key firmly clutched in my hand, I turn on my heel, anxious to get going. Jonah and Cleo watch me leave, their unique eyes piercing my back as I hurry down the slotted pier. The sandy path begins here, and I step onto it, searching for Jack.

Turning to the left, I find the path bathed in sunlight. There are birds hopping in and out of a small puddle and, to the right, the dark nose of a deer pokes through the bushes in search of loose berries. A tap on my shoulder causes me to almost jump out of my skin.

Jack is standing behind me cleaning his sunglasses with the edge of his shirt. "How'd it go?"

"C'mere." Grabbing his forearm, I yank him toward the boat hut. "You gotta see something."

"Hey! What's up?"

Even though only a few minutes have passed, everything feels different as we approach the hut. There is an emptiness that I sense even before we reach the vacant counter.

No cats. No Jonah.

"*Hello?*" I call out. "They were just here."

"Who?" Jack straightens the *Gone Boating* sign.

I have to lean all the way across the counter to get a better look inside the dark shack. There's not even a loose pen or slip of paper anywhere on the floor. *And where are the keys for all the other boats?*

"Monty! Cleo!" I click my tongue like Jonah did that first night, calling the cats.

"Who the hell are Monty and Cleo?" Jack looks around, confused.

"These big white cats." I raise my hands wide like a fisherman exaggerating the size of his catch. "They were sitting on this counter."

"A couple of cats rented you a boat?"

"No, this guy named Jonah was here, and he had two cats." Scanning the area, I continue to babble. "And then one of the cats jumped into the water . . ."

"Cats hate water, babe."

"Not these cats. These are *swimming cats*." I whisper the last two words the same way Jonah did.

Jack eyes me with concern. "Hey G, you feeling okay?"

I start out slowly, my voice low. "Look, the other night I dreamed about this guy named Jonah. Well, I *thought* it was a dream, but now I'm not so sure. Anyway, the same guy from my dream . . ." I pause. *Is my husband going to think I'm crazy?* "He, uh, just gave me this key." I dangle it in front of Jack, and he pulls his eyebrows together, confused. "Or maybe I'm just having a sun stroke or something." My hand flies to my face and I cover my eyes, trying hard not to cry.

"All right, calm down, calm down." Jack pats the air, sensing my building hysteria.

We stand together in silence for a few minutes, Jack giving me time to collect myself. Actually, I'm trying to work through the details. If Jonah really *did* rent me this boat, then that would mean he's a real live person. And here I am with this key, which Jack can see. Which means that this Jonah guy was in our bungalow the other night and it was not a dream.

Then again, maybe Jonah is just an extension of an intuitive vision. But these recent experiences are nothing like the usual visions. I've never interacted with the people in my intuitions, never had a conversation or retrieved an object like this key.

I curl my fingers around the metal key and try to feel the energy. Nothing. Of course I can't summon the visions to appear; they just drop in whenever they want like an inconsiderate neighbor. Opening my fingers and only half expecting it to still be there, I flip the key in the sunlight looking for some kind of marking.

"I've got no idea which boat this key belongs to," I admit, breaking the awkward silence between Jack and me.

"We'll figure it out." Jack rubs his head, and I get the feeling that he's been running through a few choice scenarios of his own. "Let's get going, I think a boat ride will do us both good." He slides on his sunglasses, covering his eyes and hiding his concerned expression.

Walking up and down the pier, we read the names of the boats out loud, "*Irish Wake. Marilyn. Island Time.*"

Then I see it. *Ruby.* It's a pretty little motorboat.

"This is it." I point.

Jack doesn't question me but just jumps into the small boat and slides the key into the ignition. A perfect fit. He tinkers with the outboard engine, and it sputters to life while I untie the ropes and help him navigate out of the slip.

Soon there is nothing but ocean surrounding us as I squint back at the tiny mound of Cernunnos Island, still freaked out by the Jonah meeting. In an effort to shake it off, I pull my hair loose as if that might expel the obsessive thoughts. The strong wind picks up the long strands, blowing curls wildly around my head, and the breeze tickles the nape of my neck. Though it feels great now, I know it will be a bitch to comb out later. Taking another deep breath, I pull the salty air deep into my lungs.

Yes, this was a good idea.

The seagulls swoop overhead in the cloudless blue sky, and the sun reflects off the water like tiny stars. There are no boats in sight as we cruise further and further out. A short time later, Jack points to a giant rock formation and we start heading toward it.

"Looks like a grotto!" he shouts over the wind.

The tall, jagged rocks with scalloped edges jut out of the water and reach for the sky in a high arc that climb several stories high. As we approach the stone structure, two separate arches become distinct, but they are almost identical in height and shape. From far away it looks like one big structure. But up close we can distinguish how the two distinct arches rising out of the water are like the pillars of a great bridge. I am half expecting Jack to start spewing out facts about the grotto, but he is busy maneuvering the boat through the center arch and avoiding the long, icicle-shaped rocks protruding from the low ceiling.

The moment we enter the grotto I immediately feel the atmosphere change. The air is slightly cooler, and although the waves continue to crash on the outside walls, *here* the water is still and calm. Inside the sea cave we are encircled by a combination of natural rock formations along with what appears to be man-made statues cut deep into the stone. In the sphere of sunlight spiraling through the circular dome I can see tapestry-style paintings illuminated on some of the smoother walls, and Jack points out the water markings on the paintings indicating the various sea levels recorded over time. He speculates that the grotto must have spent some time underwater and was probably only accessible at certain times of the year.

"We are lucky to have come upon it when we did." He gazes up at a mural of white-capped mountains and colorful flowers poking through the thick blanket of snow.

I am only half listening, distracted by all the nooks and crannies visible through the shadows as we float by the enchanted hallways cut into the multicolored coral. I inexplicably feel the urge to bow my head in front of a huge granite statue of a black winged horse. Pitching forward and leaning over the side of the boat, I pierce the glassy surface with my fingers and trail my hand through the clear blue water. *It feels warmly inviting.*

"Let's drop anchor and take a swim," Jack suggests.

I lift my palm letting the water run through my fingers. "You must have read my mind."

Moments later we are holding hands at the bow of *Ruby* and preparing to jump where it looks deep enough for a plunge. "One . . . two . . . *three.*"

My toes break the surface, and at the last moment I open my mouth to say something. But everything quickly closes in around me and I sink like a stone into the thick, salty water of the grotto. The whole scene reminds me of the time we spent in Capri, and I try to remember the name of that grotto as I kick my legs and rise upward.

Jack and I pop up at the same time, and something whizzes past me. Under the water I feel something brush the back of my legs. Stretching my arms wide, I swat at my calves and search for the source of the movement. I scan the water, trying to see below the surface. There, pulling themselves onto the shore and shaking the seawater from their long, white fur, are the two cats.

Slapping the water to get Jack's attention, I whisper, "It's Monty and Cleo!"

"Those? On the shore?" He scrunches up his face.

I'm annoyed at the face but thrilled that he can actually see the cats. "Remember? I told you how Monty jumped over the railing?"

"You think he swam all the way out here?"

I ignore the question and continue to tread water, watching the cats climb the grotto walls and settle into little ledges built into the coral. Cleo vies for the higher seat but Monty defends his perch, and I smile as they exchange harmless paw slaps before Cleo resigns herself to the lower level. The two of them preen themselves on their coral thrones, their purring echoing through the grotto like soft staccato wind chimes.

Carefully climbing out of the water and onto the shore we slowly approach the cats. "Monty . . . *psst, psst.*" I hold out my hand, palm up, in what I believe to be a nonthreatening gesture.

Monty stops mid-lick to stare at me in disbelief. His face seems to be asking what the hell I am doing all the way out here.

I might ask you the same question, little fella.

He cocks his head to the side, and I do the same, prompted by the way he seems to be listening for something. Then I hear it: the sound of running water like a distant waterfall. Feeling drawn to the sound, I begin to make my way along a series of ramps, aware of Jack's hesitation behind me but unable to stop myself. I feel like a tiny magnet being drawn to a much larger magnet, completely outranked and unable to resist.

On the third ramp, voices begin to take shape, and I realize that it's not water at all but words, as if someone whispering, or more than one person whispering. It actually sounds like arguing. I try to make sense of the hushed phrases, something like, ". . . Won't . . . not . . . without him . . ."

Jack grabs my arm. "Let's get out of here." His eyes are wide.

I'm sure he's right but feel compelled to keep moving toward the whispered voices. From where I stand, I can almost see into the entrance of what looks like a hallway carved into stone. It's unmistakably where the urgent sounds are coming from. We enter the hall and I lean forward, and there, on the far wall, are two elongated silhouettes, one of a woman and the other a man. The woman is shaking her long hair from side to side, and the man, tall and lean, is holding up one ringed finger as if trying to make a point.

I press my body flat against the wall and jerk my thumb toward the two, indicating that Jack should take a look for himself. He leans over, and I watch his body tense and then relax.

"This must be where they hang out. Those deer we saw." Relief is visible on his face.

Deer? What about the man and women arguing? Confused, I take another look. Sure enough, where human shadows had been visible just a moment ago, now the dark outlines are of two deer shuffling their hooves in the sand. I shake my head, losing confidence in my judgment of what my eyes just saw and thinking, *Have the deer been the source of the sounds all along?* But the shuffling is creating a different, much softer sound than the urgent whispering I'd heard.

I don't stick around to see what will happen next. Instead I turn on my heel and head back to the ramps faster than I've moved in a long time, glad that Jack is running too.

"What's up?" He pants, catching up to me. "They're just deer!"

I don't answer. I'm not ready.

We pass Monty, who is creeping along the next ramp with Cleo balancing on the railing above him like a gymnast. They stop when they see us and watch us pass as we continue onto the beach and into the water, making our way back to the boat in a matter of minutes. I'm on deck in seconds, grabbing my towel and breathing hard.

"Hey, come on, tell me why we had to tear back here so fast," Jack insists, on deck himself now.

"Just get the engine started, could you?"

He's dripping water but seems to understand that I'm borderline hysterical and wordlessly starts the engine. As it chugs into action, he turns us around and then grabs his own towel, eyes me nervously, and asks again why I took off back there.

I wrap myself in my towel, feeling cold, and sit down on the side bench. "I . . . guess I just got spooked."

But truth be told, I am starting to get worried. Maybe we should consider finding a doctor to run some tests. There might be complications that appear months after a head trauma, hallucinations and confusion and such. But I bite my lower lip before stupidly blurting that thought out. *Where the hell would we find a specialist out here?*

Despite my best efforts, though, I am unable to stop myself from looking back. On the beach are two deer, and they're watching our departure with great interest. Then, without warning, the doe takes off, up the side of the grotto like a dog chasing a train. She reaches the top with a series of zigzag patterns and stands cinematically on the highest arch as I watch her slowly shrink and then disappear from sight.

I close my eyes and pray that Jack has seen the same thing. But he probably hasn't, because he's not looking back. Daring to peek over at him, I see that he's staring straight ahead, sitting at the wheel, steering the boat away from the grotto and, I hope, back to reality.

When we reach the safety of the bungalow I make a beeline for the wine rack. Although it was still light out I justify that it is happy hour somewhere and I could use a drink. After I struggle with the bottle for a few moments, Jack takes it from my shaky hands and eases out the cork. I find the goblets sitting upside down on a towel, washed and left out to dry along with our breakfast dishes, *courtesy of the cleaning lady,* I suppose.

"The wildlife on this island is supposed to be insane—but cats and deer in a grotto?" Jack shakes his head. "Gotta say, I wasn't expecting that."

Yeah, me either.

Carrying the filled goblet back to the bedroom, I take a long swallow before balancing the glass on the dresser and peeling off my wet bathing suit. Exchanging the wet suit for the comfort of the soft brown robe I empty the goblet in two more swallows. When I hang my bathing suit in the bathroom I glance toward the old-fashioned tub. I'm tempted to run a bath, to do whatever I can to distract myself from thinking, but then my stomach makes a gurgling sound.

First food, then a hot bath, and then a long talk.

We find a room-service menu tucked into a kitchen drawer, and I place an order via an automated system, ordering small pizzas smothered in mushrooms, peppers, onions, olives, and fresh basil. *My mind may be gone*, I joke to myself, *but my appetite is still healthy.* The computerized voice politely explains that our food will be set up on the deck within the next thirty minutes.

So far, Jack hasn't commented again about my erratic behavior in the grotto, and I'm grateful. He's good that way, never pressing when he thinks I'm upset. But he does think I'm upset. I can tell by the worried look on his face and the way he keeps stealing glances at me.

While waiting for the food to arrive Jack goes into the bathroom and I refill my goblet and position myself behind the long curtains, half expecting to see Roscoe bring the tray but prepared for pretty much anything after today's adventure in the grotto.

"Hey, did you bring Q-tips?" Jack's voice calls from the bathroom.

"Yeah, yeah, in the toiletry bag." I don't risk taking my eyes from the window.

"I looked there."

"They're with the cotton balls."

After a minute. "Nope, not there."

Getting irritated now I enunciate each word. "In the plastic zippy thing."

I pause, during which I hope desperately he finds them.

"No luck."

Letting out a loud sigh, I reluctantly give up my lookout position and grudgingly go to find the Q-tips, which I know I will in two seconds. I do just that and hand them to Jack, knowing that my lips are tight with irritation and hoping he just won't notice. Then I quickly check myself in the bathroom mirror just to make sure I haven't myself turned into something like maybe a deer.

When I return I find the table covered with platters of food and a vase of tall fresh flowers. Is that possible? I wonder. That fast? *How long was I gone, two minutes? Three?* I pull open the door, step onto the deck, and stare down the steps, but the dark path is still and quiet.

"Oh, good, the food's here." Jack startles me, and I flinch in surprise. "Man, you're awfully jumpy today," he mumbles.

We eat in silence, and when the wine is gone we open another bottle, killing the rest of the afternoon with food and drink until the deck glows with the setting sun. Soon we are blanketed in darkness and I rise from the table feeling a little unsteady, the goblet almost slipping from my hand. "I'm gonna run a bath," I announce, slurring slightly. After a quick beat, I add, "Why don't you join me?"

Practically stumbling into the bathroom and toward the antique claw-foot tub, I turn the dial to full blast and shake crystallized sea salt and foaming bubble bath into the warm water like I am seasoning a pot of broth. Clicking off the overhead light, I opt instead for candlelight. Since the accident it seems that bright light bothers my eyes. I'd assumed it was because the light I saw after the accident was so incredibly bright it affected my sensitivity to all artificial light. But light sensitivity was the least of my problems. Being in a car accident that left me dead for nine minutes had other side effects as well.

It had been raining all that day. The roads were covered with wet leaves. It was late autumn and we were on our way home from a particularly cranky client in Connecticut. I was driving the Jeep Cherokee. Most of the time we utilized mass transit, but it was easier to drive to clients outside the city, so Jack and I paid a small fortune to keep the Jeep in a garage for those trips out. I'd been plowing through the wet, slippery leaves and was relieved to finally merge onto the parkway, anxious to get home before it got too dark.

Music cranked through the speakers, and we instinctively started singing along with the boys of Lynyrd Skynyrd. We loved blasting music in the car and singing at the top of our lungs. Jack with his wonderful singing voice was able to transition from Frank Sinatra to Axel Rose with very little effort. He was a natural, just like his dad. He leaned forward in the passenger seat and twisted up the volume knob, and we sang in our best fake twangs about a man named Curtis Lowe.

Suddenly the inside of the car was flooded with light and the deafening sound of screeching tires and crunching metal. I can't even remember if I screamed.

The car flipped several times, end over end, and it felt like my head was rattling around like a coin in a wooden box. The airbags exploded, blinding us from the chaos, and my body filled with panic and hot pain. The flipping finally stopped, but the radio continued to play as Curtis earned the status of the finest picker to ever play the blues.

I felt my heartbeat slow and eventually stop and then the sensation of being lifted as if I had stepped onto a high-speed elevator and hit the button for the top floor. Like a snake lifting out of its shed skin, I felt myself rising, happy to leave the shell of my battered body behind. I drifted through the air and came to a stop about a mile above the wreckage. Sirens blared from far away, but I just looked down, observing the scene from high above.

Time seemed to stop, not go faster or slower; it just seems that time no longer existed.

Looking down, I saw that the Jeep was upside down on a lower embankment just below the overpass and the tires were still spinning. Through the cracked windshield I could see airbags splattered with blood and two lifeless bodies in the front seat dangling like rag dolls from their seat belts. I felt a detachment to the battered bodies below and wondered what lay above. I was turning over in midair, weightless and buoyant, as if I were floating in a giant pool of water.

Above me was a vortex of light so bright it reminded me of the sun; yet it didn't hurt my eyes to look directly at it. I was overwhelmed by a sense of peace and love and felt myself drawn to the brilliant light. I could see deeply into it and could identify a breakdown of millions of tiny little lights making up the larger whole.

I was able to see a full 360 degrees around me without turning my head, and there was a low buzz of mental chatter from the floating jellyfish around me. These orbs of light were connected by a gold ribbon as delicate as a piece of thread, and the strongest, most powerful presence hovered just over my left shoulder.

I remember two figures drifting toward me, their slender, transparent bodies seemingly formed of glass with spidery veins. These figures were tall (ten feet tall at least); their faces with no features were only a pool of brilliant light. Near their chests, intense light and this radiating glow gave them the illusion of wings. I felt myself smile, identifying what must be angels and understanding all the winged interpretations that people have given throughout time.

I sensed a distinct personality in each of the glowing creatures, and my eyes widened as I began to realize that they were communicating with me silently. This is surely telepathy, I told myself as their words took shape inside my mind.

It is not your time.

You need to go back.

No! Why? I don't want to go back, I want to stay here! I was arguing like a stubborn child, only half-amazed that I could do this telepathy thing myself, when I sensed the familiar tone of Jack's deceased parents, or at least the *spirits* of Cory and Dan. A smaller shape peeked out from around Cory's legs, and even though I never met him, I was certain this was Jack's little brother, Sean. He, too, appeared as a faceless figure, but just as his parents had done, his young and innocent personality emanated from the light.

He murmured simply, in a voice I did not hear but felt, *Jack needs you.*

That's when I realized that Jack was not with me.

It hadn't occurred to me that he wouldn't be here, or at least nearby, hovering over the accident. That he wouldn't be sharing this peaceful place with me, given that we had crashed together and there we were below, both of us hanging lifeless and released from our heavy, living bodies. But when I scanned the area, I neither saw nor sensed Jack, not as I knew him and not in any of the floating orbs. I redirected my focus back down to the accident below.

I remember seeing smoke coming from the Jeep. Two police cars, a fire truck, and an ambulance had arrived on the scene, and emergency workers were scrambling with fire hoses and jaws-of-life while trying to keep bystanders at bay. I hovered over the accumulating traffic, watching it snake along the highway for miles as rubberneckers tried to get a glimpse of our bodies being strapped to the stretchers. EMTs quickly and efficiently loaded the ambulance and made their way through the sea of cars, red lights blaring.

Hovering just under the roof of the ambulance, I continued to survey the scene but still felt detached, wrapped in the warmth and peace emanating from the light above.

Jack was already conscious, and he was screaming my name as he tried to rise from his stretcher. One EMT was attempting to subdue him while the other worked tirelessly on my lifeless body. He was performing CPR and then applying the electric paddles, cursing and sweating with the effort.

"Come on, lady! Don't go anywhere. Come on now!"

The heart monitor kept flat-lining, and Jack became more frantic and inconsolable. They eventually gave him a needle to sedate him, and when he fell back onto the stretcher I felt his anger and sorrow flood into me.

That's when I felt myself falling. I was being sent back to my body, or I had chosen to go back. I couldn't really tell which but somehow knew that I should enter through the soles of my feet. As I felt my way back into the assaulted shell of my body, it felt empty and cold like a house left vacant for too long.

The first thing I felt was pain. Then blackness.

Hospital. Fear. Whispering. Confusion. Needles. Dizziness.

When I finally did open my eyes I was aware of the beeping of machines and the unmistakable, sterile, antiseptic smell of a hospital. A nurse with deep lines in her forehead and crow's feet around her mouth (like a long-term smoker) came to the edge of the bed and peered down at me with weary eyes. I tried to speak but quickly realized that I had a tube down my throat. I must have looked panicked, because she placed her hand on my arm, apparently in an effort to calm me.

The moment she touched my skin I had a vision of this woman in her work scrubs standing in a storage closet taking long, deep swallows from a battered *Charlie's Angels* thermos. The vision was accompanied by a sudden sense of despair, and when she removed her hand the vision melted away.

However the feeling of sadness lingered.

When she adjusted my IV another vision came into focus: the same woman at a liquor store buying a bottle of booze with quarters and dimes. This time the emotion was shame.

She snatched her hand away, and the vision crumbled like sprinkles shaken off a giant bakery cookie. Stepping back, she eyed me suspiciously. It was as if she could tell I was able to pick up her emotions, the ones closest to the surface. It wasn't as if I were doing it on purpose. I had always been tuned into my sixth sense, maybe slightly more intuitive than most, *but nothing like this.*

With a raised eyebrow the nurse reached for my chart, flipped the metal cover, and clanged it loudly against the railings of the bed. With the metal-to-metal connection I was able to receive a rundown of my injuries as if she were reading aloud, *multiple cracked ribs, broken collarbone, internal bleeding, punctured lung . . .*

Yikes, no wonder it hurt when I tried to move. As she scanned the chart, the narrative continued, *head trauma, brain dead for nine minutes . . .*

She stopped suddenly, looked at me with an expression I couldn't decode, and scurried from the room like a gecko chasing a scrap of bread. As her footsteps faded so did the overwhelming, desperate need I had for a drink.

As soon as I was able to speak I recounted the story of my out-of-body experience, picking it up in midsentence as if I had been repeating it over and over in my head like a phone number I didn't want to forget. The words spilled from my lips like a waterfall, and I was sure the nurse with the drinking problem would find it fascinating, even enlightening, but instead she just cocked her head to the side and uttered one word.

"Diablo."

Devil. I recognized the word from when Valentina used it to describe the cranky old man at the produce stand, the one with the reddish goatee. This nurse thought I saw the devil or communicated with some kind of demon. Or maybe she thought I was in fact the devil. But there was nothing sinister about the beings I had seen, although the nurse's adverse reaction did make me consider (for the first time but certainly not the last) that I might want to keep the whole thing to myself.

Jack had suffered a mild concussion and a knee injury and was released from the hospital after only a few days. After that he came to sit with me every night during visiting hours, and one night I mustered up the courage to tell him about my experience. If anyone was going to believe me, it was going to be Jack.

I probably should have waited until we got home so we could have had more privacy, as the whole time I kept stealing glancing at the door, waiting for a nurse to come bustling in, and I could hear murmurs of conversations from patients and visitors courtesy of the paper-thin walls. But I already felt like too much time had gone by, and the memories were fading with each passing minute. *If I didn't get it out now I never would.*

Jack listened, shifted in his chair and opened and closed his mouth a few times like he might interrupt me. When I finally finished I was actually out of breath and Jack just patted my hand. "The brain is a funny thing. Can play tricks on you during extreme stress." It was like he was comforting a small child describing a monster she saw under her bed.

Hurt and angry by his reaction, I got defensive. "I'm not the only person to describe a bright light, you know?"

"True, but scientists seem to think that's simply due to lack of air to the brain." He bobbed his head up and down, reassuring the little girl that there were no such things as monsters.

I struggled to sit up and continued to argue my point, trying to find words to describe the surreal things I had seen, especially Jack's parents and little Sean. I thought for sure I could convince Jack when I told him that part, but especially when I told him that part, he seemed to shut down. I had no idea we had such different viewpoints on life after death. Since we had so much in common in this life I never considered that we could be on such opposite sides of the fence about what happens in the next.

Then he dropped the Catholic guilt on me.

"Sean and my parents are in heaven." And added with a touch of distaste, "Not floating orbs of light."

Unable to keep the irritation out of my voice, I challenged him. "What did you see after the accident?"

After considering for a moment he leaned forward. "Nothing. Nada. I remember singing in the car and then waking in the hospital."

"You don't remember what happened in the ambulance?"

"Don't tell me *you* do?"

"Yes, I was hovering. I saw the EMT give you a sedative because I kept flat-lining and you were freaking out."

Jack stared at me for a long moment, his eyes dark and unreadable. Then he let out a sigh and said, "Look, I believe that you believe it."

Wow. The equivalent of "Let's agree to disagree." I was confused but not motivated to push the subject any further. So we left it at that.

Yet I still found myself desperate to find others who might have had similar experiences and begged Jack to bring a laptop to the hospital. One night he reluctantly tucked the thin, silver laptop into the waistband of his Dockers and covered it loosely with his shirt. After closing the curtain around my bed, he pulled it out with triumph.

"Does it have Internet access?" I blurted out, immediately feeling ungrateful.

"You're not thinking of checking your e-mail are you?"

Furthest thing from my mind actually. "No, I just miss YouTube." I lied, although I did kind of miss YouTube.

He pulled a wireless modem from his back pocket, and I sat up quickly to retrieve it before wincing in pain and regretting the effort.

"Easy, I'll set it up for you." He slipped it into the drawer of my nightstand. "There. Don't get caught with this thing."

After the nurse's last rounds, I'd pull the laptop from its hiding place and perform countless web searches on near-death experiences. These queries always rendered all kinds of strange results that motivated me to clear my browser's history after each session. I quickly learned there was much controversy around near-death experiences, or NDE, and skeptics (like Jack) insist that it's just a chemical reaction when the brain is deprived of air for a certain period of time. However, many survivors describe having an out-of-body experience and communicating with deceased loved ones.

Check and check.

But it was the aftereffects of an NDE that I was most interested in reading about. Some survivors described enhanced intuition and feeling as if they were now using their whole brain instead of just a portion of it. Some studies actually confirmed that NDE survivors had more activity in the frontal lobe. Many of the survivors came back with a distinct sense of purpose, and others described psychic abilities that seemed to develop after the experience. One survivor came back with the ability to read auras, one woman was able to reconstruct crime scenes, and another guy just claimed to be more patient with his kids.

In the months following the accident I kept waiting to go back to my old self but would feel myself flinch whenever a pedestrian on the street brushed up against me and unwittingly shared intimate details about themselves. Pulling the door handle of Starbucks practically knocked me to my knees with all the energy on the metal knob and the blinding flurry of images and emotions it generated. I had hoped that this super sensitivity would diminish over time, but in reality it only seemed to be getting stronger.

Jack nudges the bathroom door open with his foot, his arms filled with another bottle of wine, my cell phone, and the portable speakers. I choose a playlist of classical music, and quiet string melodies echo off the marble walls as we drop our robes and climb into the steaming bath. We slosh through the bubbles, settle at opposite ends of the tub, and drift in the coconut-scented water. We are quiet for a long time, commenting only on the music or the temperature of the water, just like at dinner when we spoke only of the wine and food. It's what most therapists would call avoidance, and I was becoming an expert at it.

But eventually I ease into the topic. Jack saw the deer in the grotto, but I saw so much more.

When I tell him what I saw he shakes his head doubtfully. "You've always had a vivid imagination, Gwen. And ever since the accident . . ." He trails off.

I try to keep the irritation out of my voice as I explain, "My newfound ability is not a free-for-all to explain away all the weirdness in the world. And it doesn't work like that. I've never dreamed of a person and then actually met them!"

"Well, you didn't exactly meet this Sebastian guy."

"That's what I'm trying to tell you. I think that was him in the grotto."

"And what about the other person you saw?"

"Ruby," I say the name softly.

"Like the boat?" He shakes his damp hair. "Okay. Well, you haven't met her either."

"I'm telling you the man and woman in the grotto were Sebastian and Ruby from my dreams."

"But I didn't see a man and woman. I saw two deer."

"This is where it gets weird." I kick the water, staring at my toe.

"Oh, okay, tell me the weird part." He can't seem to keep the sarcasm from his voice, and I feel my irritation growing.

"Forget it." I place my hands on either side of the tub and start to heave myself up, thinking once again that I should learn to keep these things to myself. *No more sharing on this little vacation.*

"C'mon, tell me." His eyes soften, and I spot the familiar crinkle at the corners.

He seems to be sincere, and I've been pussy footing around long enough, so I settle back down and take a deep breath. "Well, I think the deer you saw were . . ."

"Yeah?" He rolls his hand, motioning for me to continue.

"Sebastian and Ruby . . . but just . . . in their deer form." I say each word carefully and brace myself for his reaction.

"What!" He slaps the water in surprise, and one foamy bubble leaps up and lands on his forehead.

I press on. "Once I dreamed of them in their human form, and once I dreamed of them . . . well . . . morphing from the shape of a deer." I twist a chunk of wet hair around my finger and grimace.

Jack starts to laugh and then stops himself. "Gwen, you do realize how crazy that sounds?"

I nod silently.

"Okay, let's Google the phrase 'humans morphing into deer' and see what the experts say." He reaches for my phone near the tub and switches to a browser.

"There's no Internet here, smarty-pants." Annoyed now, I grab for the phone and in my haste accidently switch to camera mode. The first picture appears in the glowing LCD panel, an aerial shot of the island, the one I took from the plane that first day. I hadn't noticed that the water surrounding the island looked inky, as if something large and powerful hovered just beneath the surface. With a drunken intensity I start flipping through the other pictures, curious to see what else was captured by my camera's eye.

Next photo. The trio of deer on the beach that first night, the graceful black doe in the center surrounded by two powerful bucks.

Next photo. Twelve sets of glowing blue eyes staring expectantly from the dark beach.

Next few photos. Blurry, streaks of the great blue heron crossing the path looking more than ever like a blue winged fairy.

Next photo. Jack on the beach with his movie star sunglasses; then the headshot of the two of us. *It's hard to believe that was only yesterday.*

As the next photo materializes on the tiny screen my mouth falls open. Instead of a beautiful white cat at my feet, an old man sits cross-legged on the pier, his legs curled into the lotus position. His thick white hair flows over his shoulders and comingles with his long beard and mustache. He smiles up at me with two different-colored eyes. One eye is amber, and the other eye is pale blue.

Seeing my stunned expression, Jack reaches for the phone as it slides from my fingers and lands in the tub with a soft splash.

DAY IV:

Myths and Legends

Flying from the bathroom and down the long hallway I leave a trail of soapy footprints on the thick carpet behind me. Jack follows into the living room, waving the wet phone at the back of my head.

"What? What is it?" He catches me and spins me around, "What did you see on this thing?" He shakes the phone, and it spritzes water like a wet dog emerging from a lake.

I perch on the edge of the couch and pick invisible lint from my robe while confessing. "I saw an old man," I say, mumbling the last two words.

"An old what?"

"An old man! I thought I took a picture of a cat, but no, it was an old man." His face is confused, eyebrows drawn together. But he doesn't say anything, so I continue. "Through the lens, I swear I saw a big white cat."

Jack lowers his head and continues tinkering with the cell phone. He wraps it tightly in a towel and presses down firmly to soak up the excess water.

"You're telling me that you snapped a picture of a cat." He stops squeezing and looks up at me. "And it came out like an old man?"

I meet his eyes and nod slowly.

"Come on!"

"You didn't see it!"

He can tell I'm pissed and tries to backpedal. "Look, maybe it was a blotch on the lens. Like one of those ghost photos. You know the floating orb thing."

"It wasn't a blotch, Jack. And it wasn't a ghost and it wasn't a fucking orb." Frustrated, I slap my thighs. "It was an old guy disguised as a cat. I don't know. How would you explain it?"

After considering for a moment he suggests, "Faulty technology, schmootz on the lens. I'm sure we could find hundreds of plausible explanations on the Internet."

Once again I need to remind him that he took me to a place with no Internet.

"Wow, you hosed this thing." Tipping the phone back and forth we see water appear at every seam. "It won't turn on."

"It just needs to dry out. I've dropped it in water before."

"Have you?" He wraps it in a paper towel.

"Sure, when I first got it. I dropped it in the toilet."

"Well, that explains it! You can't expect the camera to work properly after dropping it in the toilet!"

Still feeling the effects of the wine, I let myself slip from the arm of the couch and melt into the soft cushions below. Cupping my hands over my face I try to think. I must be picking up the energy from this island. And if that's the case, then I need to learn more about this mystical place. *But how can I research anything without the Internet?* I feel trapped like in the hospital after the car accident, desperate for information. But this time Jack can't sneak me a laptop, and not even Jack can find a wireless card strong enough to pick up a signal on this isolated island.

"I wish we could Google this Cernunnos creature." I mumble, "Maybe he was known to turn into a cat under the full moon or something."

Jack stops fiddling with the phone and flicks his palm toward the ceiling, "Well, maybe the answer lies in these old books."

I figure he's probably kidding but ask him to give me a boost anyway.

Minutes later I am balanced on Jack's shoulders scanning the high shelves and trying to comprehend the words etched into the spines of the old books. Some are written in foreign languages, and others are simply untitled. One book catches my eye, a long purple volume lying sideways on top of the others. Angling my head to the right I mouth the words on the spine.

"*Cervus Veneficus.*"

"Greek, maybe?" Jack calls from beneath me, slightly out of breath.

There appears to have been a subtitle once, but the letters are all but worn away. I can tell that Jack is getting fed up with this chicken-fight pose, so I grab the book by the edges and carefully pull it toward me. It releases a cloud of dust that blows into my face and makes me cough in surprise. The book is heavier than I expected, and I have to slide my other hand under the weight of it, careful not to tweak my back in the process. As I balance the oversized book with both hands, Jack lowers me to the ground.

Sitting on the couch with the big purple book perched on my thighs, I trail my finger over the raised gold swirls and my heart begins to quicken. Carefully I untie the thin gold ribbon that binds the volume together and flip open the cover with a soft whisper. A brilliantly colored painting consumes the inside flap and sweeps across the first page in various shades of reds, blues, purples, and greens. The paint still looks wet with layers of thick gooey swirls like a da Vinci painting. Bold strokes of paint illuminate an island blanketed with trees, flowers, waterfalls, and an elaborate white castle cut high into the cliffs. The looming grottos reach for the clouds; the scalloped edges of the island are surrounded by sandy beaches, so white they glisten like pearls. Pink dolphins and cats of white and black dance in the water's edge, and I lift the book close to my face to examine the drawing more closely. Studying each white cat before moving to the next I don't see anything out of the ordinary. No old men swimming in the surf here.

Written over the drawing are four words in an elaborate script: *Playground of the Gods.*

The book is oversized like an artist's sketchpad, and the pages are thick and yellowed like old parchment paper. I figure that it's hundreds of years old, and Jack suggests that it might be made of vellum or lamb skin, said to last forever. The black ink is faded in spots, but the same flamboyant calligraphy appears on every page, a distinct swirl to the S's that remains present throughout the entire book, which leads me to believe that the whole thing was written by the same person. Some of the text is fading, but the artwork blooms with vivid colors like well-preserved hieroglyphics. Detailed sketches often accompany large passages, a mixture of elaborate paintings in full color. Some are simple charcoal line sketches, and others are just curious doodles that occupy many of the margins.

Not sure where to begin, I turn to the table of contents, an unexplained anticipation growing inside of me like a puff of smoke swirling around my lower abdomen. The book is separated into two parts. The first is titled "Myths quod legends" and the second "Alica quod ritus." Jack taps the word *Cernunnos* in the table of contents, and I jump in surprise and then turn to the designated page. We start reading aloud at the same time, *"Cernunnos was a horned god who reflected the seasons of the year in an annual cycle of life, death, and rebirth."*

"Let's read to ourselves." Jack suggests.

Some cultures honor Cernunnos in his ancient Celto-European form as the guardian of the forests, the defender of the animal tribes, the source of the deep forest wisdom, and the masculine half of creative energy.

There are three drawings of Cernunnos. Earlier I had suspected that he might have haunted the island in the shape of a cat, but there is nothing feline about the man who dominates the next three pages. Cernunnos is tall and muscular, always shown with an archer's bow. His face is partially hidden in shadow, and in one drawing he appears with long brown hair spilling from the dark hood of his robe and sapphire blue eyes staring off the page with a fixed intensity so powerful that it makes me squirm and look away. In the next drawing he is mostly human with one small exception—tall deer antlers poke through his long, shaggy hair and spiral up toward the sky. The last drawing is the most bizarre, as he appears with the upper body of a man and the lower body of a deer. He is reclining against a tree, his flesh melding with the twisted roots and branches, and it's hard to tell where the tree ends and he begins.

Before the oceans were blue, Cernunnos cherished Playground of the Gods and spent much of his time on this island known as PoG. It was a place where great blue herons walked the beaches, purple-winged dragonflies buzzed through the air, and pink dolphins danced in the surf. It was home to many magical creatures, including a coven of shapeshifters known as the deer witch. At this point Jack pulls away and says, "I'm going to bed."

"No! Look at this drawing!" I show him the next page, but he just glances down and starts to walk away.

"Wait, listen. *Upon each blue moon the whole island would sink suddenly and violently into the sea. With the explosive power of a reverse volcano the island would settle onto the ocean floor and the rolling hills and forests would remain dormant under the sea, fully intact like the city of Atlantis, awaiting the next blue moon."*

"Okay, that's enough."

"Are you kidding me? This stuff is fascinating." Tucking a loose curl behind my ear I scan the next page. "It feels so familiar."

"It sounds like that crap you hear on those paranormal podcasts you listen to. That's why it's familiar to you—probably got stuck in your subconscious. I'm going to bed," Jack repeats. "Are you coming?"

Not able to draw my eyes from the page, I shake my head. I hear him trudge down the hallway with a loud sigh. Then I hear him drain the tub, flush the toilet, and run the water. Finally the light goes out in the bedroom, and I stretch out on the couch and arrange one of the velvet pillows under my head. Resting the big purple book on my stomach, even though it means portions of text will be blocked by my boobs, I stay up for hours reading and rereading the myths and legends of the deer witch.

A deer witch is a shape shifter who possesses the power to transform into the shape of a deer. These immortal creatures have heightened abilities in all six senses present in both human and deer form. The eyes of a deer witch are usually blue or green like the ocean, and they will often cover their eyes when trying to hide their true nature. These creatures have the ability to breathe under water, communicate via telepathy, and visit others in the dream realm. Each cervus veneficus is also gifted with an elemental power of aer, flamma, terra, or aqua.

Aqua. I could probably use some aqua after all that wine I guzzled last night. Don't they say you should drink one glass of water for every glass of alcohol to avoid a hangover? I try to figure out just how many glasses of wine I consumed but give up, telling myself flatly that if I don't get up and drink some water now I'll regret it in the morning.

But I can't peel myself off the couch or interrupt the rich history described in the book, which dates back to the sixteenth century. Legends of the deer witch actually date back much further than that, but the mid-1500s is when someone apparently started writing it all down.

Thumbing through a section on genealogy I stop at a pyramid titled *Hierarchy of the Covens.* At the very top of the triangle are the words *Ancient Times: Coven of Cernunnos,* and then I scan from top to bottom, reading the labels on the other five slices:

16ᵗʰ Century: (Air)—Renaissance—Coven of Light
17ᵗʰ Century: (Water)—Magic—Coven of Rain
18ᵗʰ Century: (Fire)—War—Coven of the Dark Moon
19ᵗʰ Century: (Earth)—Knowledge—Coven of Trees
20ᵗʰ Century: (Fire)—Rebellion—Coven of Flames

There are chunks of text that are candid and intimate like a diary, while others are written like an official record of people and events. Carefully turning the thick, worn pages, I stop at full-page sketch titled *Ruby and the twins.* A woman with long dark hair sits on a throne and gazes down at two babies nestled in her lap, the infants curled together like seahorses sleeping peacefully.

The caption reads, *Ruby was goddess of the woodland governing wild animals, the tides of the ocean, and the phases of the moon.*

Oak groves and night-blooming jasmine were especially sacred to her, and the borders of the pages were decorated with sketches of what I assumed were these, her favored plants.

Ruby spent summers on Playground of the Gods, and Cernunnos quickly became infatuated with her. But the shadow creatures, who some say had great influence over Cernunnos, disliked Ruby and forbid the union. Legend suggests that Cernunnos defied the shadow creatures and seduced Ruby under a full moon, and the forbidden lovers reunited at every blue moon for centuries after that.

Cernunnos and Ruby would sit together, high in the forests, draped in the moonlight and cupped in the branches of her favorite tree. Cernunnos's fingers would tickle down her spine while he constructed a flawless braid, and he would often slip the king's ring from his own index finger to secure the ends of her long silky black hair.

On one particular blue moon the rumble from the earth seemed more sudden and violent than any of the others that had come before. The trees around Cernunnos and Ruby were sucked back into the earth, and the couple was jostled through the air and separated by the commotion of the sinking island. Ruby was enveloped by a powerful wave and swept underwater where she was pursued by a band of shadow creatures who took the shape of the blue-ringed octopus and chased her for miles, some say in an effort to disorient her from the site of the rising.

Ruby eventually washed ashore on a sister island where her belly swelled with twin baby boys. One was born with golden hair, and the other's was fiery red. Some claim that Cernunnos was a figment of Ruby's imagination, while others insist that he was real.

It was said that a serpent was sent to the crib of the sleeping twins in an effort to destroy the random strain of royal bloodline. But the blond one set the slithering creature on fire with a flick of his tiny wrist, and Ruby pulled the boys from the burning crib in the dead of night. The three of them were forced to go into hiding for centuries after that. The trio is said to only make themselves visible in the physical world during the blue moon when they are searching for PoG.

I am relieved to find these stories of Ruby, Sebastian and Jonah, as they seem to confirm the idea that I am picking up the energy of the island's folklore. It's like this book is the key to making sense of my recent dreams, both daytime and nighttime dreams.

With glassy, voyeuristic eyes I am compelled to turn the old pages and watch the boys grow from scrappy little boys to interesting young men where they seem to stop aging somewhere in their mid-twenties. *That must be nice.* I smile as I examine a drawing of a young boy, his face framed with dark red curls, his eyes wide and excited, and his knees bent in a deep crouch. He is pitched forward on a cliff high above the ocean, and there are small figures in the water below, their mouths shaped into tiny Os. The book documents the various attempts made by Ruby and the twins to raise PoG and reunite with their magical father. But from what I can tell PoG has not risen and Cernunnos has not been seen since that last night when they sat together in the trees.

Listening for a moment I identify Jack's snoring from the back of the bungalow and yawn so wide it makes my jaw pop. Shifting my position on the couch I flip the pages forward to read about the other members as they join the coven. I can practically hear the text being read aloud like an audio book, one where the narrator does *all* the voices.

Bridget Ellington, born 1542, rarely went anywhere without her two sisters Emma and Lucy. Their father was a wool merchant, and their mother died during childbirth with baby Lucy. Bridget and Emma were sixteen months apart and much closer in personality and demeanor than their lone-wolf little sister.

All three Ellington girls were interesting looking and musical, and they attended school with Katherine Howard, who was often invited to the court of King Henry the Eighth. Katherine would extend the invitation to the Ellington sisters, and they would spend the day rolling each other's hair and brushing their skin with rouge in the hopes of catching the eye of a viscount, a marquis, or a duke. Their schoolmate ended up catching the grand prize, the eye of the king himself. But after Queen Katherine's tragic demise, the invitations to the king's court abruptly ceased. Lord Ellington, a man strapped with three unmarried daughters, grew older and wearier with each passing year.

It was Lucy who finally attracted the attention of a wealthy baron who agreed to take her as a mistress. He lavished her with luxurious gifts, including a trip, for her and her sisters, to a private island, a popular European getaway known at this time as "Facula Isle."

The Ellington sisters were on the private island only a short time before noticing that their already long hair seemed to grow even longer in just a few days. And after arriving on the island Bridget immediately fell ill, sleeping for days, eating erratically and speaking obsessively of an angel, a beautiful blond angel visiting her in her dreams.

Emma and Lucy thought she was mad with fever until they found themselves roused in the middle of the night and persuaded to participate in a full-moon ritual. In a trance Bridget coaxed her sisters to the beach, where the beautiful blond angel appeared from the flames of the bonfire. He filled a glass bowl with water and placed it under the light of the full moon, and Bridget, Emma, and Lucy all took turns passing the bowl and drinking the moon water.

Bridget had agreed to become a changeling with one condition, that her sisters be allowed to transform with her. Apparently it was very common for gene carriers to run in siblings, especially sisters. The next few pages are dedicated to sketches and drawings of the three girls in various poses, dressed in elaborate costumes throughout the centuries.

Turning to the next section I find myself staring into the blue eyes of a majestic black stallion and am reminded of the statue in the grotto. *Was this the same creature?* Long feathery wings extend from the animal's back, and his hoofs barely touch the ground as he gallops across the page. The passage accompanying the drawing is dedicated to a shapeshifter known as Gabriel who occupied the island during the seventeenth century.

Gabriel was from a magical bloodline, some say the same ancestry as Morgana le Fey, and he too studied with the great Merlin. It was believed that Gabriel could assume many shapes, though he preferred a black winged horse or that of a deep brown buck.

Gabriel sailed the Spanish seas for many years before discovering an isolated patch of land that drew him through the waves like the pull of a beautiful woman. The island was abandoned at this point, the exclusive getaway forced to close its doors after war and disease spread throughout Europe, but Gabriel was drawn to the raw magic embedded in the earth and trickling through the ground water. Gabriel settled on the island for many years, where he perfected his magical skills, performing countless rituals and infusing the land and surrounding waters with his intense magical essence.

After becoming a changeling, Lucy still frequented the island in her deer form as it was the only place that still germinated her favorite kind of berry. One morning she was indulging in the sweetness of the iridescent purple fruit when she spotted Gabriel bathing in the sea. His olive skin, coal-black beard, and devilish good looks reminded her of her wealthy lover, the only thing she missed from her former life. Morphing into human form, she approached Gabriel one night while he slept on the beach, her elemental fire indisputably drawn to his elemental water and they made love in the sand that night and the next, (guess it's true what they say about opposites attracting). *On the third night Lucy prepared a full-moon ritual to initiate Gabriel into the coven.*

Feeling myself slip into sleep a few times I catch myself mid-head-roll and shake it off, determined to keep reading. I have the distinct feeling there is much to learn, and in an effort to save time, I skim through the section on war (never one to watch the military channel) and jump ahead to the stories describing the Coven of Trees.

Willow was the only daughter of the tribal chieftain and adored by her tribe even though they loathed and feared her powerful father. When Willow's husband was killed in battle she was left alone to care for their young son, Choovio. After a planned coup, members of the tribe scalped the chief in his sleep while his daughter and her son lay untouched in the next tent. Even though Willow was grateful she and Choovio were spared, she could not accept the savagery of a tribe that slaughtered her father in the dark of night and then named a new chief in the morning sun.

Willow and Choovio alienated themselves from the tribe, spending most of their time in the woods and preferring the company of animals. They were spiritual people connected to Mother Earth and spent their days nurturing the trees and flowers. It was during this time that Willow planted a variety of flora, breeding rare mixtures of seedlings with the rich magical soil left from the days of Gabriel. She would toss together sunflower seeds and rose petals to create tall decadent rose flowers for Choovio to sit under. The thick stem of a sunflower supported giant yellow roses that would dangle over the small boy and provide shade.

One afternoon Jonah found himself dream walking and stumbled upon Willow and Choovio napping under a cherry-magnolia tree. There is a painting of Jonah brushing back a curtain of pink and white magnolia flowers dangling from the long branches of a cherry blossom tree. The tree limbs conceal Willow and Choovio in a bubble of flowers that remind me of the big sparkly dress of Glenda the good witch. *Jonah was immediately attracted to the strong elemental powers of earth inherent in both Willow and the boy, something the coven desperately needed during this period in its history.*

Rubbing my forehead I can't believe I'm actually considering these tall tales to be true. There is probably a core message running through each one, based on some version of the truth, but these stories have surely been elaborated and enhanced over the years of oral storytelling before they were committed to print. Some of them read like fairy tales, but the alcohol and lack of sleep are making me punchy and apparently impressionable, especially since many of the characters bear a striking resemblance to people from my recent dreams.

And thinking back, I have always been open to the idea of the spiritual world.

I remember that on my fifteenth birthday, Valentina gave me a Ouija board, not the Parker Brothers edition sold at most Wal-Mart stores but rather an ancient-looking board wrapped in a sheer silk pouch. Intrigued, I remember running my fingers over the flat board marked with letters, numbers, and other symbols. In the upper left hand corner was an elaborate carving of a sun to represent YES and in the other corner a crescent moon for NO. The wood was well worn but had been polished shiny and smooth. I unwrapped the planchette from an old lace handkerchief and examined the small heart-shaped piece of wood used to spell out messages from the spirits.

I decided to use my Ouija board to summon the ghost of Anne Frank.

After reading *The Diary of Anne Frank* for the umpteenth time I had questions about what it was like to be holed up in cramped quarters with Peter, the boy she had a crush on. I'm sure there are better ghosts to summon and more important questions to ask, but I was a teenage girl and my hormones were kicking in like crazy.

In need of more bodies to properly conduct a séance I invited two sisters, Tabitha and Madison, who lived on my block. They looked exactly like Barbie dolls with straight blond hair and small perfect white teeth that reminded me of Chiclets. We all got along okay, but when the two sisters fought, well, it made me grateful I was an only child.

We waited for a rainy night and huddled in my bedroom studying the underbelly of the board, where the instructions were carved deep into the wood. Madison covered the lamps with scarves, and Tabitha lit white candles and placed them around the room. Sitting cross-legged on the floor with the Ouija board balanced between our knees, we gently placed our fingertips on the indicator and waited.

Closing my eyes and taking a deep breath I asked, "Is there anyone here with us tonight?"

The room was still.

Rain continued to pound against the windows, and almost on cue there was a bolt of lightning. The flash of light bled through my closed eyelids, and I popped one eye open to examine the room. Tabitha was chewing on her lip or a wad of gum, and everything was draped in shadows and flickering in the candlelight. The clap of thunder that inevitably followed still made me jump in surprise. Taking another deep breath I become aware of the smell of perfume-masked cigarette smoke that always seemed to cling to the blond sisters.

I tried to breathe through my mouth. "We respectfully request the spirit of Anne Frank to join us."

The room was quiet.

A muffled sound at the edge of my consciousness crystallized into a suppressed giggle. It was coming from one of the sisters, but I couldn't tell which one. *It didn't matter.* The giggle grew in volume and intensity, and it wasn't long before the other one started giggling too.

I immediately regretted my choice of séance partners.

This was never going to work with these two laughing hyenas. Deciding to have a little fun with them, I pushed the planchette to the right. Both Madison and Tabitha jumped with surprise, and two sets of scared eyes snapped open as one of them mouthed the words, "Holy Shit!"

I pursed my lips in a "Shhhhh!" and then whispered, "Is this the spirit of Anne Frank?"

After a dramatic pause I nudged the indicator to the YES position and then snapped it back to the center. At first I was just fooling around, but then an eerie silence enveloped the room. The hairs on the back of my neck snapped to attention like long strands of grass reaching for the sun. Madison's chin dropped to her chest as if she was sleeping, but Tabitha's eyes were open wide, transfixed on the board.

I continued to quietly ask questions, no longer forcing the movement but just watching with awe as the heart-shaped piece of wood glided across the board in swift strokes. At one point I ask outright if Anne ever had sex with Peter, and the glass peephole circled around the sun several times before settling on the word YES.

Ah-ha! I knew it!

When I asked why the steamy details weren't included in the diary a burst of energy shot through the wooden indicator and quickly zipped between the O and T several times. Then a gust of wind blew open the window, and the white curtains flapped wildly into the room like a surrender flag. We all flinched in surprise, letting the Ouija board crash to the floor with a loud crack.

"I need a cigarette," Madison breathed, and Tabitha nodded in agreement.

Months later I found an article at the library about Anne Frank's father and how he admitted to deleting certain entries from the diary before it was published. Apparently he had been advised by the publishers that his daughter's candor about her emerging sexuality might offend certain conservatives and suggested cuts.

I flashed back to that night with the Ouija board. I thought about the indicator whipping between the O and the T and decided that Anne must have been trying to spell out her father's name, *Otto.*

Back on Cernunnos Island, the living room is slowly lightening in the early morning sun, and it turns out that I was wrong about never seeing the sunrise during this vacation. But I'm not exactly watching the sun rise; I'm awkwardly arranged on the couch, dog-tired and unable, *or unwilling*, to put the big purple book down. The nagging feeling in the pit of my stomach propels me to keep going like a tiny poking finger telling me that I'm missing something obvious. Still not exactly sure what I'm looking for, I flip back to the beginning.

One of the very first drawings is labeled *The Majores*, and I examine the full-page sketch with eyes that complain about opening every time I blink. I am afraid to fall asleep, fearing that somehow my time with this book is limited. I can almost feel the sands of time drifting through the hourglass and settling at the bottom in an uneven pile.

I force my eyes to examine a drawing which is so old the edges of the page are curled and browning. A stately looking man and woman smile at each other in profile. The elderly man's half face shows one bushy white eyebrow as he gazes at a woman who has presence like Princess Diana but is gracefully older. The woman's face is upturned and smiling, and she has deep dimples and a long white braid coiled like a snake on top of her head. The black charcoal drawing is etched deep into the page, and the eyes provide the only color; the visible eye for the woman is blue, and the man's eye is golden amber.

My eyes are so tired that they go in and out of focus and the unusual headshot blurs into the face of a cat, staring at me with two different-colored eyes.

It hits me like a shot of static electricity. *This man is Monty.* The old man on the pier with the mismatched eyes—I've found him. I think about getting up to see if my phone dried out so I could compare this image to the photo I captured but can't rally the strength to move off the couch.

Then I try to decide if it's good news or bad news to be visited by the Elders. Part of me is afraid it might be like getting called to the principal's office, but the other part thinks it might be like finding a golden ticket in my Willy Wonka chocolate bar.

I continue to read. *Monty and Cleo harnessed the gift of sight as well as the ability to assume many shapes, though they preferred the form of a white cat as it was recognized and respected throughout the spirit world. The Elders serve as spirit guides to some of the oldest, most powerful covens. They were extremely loyal to their subjects and Monty and Cleo have been serving Ruby since she was a little girl.*

Not sure which was heavier, the book or my eyelids, I rub my eyes, dry and itchy from dehydration, and the lids finally snap shut like the shade on a peep-show window. The last thing I remember is the big purple book falling across my face as I finally lose the fight to my body's insistent need for sleep.

When I open my eyes, Sebastian is smiling down at me. He is sliding his sunglasses down his nose and peering over the rim with those brilliant blue eyes.

I jump up and knock a couch cushion to the floor.

"Are you a Virgo?" He smiles.

"What?"

"You sort of remind me of Choovio, and he's a Virgo."

I look around for the book and realize that Sebastian is holding it casually with one hand like it weighed nothing, even though it took me both hands to lift it. "No, I'm a Gemini."

He freezes, his eyes fixed on me intently. "Air," he whispers, barely opening his mouth.

"Do you need air?" I ask, misunderstanding. *How could a deer witch need air?* I just read that they could breathe under water. He continues staring, his appearance frozen and unchanging like his expression was carved into the face of a statue.

"Your element could be air." He says each word slowly and then closes his eyes and speaks in a velvety whisper, "Is that your sun sign or moon sign?"

"No idea."

"Quickly, tell me the date and time of your birth." He takes a step toward me and claps his hands together.

"I was adopted," I say by way of explanation, but when he cocks his head to the side in a questioning manner, I add, "Never saw my birth certificate."

"This is all very interesting." Sebastian runs his forefinger and thumb down either side of his chin. "The position of the moon is actually more revealing than the sun. Something the humans can't seem to get through their thick skulls."

"I celebrate my birthday on May 24, but you never know how accurate gypsies are about birth records."

"Gypsies?" He raises one eyebrow, something I have never been able to do but always wanted to.

"That's right." I nod. "Some hack detective told me I came from a band of gypsies traveling throughout Europe."

Sebastian's hypnotic eyes shine like large drops of water on his flawless white skin. "Well, that could mean ..." He stops himself, shakes his blond mane, and begins again. "Well, my dear, you've been reading the part about myths and legends all night."

Thinking he might be impressed but feeling like there might be a "however" coming, I say, "So?"

"Don't you think it's time to move on to *Alica quod ritus?*"

"Yeah, right, except, I don't know what that means."

He flashes a crooked smile. "I guess your Latin is a little rusty." Then he adds, "It's only one of the oldest languages in the world."

"Never paid much attention to Latin in school; didn't think I'd have much use for it." I shrug.

"*Alica quod ritus* means spells and rituals." He waves the book in the air, making the pages fly by as if he were hanging it out a car window. "You have been studying the past all night, my dear. It's time to look forward." He stops on a particular page and reads aloud with a grand accent, enunciating each syllable. "Thou shalt collect a large bouquet of night-blooming jasmine, a rare flower with a lush, erotic fragrance that only blooms in the light of the full moon."

"Gwen, are you still up?" Jack calls from the bedroom, piercing the dream like an echo in a canyon.

Sebastian arranges his sunglasses on his perfect face and takes a slight bow. "I must bid you adieu."

His long blond hair spills over his shoulders as he bends forward. When he rises he drops the book casually on the cocktail table, where it lands with a soft thump. I watch as he moves nimbly toward the fireplace, bending and folding his long limbs under the stone mantel before disappearing up the chimney.

Waking with a start, I find myself on the couch and push myself up to a sitting position with a grunt. I squint into the sun and groan. *Oh man, I must have stayed up all night*, because instead of pale light streaming through the thin curtains, this looks like full morning sun. I try to scrutinize the strange clock on the mantel, the one with three rings around the standard clock face. I remember reading something in the book about a similar clock used to track the solar holidays and map them to the phases of the sun and moon. I believe the name of the clock was the Ginsberg, *no*, the Gansberg clock. I rub my head and try to remember the details of my most recent dream or dreams—certainly there was more than one. I look around for the book to see if that too was part of the illusion. But sure enough I find the old book lying in the center of the cocktail table open to a drawing of a large white flower with a long crooked stem. Leaning forward to examine the exposed page, I feel my stomach lurch and painfully try to remember how much wine I drank.

Let's see—I remember opening a bottle when we returned from the grotto. Then we had another bottle with dinner, so that's two. No wait. I suddenly flash back to Jack kicking open the bathroom door with his foot because his hands were full with, among other things, a third bottle of wine. *Good God, that's three.* And there are only two of us! That means we drank more than a bottle each. Not to mention the fact that alcohol seemed to have a greater effect here like drinking cocktails at high altitudes.

"Ohhhffff."

I feel terrible. My stomach is sour, and there is a vise around my forehead connected to a sharp pain behind my right eye. Rubbing my scalp, I hoist myself off the couch and stand at the kitchen counter carefully swallowing a large glass of water. Once I'm sure it will stay down I stumble through the morning-lit bungalow and climb into the big bed, sliding in next to Jack, listening to his breathing, slow and steady. I'm careful not to wake him, because I'm in no mood for another day of fun-filled activities. *I don't care what the little notebook says; no zip-lining or snorkeling for me today.* I just want to sleep. More accurately, I need to sleep. I feel exhausted, drained, and achy. Curling up in the warm bed and molding my body against Jack I breathe in his warm familiar scent and close my eyes, waiting for sleep.

But sleep won't come.

My mind is overflowing with fantastical characters and stories, and I can't tell which ones I dreamt and which ones I read about in the big purple book. It's like trying to piece together snippets of a drunken conversation, perfectly clear at the time but in the morning only bits and pieces come back in no particular order. And it seems that physical distance from the book is making it difficult to remember any of the stories inside. I consider getting up and sneaking the book back into bed with me, reading it under the covers with a flashlight like an adolescent boy with a *Playboy* magazine. But my body protests any idea that does not include sleep, and soon my mind concedes.

My conscious mind, that is.

My subconscious mind snaps right back to the fantasy world of PoG as if I could articulate in my sleep what I could not comprehend while awake.

In my dream I am seated at a long table surrounded by eight wing-backed chairs. I get the impression that we are in a castle. The room is circular, and the walls are made of stone with floor-to-ceiling mirrors lining the back partition. Monty and Cleo are dressed in white hooded robes, and as they pass through the center of the room the mirrors show their reflection as snow-white cats.

Candlelight dances across the familiar faces at the table. Ruby is seated at the head, her back tall and straight, and directly across from her a throne-like chair sits empty. On either side of Ruby are Sebastian and Jonah, the two heirs to the empty throne, and they are both smiling those magnetic smiles that could charm the lock off any girl's chastity belt.

Jack is at my side, and Willow, the earth witch, pours wine for us. Gabriel, the magical creature who could assume the shape of a winged horse, takes the seat across from me after removing his jacket and hanging it on the back of the chair. Music and snippets of conversation drift from the next room. I keep trying to catch Jack's eye, but he is engrossed with something, staring down at his lap like he is reading a newspaper or texting under the table. Gabriel is directly across from me, a Cheshire cat smile playing on his dark features.

I wonder what the hell they are all smiling about.

When I open my mouth to ask a small bubble escapes from my lips. I clamp my mouth shut, confused, and try again. This time a stream of bubbles sprays from my lips and the bubbles drift upward, rising lazily through the thick air. I drop my head back to watch the bubbles ascend slowly upward and realize that we are under water, so far down, there is no light visible from the surface. If it weren't for the candles we would literally be in the dark depths of the sea.

Just then three girls burst through the double doors with a charged energy and spill into the room with an air of excitement. They wear heavy corseted dresses prompting images of medieval times and hold long sticks attached to feathered masks, which they use to cover their faces. Sebastian rises and greets the masked girls and then leads them to a velvet couch before positioning himself behind an artist's easel. Two of the girls have dark hair spilling past the edge of their masks, and they arrange themselves on either side of the third girl, who has ringlets of soft blond curls. Sebastian makes a production of blending several colors in the center of his palette, and then with wild strokes he begins outlining the girl's figures on the oversized canvas. Every now and then he waves his paintbrush high in the air, demanding that they be still. Small bubbles escape through the holes of their masks as if they are giggling.

Gabriel suddenly appears at the back of my chair and lends his arm in an old-fashioned gesture, the ruffled sleeves of his ivory shirt draping over his dark graceful hand. I instinctively look for the tattoo and am rewarded with the edges of the familiar oval peeking out from under the old-fashioned stitching of his shirt. Jack is still occupied with the reading material under the table, so I stand and join Gabriel. Instead of leading me toward the party, he leads me through the French doors and out into an expansive garden with rows of tall colorful trees. Willow is close behind, dancing around us like an erratic butterfly, picking flowers from the trees and collecting them in the material of her upturned dress. She focuses on one flower in particular, gesturing and pointing with conviction at the tightly closed bud, but I am too distracted by the circular tattoo on the inside of her left wrist to take notice of the flower.

What was the meaning of these tattoos, and why were they so similar and yet distinctly different?

Gabriel whistles with his fingers, and six large stallions appear, three black and three white. They come galloping through the garden breathing bubbles from their snouts, and the horses stand in anticipation before us, alternating, black, white, black, white, black, and white. The music from the unobserved party floats through the open doors, a string quartet playing louder now, and the horses perform a series of synchronized movements while Willow leaps from one horse to the next, balancing effortlessly on their backs. The horses wear straps of feathers and sequins that remind me of circus animals. At the end of the dance, they bow their heads as Willow weaves flowers into their manes, darker flowers for the white horses and lighter shades for the black-haired stallions.

I turn toward Jack who is framed in the archway, his face showing confusion, then fear, and finally understanding. He opens his mouth to say something, but only bubbles escape from his trembling lips.

Waking in the big bed it takes me a full minute to remember where I am. First I imagine that I am in our downtown apartment or asleep on the couch in the office, and for another odd moment I think I might still be in the hospital. Slowly acclimating myself to the bedroom of the bungalow, I grope the sheets for Jack and find him gone. I try to lift my head but feel *terrible*, groggy and weak. So I flop down and fall back asleep almost immediately.

When I wake again Jack is gone. *Or maybe he never returned.* I rub my eyes, trying to determine how long I've been asleep, finally deciding that I must have been sleeping for hours. But I don't feel the least bit rested. Instead I feel sluggish and achy like I'm trying to fight off the flu.

After a few false starts I eventually drag myself out of bed and move like a bear coming out of lengthy hibernation. I stumble into the bathroom to pop two aspirin, brush my teeth, and wash my face. As I run a wet comb through my hair, it seems to take longer to drag the teeth through the curls, and I wonder if my hair had grown in the past few days. Yanking my mane into a side ponytail and pulling on a pair of yoga pants and an oversized top, I venture from the bedroom in search of Jack.

Stopping in the kitchen to drink another glass of water, I wonder again if I could be coming down with something but convince myself it's just a nasty hangover. There is no sign of Jack anywhere in the kitchen, no dishes in the sink, no note on the counter.

As I pass through the living room I notice the crumpled pillows on the couch and memories from last night begin to take shape, emerging from the sludge that is my brain today. The pillows, usually pristine and arranged, are now in disarray as if to accommodate a sleeper, and I vaguely remember staying up all night and reading strange stories from an old purple book.

I glance around, suddenly anxious to continue my reading but don't see the book anywhere in the living room. After a sideways glance at the fireplace, where an odd memory tickles the edges of my mind, I glance at the unusual clock and then scan the high shelves, thinking that maybe Jack put it back. But I don't see the large volume sitting with the others. *Where the hell is it? More important, where the hell is Jack?* I stop and listen for a moment. The bungalow feels empty.

Panic starts to seep in as I walk through the rooms again, a little faster this time, calling Jack's name. Just as I am trying to figure out how to call 911 on an island with no phones, I hear Jack calling from the deck, "Out here!"

Releasing a loud sigh of relief, I follow his voice out onto the deck and find my husband seated comfortably in one of the lounge chairs watching the sun slowly drop in the sky.

"Hey you." He smiles when he sees me, but the smile does not reach his eyes.

"I slept through the whole day?" Surprised to see the sun dropping in the sky, I have no idea what time it is, and even though I figure it's late in the day, sunset is not my first guess. I scratch my head and try to comprehend how I wasted a whole day of vacation.

"That's what you get for staying up all night with that book." I sense an edge to his words.

Speaking of the book . . . I am tempted to ask him about it but decide it's not the right time. "It was an interesting read, from what I can remember." I fish for information and try to get a handle on his mood.

"I'm not sure filling your head with all that crap before bed was such a good idea."

Oh okay, he is definitely annoyed. I didn't care for his parental tone but now that I know he disapproves I will just need to be more clandestine about it.

"Okay, no more ghost stories," I lie and settle into the other lounge chair, pulling a towel over me, more for comfort than warmth.

Watching the bird shadows hop across the sand I react to a sudden splash of what I imagine is a fish leaping from the water. *Or maybe a pink dolphin?* Bizarre images from the book are slowly taking shape in my mind like a rising mist. As darkness closes in over the deck, my fogginess morphs into a new feeling of purpose, and it leaps up in my belly like a hungry lion.

I need to find that book.

Keeping my face impassive I try to tame the lion, which is generating a hunger, not for food, but for knowledge and freedom and the strange desire to drop to all fours and run full-speed through the sand.

DAY V:

Full-Moon
Menu

After I'm sure Jack is asleep, I slip from the high bed and creep through the bungalow in quiet search of the big purple book. I dig through each closet and drawer, pick apart every shelf, even probe the zippy parts of our luggage. And when I become truly desperate I find myself rustling through the kitchen pantry, ripping open packages of food, even though it was highly unlikely that Jack had managed to hide the oversized book among the cereal boxes.

What I did find in the kitchen was interesting though—my cell phone tucked away in a box of crackers.

Closing my eyes I try to replay the events of the night before. After dropping my phone in the tub, I remember Jack wrapping it in a paper towel and leaving it out on the kitchen counter to dry.

Yet here it was, minus the paper towel, shoved deep into a box of *Mary's Gone Crackers*. Powering it on and switching to the camera roll I scan through the tiny thumbnails, anxious to review the picture of the cat on the pier. But the last picture on the roll shows Jack and me on the beach, cheek-to-cheek, looking like a happy couple on a perfect vacation. No matter how many times I hit the refresh button, the same photo keeps displaying on the screen.

Where was the picture of the cat that turned into an old man?

Suddenly, something occurs to me, and I select the trashcan icon. Sure enough there in the trash are two photos. *Ah-ha!* Jack must have deleted the controversial cat pictures while I was sleeping. Maybe he thought I would forget about them—out of sight, out of mind.

But he forgot to empty the trash bin, a common mistake—*but one unlike Jack.*

I select the magnifying glass and zoom in on the first deleted photo, the old man with crinkly eyes of blue and amber, the man I now recognize as Monty. The other picture shows the same old man swimming lazily through the waves, his long white hair floating in the water around him. Slowly the stories are coming back to me, but I want nothing more than to reread the section on the Elders. I curse under my breath, frustrated that I can't find the damn book. After a few hours, I finally give up and tiptoe back to the bedroom.

After another few hours of restless tossing and turning, I finally sit up and stretch in the afternoon light.

Jack emerges from the bathroom, drying himself with an oversized bath sheet. "Hey, let's grab a late lunch."

I rub my stomach and complain of a bubbly, gurgling, nauseous feeling. "Hmm, not sure I'm ready for restaurant food." Even though I spent the better part of yesterday eating nothing more but toast and tea, my stomach still feels assaulted and unwilling to recover.

"Warm bread always makes you feel better."

My stomach growls in response, and the thought of warm bread is enough to motivate me out of the bed and into the shower.

I am determined to wear one of my new outfits, aware that we are nearly halfway through the vacation and I still have piles of unworn clothes. Slipping on a white crinkle skirt and a sleeveless cornflower-blue blouse, I tie the long tails of silky material that show just a hint of flesh between the skirt and the top. Looking in the mirror I suck in my stomach and remind myself that I need to get my tummy tan while I'm here. *All body parts look better when they're tan*; something Valentina used to say as if it were hard science.

In pursuit of a more comfortable bra, I yank open a drawer, and when it protests with a loud groan I stop mid-pull and flash back to last night. You'd think I'd have all the creaks memorized by now after all the time I spent rummaging through the bungalow in search of that book.

Now here it was almost two o'clock in the afternoon, and the headache I had developed from the effort has thankfully been downgraded to a dull throb. But an inhuman noise is emanating from my stomach, apparently inquiring about that warm bread. I am getting impatient and Jack is taking *forever* to get ready. I just want to get to the restaurant so we can have a civilized conversation about the book and the phone.

"Come *on!*" I whine into the bathroom.

"Don't rush me." Jack sweeps a tiny dot of gel through his hair, using his fingers to smooth back the sides. Watching him in the mirror I wonder if his hair might have grown in the past few days; *it looks awfully full.* Must be the salt air, I tell myself.

Out on the sandy path the birds whistle and coo, the sunlight warms the back of my neck, and I am thrilled to finally be out of the bungalow. After more than twenty-four hours of isolation, I am looking forward to seeing Roscoe, someone both Jack and I can agree is real.

I skip a few steps trying to keep up with Jack. Several tiny steps with my short legs are equal to one of his longer strides, and I am trailing behind like a baby duckling.

Still feeling out of it, my mind is in worse shape than my body, because after discovering the deleted photos I am pretty sure Jack thinks I'm losing it. He may have always suspected that I was a bit unconventional, maybe even eccentric, but lately I have been demonstrating textbook signs of crazy. Sometimes I feel myself boarding the crazy train but can't seem to pull the emergency break. These things I see and feel are so real that I have no choice but to acknowledge them.

A black bird, his feathers so dark they almost shine blue, makes me jump in surprise when he swoops down to snatch something in the sand at my feet. Watching him climb back through the air I can't stop the creeping suspicion that maybe there is no book at all.

Is it possible that I made up all the characters that dance around in my head like charismatic ghosts?

The sense of urgency I felt last night is still there but has settled into a low rumbling in the pit of my stomach, emanating from the tiny piece of un-tanned flesh beneath the cornflower blue top. Again I wonder about the head trauma not healing properly and tell myself I will definitely schedule a doctor's appointment when we get back home. Until then I vow to try to keep these magical musings to myself.

As we approach the restaurant we are greeted by low strands of music, and as we turn the corner to the outside bar we spot three girls arranged on a makeshift stage. A girl with long blond curls is perched behind a white piano, and there are two other musicians, one strumming a misshapen guitar and the other straddling an antique cello. The three of them are playing with a quiet confident ease, and I am relieved to see Jack smile in their direction, confirming that he sees them too.

Roscoe casually strolls across the sand, and I smile and point like I am spotting an old friend. He is wearing the same black-and-white uniform as the other day. But today his suspenders are looped down around his legs, his vest hangs open, and his white shirt is unbuttoned under a tie that dangles loose. When he sees us he buttons up and reassembles the tie and suspenders with quick, jerky movements.

He motions with his chin toward the girls. "Musicians for the Jazeera wedding."

Ah, the wedding that got cancelled.

I examine the girls on stage. Their sunglasses are decorated with tiny white pearls, and their outfits are made of silky material with corset hooks lacing up the bodice and flouncy poet sleeves. Wreaths of flowers in their hair conjure up images of fairies in a Renaissance painting, and I think they are perfect costumes for wedding musicians, *although they might be a tad warm for the beach.*

Roscoe pulls two scrolls from under the bar, hands them to us, and announces, "The full-moon menu."

Jack's eyebrows spring up, but he can't be more surprised than I am. "Tonight's a full moon?"

"Yes, sir." Roscoe pats his nametag as if to ensure that it's still in place.

The girls on stage smoothly transition to a new song, and I finger my menu, feeling a mental tug on the hem of my white skirt like an impatient child demanding attention. Jack pockets his scroll, still unopened, and asks Roscoe, "What would you recommend?"

"Well, today's special features exotic mushroom ravioli drenched in a white wine sauce and topped with edible flowers."

"Sounds great!" Jack claps his hands together and bellies up to the bar.

I nod in agreement, ask about warm bread, and slide into one of the high stools next to Jack. As soon as I'm seated I pull the thin ribbon from the scroll, unroll the parchment paper, and am tempted to drawl, "Hear ye, hear ye." The back of the menu is filled with all sorts of information about the moon. I quickly learn that a full moon technically occurs at one particular moment in time but the energy is palpable for forty-eight hours before and after, giving us four full days (and nights) of full-moon energy.

"Don't they say emergency rooms are busiest during the full moon?"

Jacks shakes his head. *His hair had definitely gotten bushier.* "Nah, they debunked that rumor."

Roscoe presents a basket of assorted breads. I'm thrilled to find it overflowing with varieties of rye, sourdough, and pumpernickel encrusted with nuts and seeds. When Roscoe passes through a black curtain, I peek in after him, unable to see anything past the dark material. *Pay no attention to the man behind the curtain,* I recite in my head, thinking of *The Wizard of Oz.*

I greedily rip open a soft seeded roll, and it releases a puff of steam. Dropping a dot of butter into the soft dough, I take a bite and practically moan. Jack was right. Warm bread always does make me feel better.

When Roscoe returns he is carrying a pink-tinted glass pitcher. "An island favorite."

The white foamy concoction is sprinkled with what looks like cinnamon. Not trusting my stomach to new things just yet, I make Jack try it first. He takes a sip, leaving a milk-mustache across his upper lip.

"Wow! Tastes like Baileys and something else." When I frown, he adds, "You know what they say—a little hair of the dog that bit you."

He fills my glass and then tops off his own. I tentatively sample the creamy coconut concoction, and it joins the warm bread in my stomach to ease the bubbling. I lean back in the stool, stir my drink with the long straw, and resist the urge to dip my bread into the glass.

The blond girl behind the piano speaks softly, but her voice rises over the surf like the cry of a sea gull. "We'd like to dedicate this next tune to the awesome power of tonight's blue moon."

Did she say a blue moon? I thought it was a full moon. I wonder what the difference is and scan my menu in pursuit of more information about blue moons. I sneak a sideways glance at Jack, who is emptying and refilling his glass like a man on a mission to get buzzed. It's hard to read his expression because we are sitting side by side, but I decide that he looks super serious.

The music shifts again as the cello player drags her bow heavily across the thick strings, her torso rocking with the effort. I close my eyes, feeling each note unearth a memory like a root poking through the soil. She creates a low and deep rumble, one that resonates in my lower abdomen and awakens the lion in my belly.

Jack has consumed four or five glasses of the island favorite at this point and pushes back his stool, mumbling something about needing a bathroom. As soon as he is out of sight, the cello player places her instrument gently on the sand and pulls something from the circular wood cutout. She moves toward me with the prowess of a panther, and I turn in my stool to watch her approach. Her long dark hair frames features that are sharp and unusual, with a thin scar that tugs on her lower lip. The faint white scar runs along her jawline like someone might have tried to cut her throat, *but missed*. She gently drops a flower on my lap, and I am struck by the fuzzy dark green stem in stark contrast to my white crinkle skirt.

"Night-blooming jasmine," she whispers, and her voice sounds like the wind blowing through trees filled with leaves.

Almost choking on my bread when I hear the words "night-blooming jasmine," I remember Sebastian reciting them to me in a dream. I can almost hear him clucking his tongue at me for taking so long to remember. *Of course I need to collect a bouquet of night-blooming jasmine.* As if in confirmation the internal lion snaps its jaws in the direction of the small white bud.

Mesmerized by the strange flower on my lap I slowly lift it toward my face, but even from arm's length, I am overwhelmed by the sweet scent emanating from the tightly closed bud. It is strong and overwhelming like walking into a store with open barrels of potpourri.

"Wow, they certainly are fragrant."

"Just wait till tonight when they are in full bloom." She turns to go.

I stroke the oblong leaf between my thumb and forefinger, savoring the velvety texture. "Wait, where can I find more?"

"Oh, they are all around." She waves her small hands in the air, making the material of her dress whoosh as she moves back toward her cello.

Jack returns from the bathroom and grumbles. "Whew! What stinks?"

"It's night-blooming jasmine." I hold up the long crooked stem and wave it at him like a magic wand.

He stiffens. "Where did you get that?"

"From her!" I point toward the wedding musicians.

It's coming back to me now, something about the need to perform a full-moon ritual. I feel an obligation to do it, and somewhere inside of me, I actually *want* to do it. But I must be careful how I present this to Jack. After all I don't want to scare him off by making it sound weird or witchy.

"Hey, what's on the itinerary for tonight?" I ask trying to sound casual.

He clumsily searches for the little notebook, and I can tell that the alcohol-enriched milkshake is taking a toll on him. *Hmm, this could work to my advantage.* I try not to smile as he pulls his pockets inside out before realizing that he left the notebook back at the bungalow.

"All I know is this: yesterday's little *sick day* got us off schedule."

I deflect the comment and keep the smile in place. "How about we do some night snorkeling?"

That gets his attention, as I knew it would. He sits up and bobs his head. "Yeah, yeah, let's do that."

I build on the momentum. "Maybe we could ask Roscoe to suggest a good dive spot."

He snaps his fingers. "Hey, I bet the grotto has some amazing snorkeling."

The grotto. Perfect.

Just then Roscoe comes bustling through the curtain with two oversized dishes and places them down in front of us with a satisfied grin. Then he makes a big production of grating cheese and grinding fresh pepper over our raviolis.

"Bon appetit!" He kisses the tips of his fingers before disappearing again.

The food looks and smells delicious, but I've lost my appetite, distracted by the possibility of pulling off this full-moon ritual. Piercing one of the triangles of pasta, I swirl it in the buttery sauce and repeat a figure-eight pattern on the bottom of the plate, trying to think. Getting Jack to the grotto tonight is just the first step. But how am I going to convince him to perform a full-moon ritual with me? In fact, I don't even know how to perform a full-moon ritual myself. Another reason I need to get my hands on that book.

I distractedly put my fork down, and it slips from the plate and lands in the sand with a soft thump. Roscoe immediately appears and presents me with a clean utensil, and when we become connected by the metal fork, I am overwhelmed by a powerful vision.

I am in a crowded bar with big band music and lots of blaring horns. Couples dance on tabletops with olive-filled martini glasses. The scene makes sense since Roscoe is a bartender and would probably retain memories like this, but there is something off about this vision.

The bar has no windows, and the wallpaper reminds me of something Jack's Mom might pick out. There's something old-fashioned about the way the girls are dressed too; it's as if they are at a costume party. And everyone, I mean *everyone*, is smoking, as in an old black-and-white movie where a surgeon comes out of an operating room with a Camel cigarette dangling from his lips and nobody seems surprised. All the girls press long skinny cigarettes to their rouged mouths, and men wear fedora hats and puff on thick cigars. I wonder how long ago these images have been ingrained in Roscoe's memory, as there isn't a bar left in Manhattan that will let you smoke indoors anymore.

When I release my grip on the fork, the vision evaporates like jagged pieces of glass sprinkled from a cracked mirror. Even though Roscoe's eyes are covered with dark glasses, I can feel him examine me like I am a curious bug, one that just crawled out from under a rock and showed its full size and potential.

Shaken by the unexpected vision, I push back my stool, and it topples over in my haste to get away. As I run toward the beach I need to quell an unusually strong urge to run directly into the waves.

I can hear Jack's footsteps in the sand behind me. "G, what happened?"

Despite my best effort to stop them, tears squeeze from the corners of my eyes. I turn to face Jack and "The fork . . ." is all I get out before the lump rises in my throat and I can't speak without squeaking.

"Ah. Another vision." He looks toward the bar, and I steal a quick glance, thankful to see that Roscoe is conveniently absent.

I nod silently.

"What am I supposed to do? I just don't know what to do anymore."

"Stop hiding the book from me!" I blurt out, surprising myself with the sudden burst of emotion that has manifested itself into anger. I always do this—keep things bottled up for so long that they eventually explode like a shaken can of soda.

He looks confused, and then his face softens. "I'm not hiding it. I'm *protecting* it."

"Protecting it from what? *Me?*" I feel my paranoia growing.

"No, look, yesterday while you were sleeping, I started to read that book."

"And?"

He takes a step toward me and lowers his voice. "And there's this full-moon ritual I think we should try."

Maybe the island favorite is stronger than it looks. "Wait a minute. The other day you were making fun of me, and now you're telling me you believe in all this hocus pocus?"

His eyes are green and excited and a little rebellious, something I haven't seen in a few years. "I can't really explain it. First I found myself drawn to that page you left open for me . . . and then I had this dream. *Two* dreams in fact." He shakes his head and looks away, embarrassed.

"You never remember your dreams." He is full of surprises today.

He scratches his head. "Yeah, well, this island is having a strange effect on me. And *you*, it's like this island's energy mixed with your heightened sensitivity; well, it seems to be enhancing your abilities."

Here I was afraid he was thinking I was crazy, and it turns out he thinks I'm enhanced. But I am still slightly suspicious. "What made you change your mind?"

"The book. The dreams. It's a combination of things, like the crazy cat picture."

"Yeah, speaking of that. Why are you deleting photos from my phone if you think I'm so special?"

He looks genuinely surprised. "I didn't delete any pictures."

"Oh and I suppose you didn't hide my phone in a box of crackers either?"

He snorts and shakes his head. "I couldn't even *find* your phone. Look, you were feeling no pain from all that wine. You could have fat-fingered the deletion yourself."

I guess it's possible that I deleted one photo by accident, but two? "And how did it get from the counter to the pantry?"

"Maybe it slipped into the box of crackers while you were snacking."

I resent the implication about my late-night snacking, but then a chill runs through me and I have one of those moments of *unexplained knowing*.

Someone else touched my phone.

Someone was also aware of my little gift, but instead of celebrating it as Jack seems to be doing, they were seemingly trying to hide all evidence of it. Come to think of it, there *was* a strange energy on the phone when I found it, but I ignored it. Trying to do the same now, I shake off the chill and focus on Jack, who is speaking passionately now, using his hands like an old Italian baker.

". . . and then the full-moon menu! It's like we were meant to be here, in this place, at this time."

"Okay, just what are you proposing here?"

"First we need to find more night blooming jasmine." He motions toward the single stem I left on the bar. "We need a large bouquet."

So I've heard. I nod and wonder if it was Sebastian who appeared to Jack in a dream.

"Then we . . . you know . . . perform a full-moon ritual."

When I don't say anything he continues, and I realize that he must be misreading my silence for opposition. In reality I am just pondering the irony. I'm worried about how I was going to convince him to do a full-moon ritual, and here he is trying to convince *me*. He certainly has changed his tune from six months ago when he seemed adamantly opposed to anything magical. Even a few days ago I would have sworn that he would have been completely closed off to this sort of thing. I never considered that this island would be affecting him just as much as it was affecting me.

"Think of it as wishing on a star or throwing a penny in a fountain." He continues making his case and even compares the cleansing ritual to the juice detox we did after the holidays. "At the very least it will give us one hell of a story to tell people when they ask, 'What did you do on your vacation?'"

"Okay, okay. You had me at night-blooming jasmine."

Jack looks relieved and smiles at me for what seems like the first time all day. "Good. Now can I finish my ravioli?"

When Roscoe clears our plates he doesn't mention the fork incident. But I do notice him flinch when I reach for the silver platter of homemade truffles he offers, probably afraid of another metal-to-metal connection. I avoid his stare and select a milk chocolate morsel covered with slivered almonds. It turns out to have a warm cherry filling, the cherry on the cake of my day as it were. Washing it down with the last of my coconut drink, I grab the flower and hop off my stool, anxious to get going. Now that we are in agreement about the full-moon ritual, there is much to do, and as usual we got such a late start to the day.

Jack and I spend most of the afternoon wandering around the lush gardens in search of the unique white flower with the crooked stem. But we can't find anything that even remotely resembles our lone sample. With the afternoon light quickly slipping away, we decide to split up so we can cover more ground. I keep the flower given to me from the cello player, and Jack finally unrolls the menu as it turns out to include a drawing of the night-blooming jasmine in both hibernation and full bloom. We plan to regroup in half an hour.

Once alone, I become lost in thought and more focused on the potential of the flower bushes around me than the path beneath me. I easily wander aimlessly through the vast gardens and soon find myself near the rope bridge.

Shielding my eyes from the sun I make out a figure standing in the center of the bridge, arms outstretched wide. I blink several times to ensure that this figure is really there, not courtesy of one of my little visions. At first I think it's a smallish man, dressed in a suit and fedora, but as the face turns toward me, I spot the red lipstick and familiar spit curls. *Is that the lady from the bar that first night?*

The suit looks similar to the one Roscoe was wearing with vest and suspenders, but she's added a long colorful scarf that hangs loosely around the lapels and flickers in the breeze like the wings of an insect. As I inch forward her head snaps in my direction and the breeze around her abruptly dies down.

"Well, well, well. Just what are you up to, *Guinevere?*" She spits out my full name like it was poison.

I don't remember telling this woman my name but reason that she may have overheard it that first night when we introduced ourselves to Roscoe. Still, I never use my full name, and Gwen could be short for Gwendolyn or Gwyneth. What are the chances she would guess Guinevere?

I try the tone I save for our most high-maintenance clients. "Is there something I can help you with?"

"*You?* Help *me?*" She tosses her head back in a high-pitched laugh that reminds me of my mother's sister, Aunt Wanda.

Then she pulls a jeweled cigarette holder from an inside pocket and expertly fits it with a long thin cigarette. She flicks the round metal lighter, and it releases a flame that licks toward the brim of the hat and almost sets her nose on fire.

But she doesn't even flinch.

I can't get a read on her mood because behind the large round sunglasses her face is porcelain white and expressionless, like someone who received too many Botox injections. Her blood-red lipstick leaves a ring mark on the cigarette, and she blows a donut ring of smoke in my direction. As I watch the donut drift lazily toward me I start to think how unsafe it is to smoke on a rope bridge. Then she is just inches from my face, and I pull back in surprise.

"You're in over your head, doll face!" she hisses. We are toe-to-toe now and just about the same height.

Not sure how to respond to this crazy lady I look around hopefully for Jack. Like a frog's tongue snapping up an insect, she plucks the jasmine flower from my hand and dangles it over the side. Cocking her head, she threatens to drop it.

"What the what . . ." is all I get out before awkwardly reaching for the flower, hesitant to venture out onto the wooden planks of the bridge.

But she lifts the stem higher, trying to provoke me further out. Alternating her other hand between her popped hip and her bee-stung lips she takes purposeful drags of her cigarette while watching my every move. I take a tentative step toward her, and a slow smile creeps across her kewpie-doll face. Sensing this is just what she wants me to do, I'm too pissed to care. *I need to get that flower back.* It's the only one we have.

Then there is the sound of rumbling that at first I think is coming from my stomach; then I consider that maybe its distant thunder. Finally I realize that it's the galloping hooves of three deer as they race across the planks, their legs pumping and making the rope bridge buck and bounce under their weight. When the woman spots the deer she flings the flower defiantly over the railing, and I uselessly clutch the air trying to save it. She clamps her cig between her lips and crouches down, hands flexed in a defensive pose. Although I realize I should probably get out of the way I can't take my eyes from the elusive flower as it floats from the bridge like a string of beads flung from a Mardi Gras float.

The first deer knocks the woman slightly off balance, the second deer forces her up against the railing, and the third deer, the one with the darkest coat, kicks her hind legs in a squat-thrust that knocks the Aunt Wanda lady clear over the side of the bridge.

I watch in horror as she flips back. It seems to happen in slow motion like a diver doing a backflip from the high board, her bare feet the last thing to disappear over the side. Rushing to the edge, I ignore the familiar sense of vertigo and search the rocks below for the falling woman. But all I see is her scarf snagged on one of the planks.

When I bend to retrieve it, a porcelain white hand covers mine and I let out a scream. To my surprise the woman is swinging from the bridge with one arm like Arnold Schwarzenegger. She continues to conjure up images of an action hero as she heaves herself over the railing, demonstrating the strength and ease of a navy seal. I stare in disbelief as she regains her footing and breaks into a sprint after the three deer that attacked her.

As they disappear through the garden, moving so quickly it looks like a film reel that has been sped up, I try to process what just happened. As soon as the bushes settle back into place, Jack steps into view, triumphantly holding up a generous bouquet of night-blooming jasmine.

I try to cover with a smile, but I'm not quick enough and he catches my stunned expression. Jogging over to me, he says, "Hey, are you okay?"

I think about telling him the truth.

Really I do.

But with the level of understanding we just shared on the beach, I figure it's best to keep the Aunt-Wanda-Schwarzenegger experience to myself. Plus I'm still only half convinced that it wasn't an intuitive vision or even a hallucination, courtesy of this island's intense energy.

"I dropped my flower over the side." I lie, figuring I could explain both the missing flower and my disheveled appearance in one shot.

But then he looks questioningly at the scarf that I find that I'm still holding, so I casually place it over my shoulders and lift the edges, sweeping my heavy hair off my neck and tying the material in a loose knot. He has no idea how many scarves I own and will assume this is part of my cabana wear if I act nonchalant about it. "I just got a wave of vertigo, and it made me drop the flower." I shrug and try my best to look like it's no big deal.

He searches my face, takes another look at the scarf, and then seems to relax. "No worries. I found a whole bunch of night-blooming jasmine growing down by the sand dunes." He holds out the odd bouquet of crooked stems topped with dozens of tightly closed white buds.

I take a step toward him, feeling totally safe now that Jack is here, and try to erase the rope bridge incident from my mind. It is getting dark now, and we stop to watch the intense full moon slip into place and light up the midnight-blue sky. We stand alone, waist-high in the flower bushes, and the whole garden is now covered in a purplish glow.

The flowers in Jack's outstretched hand instantly respond to the moonlight and begin blooming like time-elapsed photography. We watch in wonder as the tiny buds plump up like kernels of popcorn and then burst open into robust, greenish-white flowers surrounded by small berries. The fragrance is completely penetrating and gives me a head rush that almost knocks me to my knees. I can't take my eyes off the flowers and gaze down at them as I hold them at my waist like a bride's bouquet.

Silently we snake our way back to the bungalow in a single-file procession and continue like this, walking through the dark rooms and clicking on lights. I end up in the kitchen, opening and closing cabinets looking for a vase big enough to accommodate the tall plump flowers.

Once I have the thick glass vase filled with water, I turn to the flowers lying on the counter but find them shriveled up like frightened little turtles. *Oh no!* I gasp in surprise at the large pom-pom flowers that have collapsed into closed buds. In a panic, I quickly immerse them in water, afraid that they are dying. Even in the water the flowers remain tightly shut, and then it dawns on me: they need the light of the full moon, not the artificial lighting of the bungalow. To prove my theory I carry the vase down the hallway into the bedroom, slide back the doors, and step onto the deck, feeling like I am stepping onto a stage under a brilliant spotlight. The moon hangs low in the sky, reflecting in the water and shining so bright it lights up the deck like a floodlight. Almost immediately the flowers burst open in response to the moonlight. Relieved, I decide to leave the vase on the deck, but after an apprehensive look up and down the beach, I move them close to the bungalow where I can keep an eye on them.

Back inside I sit on the bed and ask Jack to cough up the book. I watch with interest as he digs a brown leather belt from his suitcase and then drags the dresser to the far side of the bedroom. He climbs on top and uses the prong on the buckle to untighten the four tiny screws from the air conditioning vent, pops off the grate, and reveals the big purple book inside.

"Great, Jack. No wonder I wasn't able to find that!"

"Well, they don't have a safe in the room, and I needed to make sure it didn't disappear." He looks down at me and seems embarrassed. "I think that was the message in my dreams, something about keeping the book safe. Or *you* safe. It's strange—I can't remember the details."

"You done good," I assure him.

My heart quickens when I see the book, and I reach for it like a mother accepting her newborn child. Tempted to refresh my memory and reread some of the myths and legends, I can almost hear Sebastian scolding me and force myself to flip directly to the section on rituals, scanning the section on full-moon rituals in particular. According to the flamboyant script, we need three things to perform a full-moon ritual.

One, we need a large bouquet of night-blooming jasmine. I glance through the sliding glass doors and confirm that the tall flowers are still safe and sound on the deck. *Check.*

Two, we need long tapered candles, preferably white or purple. Hmm, I remember seeing candles last night when I was rummaging through drawers, but in all honesty, I can't remember where I saw them or what color they were.

And three, we need a verse to recite under the light of the full moon. Apparently there are various stanzas to be used for different desires and outcomes.

Okay, that doesn't seem so bad. This process may turn out to be less invasive than that holiday juice detox.

Glancing up from the book I smile at Jack, who is busy getting the equipment situated for the night-snorkeling excursion. I watch him replace the batteries in our underwater flashlights and clean our new masks with toothpaste, an old trick to keep them from fogging up. Meanwhile I find a small apothecary table built into one of the closets.

One of its tiny drawers is filled with different-colored candles, and old books of matches are tucked into the edges of the wooden encasements. I select two tapered purple candles and an old matchbook with the words *Facula Isle* inked in cursive print.

I had wrongly assumed that we had to wait for midnight to perform the full-moon ritual. Turns out it just has to be dark enough for the moon to glow brightly in the sky. I also find out what a blue moon is. Since the full moon happens every twenty-eight days and some months have thirty or thirty one days, there are leftover days each month that add up every two and half years to create an extra full moon. A blue moon is like extra innings in a baseball game—a bonus. And the energy from a blue moon is extremely high. *Like a full moon on steroids.*

While I am busy preparing for the ritual, the lion in my belly is content and happy. The intoxicating aroma of the flowers drifts in on the ocean breeze, making me feel mellow and focused. With the flowers and candles accounted for I just need to ensure that we have an appropriate verse to recite in the grotto. I flip through the pages considering several options before settling on a general stanza dedicated to Cernunnos. *That seems appropriate.* It is noted as a cleansing ritual, a way to release things that no longer serve us. I have a backpack fit for a recon marine of stuff I want to release. Zooming in on the text, I snap a picture of the page, figuring we don't want to bring the big book out on the boat with us, afraid I might waterlog it as I've done with so many of the books I've taken into the bathtub with me.

It's getting late, and it's time to suit up, pack a dive bag, and go. I shimmy into my wet suit, a cute black shorty with yellow accents. Jack suggested the bright color so he could spot me easily underwater. Folding two clean towels, one for me and one for Jack, I slide on my trusty gold sandals. *They really do match everything.*

"Ready?" Jack walks into the room wearing his wetsuit, much more hard core than my ensemble. His is full-length, black with blue accents, and he wears a dive knife strapped securely into his ankle holster.

Glancing in the mirror I smooth my hair around the scarf, the one I acquired from the rope bridge and find that I'm still wearing. I decide to leave it on as it does a good job of keeping the hair off my face and I think it might be a good prop for the full-moon ritual, a way to ward off unwanted visions like the Aunt Wanda lady.

"Are you ready?" Jack repeats.

I turn from the mirror. "Let's do this."

Taking the flowers from the vase I shake the excess water from the long stems and carry them through the bungalow, watching them shrink in the unnatural light and then bloom again when we step outside. I'd heard of nocturnal flowers that only flourish in the moonlight but have never seen flowers react this extremely, so connected to their surroundings. I am reminded of the magical species Willow described in the book and wonder if this flower is somehow connected to that genetic family.

By the time we reach the boat dock I am overwhelmed by the strong fragrance of the exotic flowers and feel myself slip into a whole new level of intoxication. I examine Jack's eyes and find them glassy and hooded just like mine feel. *These flowers are making us high.*

In a series of dreamlike movements, we climb into *Ruby* and head out to the grotto. When we reach the arches Jack kills the motor and hands me a paddle explaining that we don't want to scare away the fish for snorkeling.

"First the ritual."

"Yeah, yeah."

The silence is eerie as we slowly work our way under the archway, and the moonlight shines through the dome and illuminates vibrant rainbow-colored coral lining the inside walls. In the moonlight this space feels even more sacred, like an empty church lit only by the light streaming from the stained-glass windows.

Following the ritual instructions that I'd memorized at this point but referred to on my cell phone anyway, I pluck the large white petals from the night-blooming jasmine and drop them into a small pile on the floor of the boat. Then I manipulate some of the petals into a large circle big enough to enclose both Jack and me. Checking the time the digital clock shows 11:34 and I wonder what the three rings of the Gansberg clock look like right now. Too worked up to wait any longer, I light both candles with the old matchbook and hand one to Jack, the Halloween glow from the candlelight dancing across his five o'clock shadow.

We begin to recite the words, reading from the tiny cell phone screen, and wait for something to happen.

Father of death, father of night
Father of birth, father of light
Cernunnos, Cernunnos, Cernunnos
Through the veil you pass with pride
As I beckon thee to be at my side
Cernunnos, Cernunnos, Cernunnos

We are supposed to repeat the phrase four times, first to the north and then to the south, the west, and finally the east.

But Jack and I spend several minutes arguing about which way is actually north. We each point out a few bright stars that all could have been the North Star. Jack fiddles with the boat's compass, but it appears to be broken. Then we spend more time debating how to pronounce Cernunnos, disagreeing about the hard C. Not sure what I was expecting, this certainly isn't it, and I find myself, not for the first time in my life, regretting my choice of séance partners.

I don't feel anything magical or any sense of release. After all the buildup this is turning out to be one big waste of time, and I blow out my candle, feeling discouraged and silly. But as the smoke from my extinguished candle drifts toward the far wall like a wisp of steam escaping from a boiling kettle, three figures slowly materialize from the dark corner.

It's Ruby and the twins, Sebastian and Jonah.

Holy crap, looks like we summoned the whole crew. My glassy eyes move from one familiar face to the next, and although the trio appears in human form, the elongated silhouettes on the grotto wall cast the shadows of three magnificent deer.

I turn toward Jack to ensure that he is seeing this too. Sure enough, his wide eyes are fixated on the three elusive figures that, until now, have only appeared to me in my dreams or when I was alone. I was relieved that Jack was here to see them this time.

Without a word Sebastian extends his arms back and lets his leather jacket drop dramatically to the sand before diving into the water. Jonah follows with a swan dive, and Ruby simply steps off the sand, dropping soundlessly into the sea. When the three of them break the surface they motion for us to join them. Their long wet hair floats around them in the water like seaweed, and their eyes glimmer like jewels in a tiara.

The boat dips under my feet, and when I turn to see what's caused it I spot Jack diving off the boat in such a hurry that he forgets to blow out his candle. I watch in amazement as the water puckers around him and he swims through the dark ocean toward Ruby and the twins.

The odd collection of swimmers, which now includes my husband, is arranged in a circle, treading water and expecting me to join them. I feel compelled to see this ritual through, so I slide off my sandals, climb down the ladder, and slowly descend into the black water.

DAY VI:

Transformation

R uby trails her long fingers through the ocean in a mesmerizing pattern, making small circles in the water. With each rotation she enlarges the circle, and the swirling water responds by increasing in size and speed. Jack and I are unable to look away, as if she is hypnotizing us with the tiny whirlpool that materializes before us. Her fingers in the water have a surreal effect combined with the trippy feeling still evident from the jasmine flowers. The circle continues to shift and grow until it resembles an oversized manhole cover made entirely of spinning seawater.

Jack's eyes are fixed on Ruby now as she lifts her arms high in the air, arching her back with the gracefulness of a ballerina. As if being lifted by invisible wires, her torso slowly rises from the water, and she neatly bends forward and dives headfirst down the watery hole, barely making a splash. I stare at the opening and wait for her to pop back up, but the water continues to spin.

Sebastian points his chin in my direction, and I give him a *"Who me?" face*. Jonah chuckles and clasps his hands over his head, pointing up toward the glowing moon. He tilts his head back, and his red curls bob in the water like sea serpents before he lifts himself up and jumps down the underwater tunnel.

And then there are three.

Sebastian, Jack, and I continue to kick our legs, and I flap my arms, inching closer to the strange circle, curious now. The water surrounding the hole is lava-lamp blue. It spins faster now, spritzing seawater around the edges like sparklers on the Fourth of July.

Jack suddenly lunges forward and in his haste kicks me under the water, knocking me sideways.

"Hey!" I flap my arms, spin around, and readjust my treading rhythm, and by the time I circle back I am surprised to find Jack pulling himself awkwardly up on the ledge. *Is he seriously going to dive down the tunnel without scuba equipment? We need our masks at the very least.* He spreads his arms wide and places a hand on either side of the watery rim, peering down. The blue stripe of his wetsuit glows in the radiating light, and his face is basked in an eerie hue. His eyes grow wide as he continues to peer down the hole.

"What is it?" I sputter, slightly out of breath, wondering what he sees.

Sebastian whispers something in a language I don't understand, and as if in response Jack calmly releases his grip, falling silently face-first down the hole.

My mouth drops open in surprise. *He is certainly taking this full-moon ritual to the extreme.*

A cloud covers the moon and blankets everything in sudden darkness. I listen for Sebastian moving in the water next to me, but it's so quiet that I think he might have slipped down the hole and left me up here to fend for myself. Then there is a low crackling, and Sebastian's face illuminated in firelight appears much closer than before. I pull back in alarm, wondering where he got the torch, and realize that the flame is coming directly from the palm of his hand. I stare in disbelief as he rolls his eyes and shrugs one shoulder. He leans in to examine my face, and I welcome the opportunity to study his expression. *Serious. Border-line stern.* Part of me thinks he might just pick me up and toss me down if I don't go myself.

In the end I convince myself that this is all part of one wild hallucination. After all, I still feel the high from the night-blooming jasmine, and clearly it is affecting Jack too. Maybe the jasmine was some kind of hallucinogenic plant like the peyote we tried senior year in college. Well, if that is the case, then I might as well enjoy the ride. There is no denying the burning in my arms and legs, and I know I can't tread water for much longer. I need to make up my mind. And fast.

Sebastian waves the flame in my direction. "Any time you're ready, princess."

Still not completely convinced but in desperate need of rest for my arms, I grip onto the watery edge and am relieved to find that it can support my weight. Despite its appearance, the lip of the whirlpool is not exactly liquid but not quite solid either. It sort of reminds me of a jellyfish. I pull myself into a sitting position on the jellyfish wall and dangle my legs down the shaft. I have to fight the undertow, so strong it nearly sucks me down like a garbage disposal and makes up my mind for me. Pushing the soles of my feet flat against the inside wall and clamping my fingers to the edge I try to hold myself steady and crane my neck trying to see what Jack saw.

Swirling seawater basked in a warm blue light circles down, down, down like a bottomless well. Sebastian again repeats the foreign phrase, and I find myself automatically tipping forward and let myself drop, feeling very much like Alice in Wonderland.

My stomach lurches like I'm descending that first big hill on a roller coaster. I instinctively close my mouth and plug my nose but quickly realize that's not necessary as the underwater cylinder is filled with plenty of fresh air.

Sebastian cruises by me, his arms and legs tucked close to his body like a luge rider at the Olympics. I, on the other hand, am being tossed and jostled like a stunt woman taking a hard tumble down a flight of stairs. My journey down is accompanied by high-pitched shrieks and plenty of profanity that bounce off the cylinder walls.

Finally I land with a squishy thump and find myself on the floor of a giant bubble. The thin membrane is about ten feet tall and six feet wide and, like the water slide, is filled with fresh air. Quickly scampering to my feet I press my hands against the thin wall, completely in awe of my new surroundings.

I am suspended deep under the sea where coral sparkles as if being lit up by a giant flashlight with vibrant shades of red, bursts of orange, yellow, green, sky blue, indigo, and sparkly white. Feeling like I've been dropped into an exotic fish tank, my eyes follow the underwater creatures as they float by and occasionally press their mouths against the see-through walls in an animated kiss. One angel fish, as large as a sting ray, makes slow circles around me as if trying to get a better look. As soon as the giant fish passes I search for the others.

I find Jack suspended in an identical bubble right next to mine and look up to find that the end of the water slide splits into different branches like fallopian tubes, but instead of two arms there are three or four options, more like a plastic hamster tunnel. I tap the walls of my underwater container with open palms trying to get Jack's attention. But the bubble appears to be made of the same consistency as the watery hole, and my banging does no good; it is like tapping on cookie dough.

Ruby, Sebastian, and Jonah are swimming in the blue-lit water outside the bubbles like fully clothed mermaids. Tiny bubbles escape their lips, and I realize that it must be true what they say about deer witches—*they really can breathe under water.* Ruby appears outside my bubble, her long white dress billowing around her figure like a watery ghost. Tonight she is wearing a gold headpiece decorated with hundreds of sapphires, not quite a crown but close. One blue teardrop jewel dangles low on her forehead, sparkling brilliantly like a third eye.

Her head is pitched forward as she searches the water below, and I am compelled to follow her gaze. Through the floor of my personal glass-bottom boat there is a giant jeweled hula hoop made entirely of glowing blue coral, the same color as the eyes of the deer witch. The ring pulses beneath me, and I realize that this is the source of the soft blue light coloring the water.

What happens next happens so quickly that it takes me a moment to sort it out. Like an arrow released from an archer's bow, Ruby drops through the water in a blur of black hair, and the white material of her dress flutters around her like the wings of a dove. She dives headfirst through the blue coral ring and the transformation begins.

Just like in my dream her arms and legs stretch like Play-Doh and reshape into long, toned deer legs, her hands and feet curling into hooves. Thick black hair grows down her entire body, and a shiny coat of deer fur replaces her flawless skin. To complete the transformation, her face pulls back and lengthens into the pointed head of a familiar black doe.

Sebastian and Jonah exchange a sideways glance and then race each other to the coral ring, moving so quickly it's hard to make out who's who. They tackle each other in the water, tumbling over and over in a blur of Jonah's jeans and the purple ruffles of Sebastian's silk shirt. But it's Jonah who gets there first, his giant antlers ripping through his red hair as he somersaults through the ring and bounces off the inner edge, morphing into an auburn deer.

It's Sebastian's turn now, and with the grand gestures of a Vegas stage magician he takes a leisurely lap around the ring, clearly showing off for our benefit. He casually lets his legs slip through the ring and then shoots his arms straight out to the side, holding his body straight like a gymnast. He pauses for dramatic effect, a devilish smile playing on his innocent face. For a moment he has the upper body of a man and the lower body of a deer, his almond-colored legs kicking the water below the ring. It reminds me of a drawing I saw of Cernunnos, and Sebastian's eyes flicker with amusement as if he seems to like the comparison to his mythical father. After a few more kicks he releases the edge of the ring and lets himself drop. Shaking his long blond mane wildly, sinewy antlers sprout through the crown of his head as his deer face pops into place with the same wide mesmerizing eyes that peered at me over sunglasses the other night in the bungalow.

Watching the whole thing like a strange dream everything seems eerily familiar, but I turn to Jack, anxious to see his take on the whole thing. It's difficult to read his expression through the saran wrap wall of his bubble, but from what I can tell he is not afraid.

He actually looks excited.

Before I can figure out what to do, the three deer witches gently nudge Jack's bubble into position over the coral ring. Jonah swims into a school of colorful fish, and they immediately organize themselves like tiny synchronized swimmers and start doing laps around Jack's bubble. Ruby and Sebastian join the fish, zipping through the water like drops of caramel and licorice.

I jump up and down in my underwater cage trying to get Jack's attention, but he is completely oblivious to me. His hands clutch and reclutch the air, making fists. *Uh-oh, this is not a good sign.* This is something I've seen him do to psych him up for a big presentation. A feeling of dread slowly spreads through my limbs.

"Jack!" I call out, jumping up and down and trying to move my bubble closer to his.

Sebastian and Jonah emerge from the school of fish and float near the top of Jack's bubble like two mischievous boys still evident in their deer form. They bow their heads and start to poke at the thin material with their sharp antlers, making small puncture wounds in the soft material. Jack nods as if he understands and then drops to his knees, pulls his dive knife out of its sheath, and stabs several holes in the floor. Tiny rips weaken the fragile structure, and seawater begins to seep in, first as a trickle and then as gushes of water like a pipe that burst.

What the hell is he doing? Isn't Jack afraid of drowning down here? "Wait!" I shout uselessly, my voice bouncing off the jelly walls. He continues to slice at the floor until it's shredded to ribbons and then replaces the knife and smiles with satisfaction as the water washes over him.

I watch as the bubble collapses like a soft contact lens and the floor drops out, plummeting Jack into the open sea. Small bubbles escape from his lips as he swims straight down toward the coral ring. I drop to my knees and stare through the floor of my bubble, watching in disbelief as he brazenly slips through the blue coral ring.

His hands are the first things to change.

Jack holds a palm in front of his face and watches the fingers meld together and curl into hardened hooves, his wedding ring disappearing into the thick black clog. His eyes widen as his five o'clock shadow spreads across his cheeks and quickly grows down his neck and shoulders. Baby antlers and small floppy ears sprout through the top of his head, and I clamp my eyes shut and turn away, unable to watch the rest of his transformation.

When I finally do open my eyes Jack is swimming before me in the shape of a handsome young deer. A sprinkling of tiny white spots cover his torso, and his juvenile face is wide and expressive. Amazingly I can still see my Jack in this strange creature before me. There is salt-and-pepper fur near his temples, and the familiar green-speckled eyes I've known for half my life stare back at me with wonder.

Alone in my bubble there is nothing left to do but wake up from this fantastical dream or join Jack as a deer.

All around me the underwater creatures redirect their efforts to me now and encourage my bubble forward. Jack and the others are using the top of their deer heads to inch me toward the coral ring, which is shining bright beneath me. I feel my bubble slowly lumber into place. There is an urgent whispering all around me. The voices are encouraging me to follow Jack's lead, and I get a wave of peer pressure times a million.

And even though I was the one who started this whole thing I am now desperately wondering how to shut it down. True, I was initially intrigued by the full-moon ritual, and even felt an obligation to try one while on this magical island, but this is way more than I bargained for. And just when I start to convince myself that I can just walk away, a cloud of doubt washes over me and makes me think that maybe we have gone too far to turn back now. Maybe Jack's decision to transform somehow made my decision for me. *Would they really let me back out now?*

Looking up to find Ruby's deer face pressed up against the bubble, I am afraid that her piercing blue eyes will pick up on my hesitation. As Jack and the others watch with anticipation, it is then that I make my decision.

I claw at the thin wall like a bear mauling a camper's tent and, in no time there is a hole big enough to swim through. But instead of letting myself drop like the others I push myself off the bottom and propel myself up, away from the glowing blue coral ring.

As soon as I leave the womb-like safety of the bubble, everything changes like turning on the lights in a haunted house and revealing all its secrets. I immediately swallow a mouth full of salty water and clamp my lips shut in a growing panic. Anxiety runs cold through my veins, and my heart pounds in my ears as I frantically kick my legs and reach for the surface, which feels like it might be a million miles away. *Perhaps I should have thought this through.* It's as if the high from the jasmine flowers has run its course, and I am instantly sober. Stone-cold sober.

I resist the urge to look back even though I'm convinced that the deer witches are pursuing me, and I anticipate a tug on my leg from Ruby, Sebastian, or Jonah, or maybe even Jack. Desperately clutching fistfuls of water and kicking my legs hard, I slowly but steadily rise. The vibrant colors of the coral begin to fade, so I know I'm headed in the right direction. My lungs are on fire, especially the one that was punctured in the accident, and I make a small noise like a frightened animal. But adrenaline and sheer determination drive me forward.

Almost there. I must be almost there.

At last I see the light of the full moon shining through the water like a lighthouse in a storm. It sends hope to my lungs, which feel like they are about to burst into flames. *Yes, just a few more kicks.* With one last push I crash through the surface coughing and wheezing with the relief of a marathon runner breaking the finish-line ribbon.

Checking myself quickly by tapping the foamy wetsuit, I am relieved to find that I am still very much in my human form. As I had assumed, the coral ring was the key to the transformation, and since I did not pass through the ring, I was still in fact human.

Jack, on the other hand . . .

No time to think about that now.

My breathing labored and loud I scramble up the ladder and search the surrounding water for the deer heads that I'm convinced are going to pop up and drag me back down. I hoist myself into the boat and with shaking hands push wet strands of hair from my face, vaguely realizing that the scarf is gone but too freaked out to care.

I jam the key into the ignition and after a few failed attempts manage to start the motor with an ear-splitting squeal. The boat lurches forward wildly like an electric bull, and I let out a loud "fuck" and pull hard on the wheel. Regaining control of the boat I pass under the wide arch, and as soon as I'm clear I press down on the throttle, increasing my speed.

The cool night air begins to clear my head and makes me start to second-guess myself. *What have I done? How could I have left Jack like that?* I consider going back for him and at one point actually stop the boat and bounce in the waves, weighing my options.

Maybe I could find Roscoe and he could help me. But how would I find him at this hour when I remember him saying that the staff doesn't live on the island? And even if I can find him how do I explain what's happened? *You see, we were just performing this full-moon ritual and got ourselves in over our heads.* It's like playing with the Ouija board and poking at the spirits and then complaining when they poked back.

Alternating right and left, I slap both cheeks in an attempt to snap myself out of it. *This, whatever this was.* Closing my eyes and then opening them again I find myself still in my dripping wetsuit, alone on the boat.

"Ready to wake up. Any time now!" I shout into the moonlit sky.

After running through various possibilities I entertain the idea that maybe I'm sleepwalking. *Yes, that's it.* I just need to get back to the bungalow, I convince myself, even going as far as to imagine my sleeping self curled up next to Jack, dreaming this whole thing. So I start the engine and head back to Cernunnos Island with a renewed false sense of hope.

After haphazardly tying up the boat I run down the path, wet and barefoot, constantly glancing back and freaked out by every little sound.

Rushing into the bungalow I lock the door behind me and pull a chair in front of it for good measure. Checking to make sure the windows are locked I turn on all the lights, still half expecting to find Jack padding around in his chocolate-brown bathrobe.

But the rooms are empty, even the bedroom.

No Jack.

Peeling off my wet clothes I drop them in a heavy heap on the bathroom floor and stand in the shower for a long, long time. I let the hot water pound down on my head as I seesaw between complete denial and loud crying jags. In my hysteria I let myself consider the possibility that maybe I never woke up from the car accident and perhaps this was all part of one wild coma-induced hallucination. I again picture Jack, but this time he is sitting next to my hospital bed while my eyelids twitch and flutter.

When I finally emerge from the shower I spot Jack's T-shirt hanging on a hook behind the bathroom door. With water-pruned fingers I pull the shirt to my face and inhale deeply, my eyes filling with tears again. It's the shirt he slept in the other night and still smells like him, warm and familiar. I slip on the oversized T-shirt, and it hangs down to my knees like a nightshirt. Pulling a strip of toilet paper from the roll, I blow my nose, wash my face, and weave my hair into a long braid just like Valentina used to.

I pace the bedroom and regret ever reading the witchy book but after some reflection decide that maybe it holds the key to getting us out of this mess. I march down the long hallway, determined to comb through the book and find some kind of follow-up ritual. I need something to uncast the spell, something to turn Jack back into himself.

Just outside the dark living room, I stop short. *Why is the living room dark?* I'm certain I left all the lights on. *Maybe it's Jack!* Hope and relief flood through me as I flick on the light.

"Are you looking for this, my lady?" Sebastian is stretched out on the couch, his long legs crossed at the ankles, and he is holding the heavy book high in the air.

"Where's Jack?" I demand, taking a step toward him.

Jonah jumps up from behind the couch and snatches the book from Sebastian's grip, spinning it on one finger like it was a basketball. Sebastian tries to retrieve it, but Jonah is dancing around the living room twirling the book and avoiding him skillfully. Ruby emerges from behind the long curtains and stealthily takes the spinning book from Jonah's fingers.

She rolls her eyes disapprovingly. "Boys, please, let's not play monkey-in-the-middle with our guest." Then she adds, "She's had a rough night."

Hugging the book close to her chest she glides across the room, the long material of her dress dragging on the floor and hiding her feet. Quickly scanning the room I realize that Jack is not with them. I feel a lump in my throat and feel myself on the verge of crying again. But Ruby appears just inches from my face, and her brilliant blue eyes act like a Valium, making me feel relaxed and sleepy.

"You are wondering about Jack." She examines my face.

I nod several times. I have so many questions but don't know where to begin. *Where is Jack now? Is he okay? Is he pissed at me for leaving him?*

"He is resting," she says simply.

"It's cool." Jonah jumps in. "It's totally normal to sleep for like twelve hours after the first transformation."

"Oh good, well, as long as this is all cool and normal," I grumble.

"You want to know if he's pissed at you." Sebastian twirls his silver rings up and down his long fingers.

Okay, they must be reading my thoughts.

"Yes, we are reading your thoughts." Ruby confirms.

"And yes, Jack is pissed at you," Sebastian adds.

I rub my forehead and try to shake the strange sensation like drinking a frozen margarita and getting a brain freeze. "When can I see him?"

"We will bring him to the beach."

"Tomorrow at noon."

"He should be done with his resting period by then."

The three of them take turns reciting each line like a rehearsed speech, one they'd recited many times before.

I plop down on the couch. "Okay, let's recap. My husband is now a deer, but don't worry, he's just resting. And oh yeah, he's pissed at me for not becoming a deer too!"

"Actually, we are all a little pissed about that."

Ruby joins me on the couch, sitting gingerly, her spine pin straight, and I am reminded of this same type of posture she holds as a deer. She opens the book and flips through the pages so fast that it generates a breeze that lifts the curtain of shiny black hair from her face. I have never been this close to her and still can't shake the illusion of a hologram. I am tempted to reach out and touch her, curious to see if my little radio frequency will work on a deer witch. *What kind of vision might I pick up from this ancient creature?*

She stops at the page with the pyramid and proffers it toward me. Moving her long fingers across the drawing on the old parchment, she points with nails dyed a dark red and sharpened like talons. "This pyramid illustrates the major covens and how the bloodline moves through the centuries."

"There are five major covens?" I look up at Sebastian for confirmation.

"Six, if you count the ancient coven led by Ruby, which is the oldest and most influential in the tribal community."

I study the pyramid and try to figure out where Jack and I fit in.

"There are thousands of gene carriers roaming the earth; some are just more in tune to it than others."

"Some go through their whole life never acknowledging that persistent little voice telling them they are different." Sebastian fusses with the strange clock on the mantel.

"It's a combination of born potential and learned skills." Jonah shrugs.

"Like the ability to sing." Sebastian tries an analogy. "While most people *can* sing, some people are clearly better at it than others."

It doesn't take me long to get used to the way they weave in and out of each other's sentences, each taking part in completing a single thought.

"How did you know Jack and I were gene carriers?"

"The most effective way is to do an identity test, what the humans call a DNA test, and you made that real easy with the towel you shoved into the trash can when you first arrived."

"Ewwww." I shudder.

"Jonah wanted to use the vomit towel, but I thought it would be more civilized to use the champagne goblets." Sebastian slides in next to me, and now I am sandwiched between him and Ruby. There is a warm energy radiating off the two of them, and I feel cocooned like being wrapped in a blanket fresh out of the dryer.

"We were most excited to find that Jack was a gene carrier, because that probably meant you were one too," Sebastian points out.

"It's very common for gene carriers to find each other in the mundane world. They are naturally drawn to one another."

Jonah can't seem to sit still and wanders into the kitchen, poking through the refrigerator. "Nice, guacamole!"

Sebastian rolls his eyes while Jonah nosily searches for something in the pantry. "Yeesss!" I catch a small fist pump when he finds a bag of tortilla chips. I try to focus on what Sebastian is saying and not get distracted by Jonah.

"Not an easy thing to do." Ruby smiles, plucking the thought from my head.

"May I please continue?" Sebastian whines and actually pouts.

"Nobody's stopping you." Jonah has my cell phone now and is snapping pictures of himself posing with the guacamole. I try to hide a smile as Sebastian shakes his blond mane and takes a deep breath.

"You see, my dear, there are four different types of deer witch, and we are each classified by our elemental power." He holds up four bejeweled fingers.

Jonah carries his snack into the living room, shoving several chips piled high with guacamole into his mouth. He offers the bowl to Ruby, and she responds with a hand held high like Diana Ross performing "Stop in the Name of Love." He drops the snacks on the cocktail table and pulls a tall ceramic mug from behind his back. He hands it to me, and I find it half-filled with dried flowers and golden tea leaves.

"I have the elemental power of earth, governed by Taurus, so I'm sort of a wizard when it comes to medicinal herbs," Jonah explains.

Ruby flicks her wrist over the mug, and it instantly fills with fresh water. "Power of water, ruled by Cancer." She sighs.

"And I have the power of fiery Leo." On the word "fiery" Sebastian dips his index finger into the tea water, and it quickly ripples to an instant boil.

Hmm, that's handy. "So, fire, water, earth and . . . ?"

"Air," the three of them say in unison.

"To find an air witch is extremely rare these days."

"Those who possess the gene rarely tap in to its true potential."

"And the ones who do develop the power usually wallow in self-destruction or find themselves lured by Atrum."

When I look confused, Sebastian translates, "Dark arts," and then Ruby lowers her voice to a whisper, "Air witches have always been much sought after for dark spells and rituals."

I frown. "What does this all have to do with me?" Testing the tea, I find it to be too hot to drink. *But it smells delicious like chamomile and something else.* I cradle the mug between my palms and let the fragrant steam spread up over my face, tempted to close my eyes but afraid that I might fall asleep.

Sebastian bites his lower lip. "Are you going to tell her or shall I?"

Uh-oh. I sit up. *Tell me what?*

Ruby's blue orbs meet mine, and I get another dose of those Valium eyes to squelch my growing panic. "When the tests came back we discovered you are stronger than a gene carrier. You are a *BloodLiner.*"

"A pleasant surprise, most *unexpected.*" Sebastian says the last word with syncopated beats.

"We ran the test twice. Once on the goblet and again on the towel just to be sure."

"Wait, how is a BloodLiner different than a gene carrier?" I shake my head.

"BloodLiners can be traced back to one of the six major covens, so their inbred potential is the most powerful, closest to the source," Ruby starts.

"A BloodLiner is a direct descendant of another BloodLiner. So when a BloodLiner mates with another BloodLiner, a gene carrier, or even a human, they create another BloodLiner," Sebastian adds.

"The power of a gene carrier is similar but slightly diluted like third cousins." Jonah munches from above.

"Okay, so somewhere in my ancestry there must have been a BloodLiner?" I ask, thinking about the years I spent searching unsuccessfully for my biological parents.

"Precisely," all three of them answer, sounding like one harmonized musical note.

"Could it be one of you guys?" I ask a little uneasily, pointing at each of them. *Was it possible that Sebastian was my great-great-granddaddy?*

"It's highly unlikely . . ." Sebastian trails off. "In any event, it is believed that you hold the key." He lowers his chin and stares up at me.

"What key?" I look slowly from one face to the next, trying to read their expression. All three of them are looking at me like a dog that spotted a squirrel.

"To the rising of PoG." Ruby answers in a low whisper, her eyes glowing.

Sebastian takes the book from my lap and opens it to the two-page spread of Playground of the Gods. He closes his eyes and runs his hand over the textured paint like a blind man reading braille.

"Let me see if I understand." I begin, carefully watching him trace the outline of the castle with his long fingers. "You believe that I have the potential to become a powerful air witch and I have the power to raise PoG?" I tap the page to ensure that we are talking about the same thing.

"Correct!" Sebastian clamps the book shut and almost snaps off my finger in the process. "You complete the circle."

Oh okay, so long as there's no pressure. "How long has it been exactly?" I take another sip of tea and feel it spread through my abdomen like a hearty soup.

"Monty says it's been thousands of years since PoG has risen."

As if on cue Monty appears at my feet and lets out a loud meow to announce his arrival. Blinking up at me and nodding his furry face he seems to be confirming this last statement. He jumps up on the couch and curls up in my lap while I move the hot tea out of his way. As I stroke his soft fur he flops his big paw over my wrist protectively and moves his eyes from speaker to speaker, apparently able to follow the conversation.

"Each century we try," Ruby starts wearily.

"And each century we fail," Sebastian finishes.

"Only once per century are the planets aligned for optimal success," Jonah explains.

I sip the flowery tea and continue to pet Monty while the musical voices of Ruby and the twins drift over me deep into the night and eventually lull me to sleep.

In my dream, I am transported to the grotto.

"Okay my fiery friend, let's try this again." Sebastian's velvety voice curls around the coral walls and washes over me where I stand unobserved. I peek around the wall and see Jack's hind legs positioned in a wide stance, his deer body pitched forward. He is standing directly across from Sebastian, who is in his human form, and on the ground between them is a small pile of stones.

Jack and Sebastian are staring intently into the mound of smooth gray rocks when suddenly a small flame sparks up from the center and flickers in the dark grotto. Sebastian bends to examine the emerging flame and looks pleased. He rises from his crouched position and rubs his hands together, placing his left palm above the fire. The orange flame responds by leaping in a high arc and reaching for his hand like a hungry tiger snapping at a piece of meat. When he lowers his hand the flame responds by retreating back to its original size.

Jack's body stiffens, and he shifts his weight as he stares down at the little flame. He tries to make the flame grow like Sebastian did, squeezing his face with the effort like he was trying to blow up a balloon. The flame flickers a few times but refuses to rise to the challenge, and eventually it dies out.

"Again!" Ruby's voice comes from the darkness.

Waking with a start I drop the empty mug to the floor with a loud crack. I am still on the couch wearing Jack's T-shirt, but someone has covered me with a blanket. My neck is stiff, and my back cracks loudly when I sit up. Sitting and listening for a moment, I decide that the bungalow feels empty.

Slowly looking around the empty room I try to separate the dream from recent events. Memories from last night quickly flood my head, and a wave of nausea washes over me. I run to the bathroom and flip the lid, pulling my hair back and preparing myself. Nothing happens, so I splash cold water on my face and try to shake it off. Standing at the sink I let the cold water run over my hands and flick it toward my face and neck. Staring at myself in the mirror I try to figure out what to do.

In the harsh morning light, I am feeling like I need to get the hell off this island as quickly as possible. Maybe I should fly back to Athens and contact the police so they could start an official search for Jack. Perhaps this sort of thing has happened before? Could it be some kind of elaborate prank organized by the locales to mess with the tourists? Not very good for return business if that were the case.

After a few minutes my body complains about the awkward position, so I place both hands on my lower back and stretch with a loud groan.

No more aches and pains.

The words pop into my head as if someone whispered them in my ear. I spin around in the empty bathroom trying to locate the source of the sound.

Your body will feel like it's brand new. You can run and swim and never worry about hurting your back, certainly not doing something silly like bending over a sink.

I recognize the voice as Jack, but he sounds so different. He sounds young and optimistic like when we first met, *full of piss and vinegar.* Hearing Jack's voice makes me long to see him, and tears burn my eyes, squeezing out of the corners and rolling down my cheeks. Pressing the towel to my face I sigh and remember something Sebastian told me last night: "We will bring Jack to the beach at noon."

Shit, what time is it? I gasp at Jack's watch, the one he left on the bathroom sink when he swapped it for his dive watch, when I see that it shows fifteen minutes past noon. Damn, I am always fifteen minutes late for everything. In a mad rush I pluck a black-and-white sundress from the closet and swap it for the old T-shirt, adding my trusty gold sandals. I am still closing the tiny tortoise shell buttons down the front of the dress while I run down the steps of the bungalow and hurry toward the beach to meet Jack.

My husband.

The deer witch.

Half walking, half jogging in an effort to make up time, I arrive at the beach around twelve thirty. My heart is pounding in my ears, and I can feel beads of sweat gathering at the nape of my neck. I look around expectantly, but the sandy beach is deserted. The virgin sand is raked to perfection like the comb marks in a librarian's hair. I examine the shoreline, sweeping my eyes up and down the water's edge, but there is no sign of anyone, deer or otherwise.

Slipping off my sandals I quickly hop through the hot sand and am relieved to reach the water's edge. Letting the cool water soothe my burning feet I scan the area again. No sign of anyone. I begin to think I have imagined the whole thing.

Which part, Gwen?

The sea stretches for miles before melting into a clear sky sprinkled with cotton candy clouds. It was easy to understand why ancient man thought the earth was flat. From this angle it looks like a boat would simply tip right off the edge of the earth. In fact, intelligent man believed that the earth was flat until some brave soul actually took a boat out over the edge to prove that there was something else beyond the horizon, a world we never even dreamed possible. So why am I having a hard time wrapping my mind around the idea of the deer witch? *And why can't I accept the fact that I might actually have the potential to become a powerful air witch myself.*

Last night Ruby and the twins told me about gene carriers living in the mundane world and always feeling different and out of place. Hasn't that been the case for me? Being adopted and an only child I have always felt like an outsider.

And there were moments in my life when I can certainly remember becoming distinctly aware of the air around me. Like that night with the Ouija board when the window blew open like an urgent whisper. Or at our wedding when we danced our first dance on the top deck and my veil whipped in the air like a playful tug. Maybe these were subtle signs of my air witch potential.

Closing my eyes for a moment I wonder about my near-death experience and my subsequent abilities. Maybe a human without the gene would have responded differently to the accident, and perhaps this enhanced intuition was due to my deer witch heritage. And stronger than a gene carrier, they say I am a BloodLiner, which would make everything more magnified and intense. My life, especially recent events, seems to make more sense thinking along these new lines.

Opening my eyes I watch the scalloped waves curl around my toes and then retreat back to the sea. Surprisingly I spot faint footprints in the wet sand. They seemed to emerge from the waves and continue up onto the beach. I hadn't noticed them until now. Is it possible someone walked past me while I was sitting here with my eyes closed? *I guess anything is possible at this point.*

I examine the three sets of tracks comprised of half-moon deer hooves that change into human prints halfway down the beach. The prints disappear into a cluster of rocks further down the shoreline. Placing my hand to my forehead and squinting toward the rocks, I make out three human forms. Ruby is out front, Jonah is pointing at something in the water, and Sebastian's head is thrown back in a laugh, one I can't actually hear from this distance.

But no Jack.

"Hey . . ." I start to call after them but then spot a fourth set of tracks.

Following these smaller half-moon deer hooves across the sand I keep waiting for them to change to human footprints, but the half-moons end in the sand dunes where I find Jack in his deer form curled behind a large rock. His head is tilted toward the sun, reminding me of his posture the first day we arrived on Cernunnos Island. *That seems like a million years ago.*

Blinking several times I try to comprehend the fact that the deer before me is Jack. I can tell he's pissed; even in deer form his body language is clear. When he senses my approach he lowers his chin but keeps his eyes clamped shut.

Figuring that I had better start off with an apology, I kneel down next to him in the sand and whisper, which seems silly because of his new gift of telepathy. But I still feel the need to speak out loud. "I am so sorry."

I can't believe you chickened out! Jack's response pops into my head like he was calling out from the next room.

"Holy shit, I thought we were going to release some emotional baggage, not turn into frigging deer!"

Jack's green eyes fly open to meet mine. Like the salt-and-pepper fur around his temples, his eyes are the same as they were in his human form, and I get a strange jolt of familiarity. Plus an overwhelming curiosity.

"Tell me. What's it like?" I lean in close, anticipating his response.

It's . . . He pauses. *Enlightening. Sure it was a bit freaky at first, but then the enhanced powers kick in and you can't believe you lived so long in the restrictive shell of human existence. You have to do it, Gwen. I don't want to do this without you.*

"Well, I'm not so sure I could sneak you back home like this." Jack lets out a surge of air, and I figure it's his version of a deer laugh.

"What about the business?" I ask, imagining Jack taking a client meeting in his new deer form. I need to literally shake my head like an Etch A Sketch to dissolve the image of Jack sitting at a conference table as a deer.

Screw it. Let them figure it out. There is defiance in his eyes I've not seen before.

Wow I never thought I would see the day when Jack would be willing to give up the business that took us years to cultivate. Even stranger, the idea is starting to appeal to me too. *Why the hell not?* I start to get excited about the idea of never having to run a staff meeting, balance the books, or settle an employee dispute ever again.

But still I have questions.

"Where would we live?"

We'd live on the beach. Travel from island to island. Jack sways his wet nose side to side when the phrase "island to island" echoes in my head.

"What do we do for money?"

Details, details. Sebastian says money is not an issue.

Looking over my shoulder I try to locate Sebastian and the others, but they are so far away now they look like tiny ants scurrying across the rocks. Apparently they are trying to give us privacy, or at least the *illusion* of privacy. I have no doubt that they are listening in with their enhanced sense of hearing. It is impossible to conduct a private conversation when deer witches are near.

Still looking toward the others I ask, "What about our family and friends?"

We can visit them in the dream realm.

The dream realm, huh? I guess that can't be much different than opening Christmas presents on web cam, which is what we have been doing for the past few years anyway with Jack's brothers and their families. I've never really had much of a family. *Jack is my family.*

Instinctively I reach out to touch the fur above his eyes. He pushes his head into my hand affectionately, and I continue to smooth down the fur around his face. I have to stop myself from wrapping my arms around his deer torso and giving him a hug.

Okay, we certainly can't go on like this. Since Jack is usually one step ahead of me on most things, I might need to trust him on this one. Yes, it might be time to follow my Peter Pan into Never-Never-Land.

Placing both hands on my knees I push myself into a standing position with a small grunt. "Okay," I say decisively. "Tonight at the grotto."

Really? Jack's almond-shaped eyes light up.

DAY VII:

In or Out

The birds cry overhead as Jack makes a whinny sound signaling for Ruby and the twins. The three of them appear in the sand dunes, their human forms taking shape from a rising mist. It is like looking at one of those posters on the boardwalk, the ones made entirely of tiny dots that you stare at until finally an image appears. They rally around me like I'm a stubborn teenager who has finally agreed to go to college.

Ruby is most excited to hear the news and starts pacing back and forth in the sand. "Good, good. Now all we need to do is wait for nightfall. It must be dark enough to see the moon. Remember, if you get cold feet . . ."

If you get cold feet again . . . Jack pops into my head, and Ruby shoots him a silencing look.

"We'll need to wait two and half years for another blue moon, and we don't have that kind of time." She begins to make a shallow trench in the sand with the intensity of her pacing.

Sebastian lies back onto the sand, his long blond hair sprawling around his head like a messy halo. "Wear something pretty!"

"Pretty but comfortable." Jonah drops to his knees and dumps a collection of nuts and berries from his upturned shirt.

He is now separating the food into two small piles, nuts and berries. Ruby takes a break from pacing to wade into the shallow waves and pull an ancient bronze pitcher from the swell of water. As she makes her way back, large drops of red liquid splash over the side and I unnecessarily worry about her staining her long white dress. Cold condensation bubbles up on the jug as she presents a pitcher of ice-cold sangria, and Jonah dumps in the pile of fresh berries to complete today's cocktail. Sebastian stirs the drink with a long stick, the tip shaped like a horse's head, and I wonder if it was carved that way or was nature's happy accident.

We lounge in the sand dunes all afternoon drinking sangria and making plans for my transformation. I ask dozens of questions, and they each take turns calming my fears. Sometimes I just think questions at them and they patiently answer each inquiry, their words negotiating with my inner thoughts.

Has anyone ever died from the transformation?

No. Although the transformation itself is a cycle of death and rebirth.

What if a non-gene carrier attempts to perform the transformation ritual?

Nothing happens. But sometimes, depending on our mood, we might show up and have a little fun with them.

It was interesting to learn that most people approached by the deer witches are loners, people who don't have deep connections to family or friends and might be open to the idea of leaving their old life behind and joining the coven. And from what I could tell it is considered lucky to be approached by a deer witch; it's like meeting a leprechaun or a genie. The encounters usually occur during a full moon, and some people suggest that it is the light of the moon that makes the deer witch visible in the physical world.

How come you can't change back into your human form? I try to direct the question at Jack, but Sebastian looks up from his sangria and answers in a silent whisper.

Patience, my dear. A changeling develops slowly; the basic powers come first, and then the elemental powers, and everything slowly crystallizes over the first year like a newborn baby.

"A whole year!" I shout, jumping up from the sand.

This might be a deal breaker. Nobody said anything about running around like a deer for an entire year. I still try to overcome the initial shock of taking the shape of a four-legged creature but reason I can switch back to human form whenever I want to, *or so I thought.* Being a deer witch in human form with enhanced powers is much more attractive to me than walking around on all fours. But then again being a deer is better than being something like a werewolf. *Who wants to be something that so closely resembled a dog?* At least there is something regal about a deer. After all, their legs are longer and they are higher up off the ground, like a horse. I cock my head and nod as if this would make it so.

"Not necessarily a whole year." Ruby's voice is low but firm. "I've seen a deer witch shift back to human form just hours after the first transformation. It all depends on the strength of the witch and the purity of the bloodline."

Jonah cracks a walnut in his fist and sprinkles the edible pieces into his mouth. "The fact that you are making the first transformation under a blue moon is a good accelerator."

"That's why Jack is developing so quickly. Already he can generate a small flame; isn't that right, buddy?" Sebastian claps him on the back like a proud father, and Jack arches in appreciation.

I think about the dream of Jack with the flame and try to figure out how long the deer witches have been visiting me in the dream realm. Probably since we first arrived on this magical island, but Sebastian's mouth curls into a guilty smile, indicating that it could have been much farther back than that.

As if sensing my silent inquiry, Ruby waves her arms in the direction of a large oncoming wave, and the water stops in midair and crystalizes into a flat-screen television. Home movies of our Italian honeymoon, the Isle of Capri, and subsequent travel up through Rome and Venice fill the projection screen.

"Wait, were you guys in Italy with us?"

"That was a radical trip." Jonah chuckles.

"Members of the coven were becoming curious about you and considered approaching you in Roma."

"But the Elders thought it would be wise to let you live in the mundane world and gain strength through success."

"And sorrow." Sebastian's eyes track a white bird as it passes overhead.

The three of them continue to weave in and out of each other's sentences just like the other night when they made me tea in the bungalow.

"When you and Jack were approaching Cernunnos Island the MCs became all a buzz."

An MC? Is that like a master of ceremonies? I picture the emcee from *Cabaret.*

Sebastian spits out his wine with laughter. "That's one way to describe them, I suppose."

"MC. Magical. Creature." Jonah flicks two berries into my glass, emphasizing each word, and they land with small splashes of accuracy even though the glass is a moving target on its way up to my mouth.

The only thing more powerful than a BloodLiner is a magical creature. These are creatures that are born, not made, such as wizards, deities, fairies, and spirit guides. Jonah thinks at me.

"I suppose you guys are considered magical creatures, yes?"

"Yes." Jonah smiles.

"What about the lady on the rope bridge?"

The three of them freeze, and then Sebastian lifts his shirt and slowly pulls a long piece of silky material from the belt loops of his jeans. "Are you referring to the owner of this lovely garment?" He waves it from side to side like a hypnotist.

To my surprise he was using it as a belt, the colorful scarf from the Aunt Wanda lady and the same one I lost during last night's ritual. Jonah grabs one end and sniffs it like a bloodhound until Ruby snatches it from them and squints at it as if she were reading something in the pattern.

"Where did you get this?" She takes a purposeful step toward me.

"From the lady on the rope bridge."

"She gave it to you?"

"Not exactly." I tell them the story about how she flung the jasmine flower over the side and how the three deer tossed her over the side after it. "The scarf got snagged in the shuffle. But now after everything I've learned, I assume she is one of your kind, right?"

"In a matter of speaking." They exchange a look I can't decode. "Did she say anything else?"

"Hmm, yeah . . . something about being *in over my head.*" I hold out my glass for a refill.

Ruby stirs the pitcher of sangria with the horse stick, and her inner dialogue is quiet for several seconds. I realize that Jack hasn't joined the conversation in a while, and I prop myself up on both elbows and look around, finding him nestled against a rock, sound asleep.

"Newborns sleep a lot in the beginning." Jonah explains. "Don't take it personally."

Ruby casually hides the scarf away in the material of her dress and refills my sangria glass. She wears a smile like a hostess who just discovered that her pot roast is burning but is determined to keep this little detail from ruining her party. Deer witches have the ability to cast an emotional cocoon around themselves and those in their close proximity, and I can feel the invisible walls around us filling with a big dose of it's-all-good. I settle back down on Jack's deer body and use him as a pillow as the afternoon drifts away.

After a few hours Ruby lifts her white hood into place and announces that it's going to rain, but I examine the clear, blue sky and frown uncertainly.

"Till tonight," she calls over her shoulder and strides across the sand with the poise of a dancer. I half expect her to pirouette in the sand.

The twins break into a slow jog toward the water, and Jack wakes with a start and looks around, confused. I pat his head reassuringly and nod toward the others. When he jumps up, his legs are a bit shaky like Bambi trying to stand on ice.

Love you, he projects back at me before steadying himself and skipping toward the others.

I watch them walk together into the waves, and the powerful swells crash against their bodies like an amateur fighter throwing punches at the reigning champion. For a moment they blend with the white spraying surf, and then they disappear under the water. Almost instantly three familiar deer heads emerge, Ruby out front with Sebastian and Jonah's tall antlers poking up toward the sky. Jack and his smallish antlers trail behind. He thinks his horns grew a little last night, and I agreed to make him feel better. But I can't really tell if they grew or not.

Like a line of ducks the four of them disappear toward the horizon, and I feel intensely lonely as I look for my gold sandals. The sky above begins to fill with clouds and then darken. It looks like Ruby was right about the storm. *It was probably foolish to doubt a water witch about something like rain.*

Warm drops of rain fall from the low-hanging clouds as I rush back to the bungalow. Fumbling with the door, I barely get it open before the sky opens up and dumps buckets of rain all around me. By the time I get inside I am completely drenched. Quickly I peel off my wet clothes and towel-dry my hair before surrendering to the comfort of the chocolate-brown robe. Stroking the arm of the smooth material I remember the softness of Jack's deer fur, soft as feathers, and wonder if my fur will feel like this.

Even softer, comes the answer.

Smiling and wrapping the robe tightly around me I collapse onto the bed and listen to the rain striking the tin roof like the metallic drums of a reggae band. I lie there for a while and try to figure out what to do with myself for the next few hours. The waiting was going to be the hardest part, and now that I'm alone I could feel the familiar doubt creep over me. The anticipation of something was usually worse than the actual event, and I recall another one of my father's plaques and recite it out loud in the empty room,

"Today is the tomorrow you worried about yesterday."

Yikes, what is my father going to say about this? And my mother? To be honest that was the least of my worries. Being adopted, I was never all that concerned with their opinions. I gave up seeking the approval of my adopted parents years ago. I found myself more concerned with what our friends and colleagues might think. *And Jack's family!* His brothers, their wives, our nieces and nephews. But I guess if he is ready to do this, then so am I. No use worrying about what people might say.

Unable to sit still I jump up and try to busy myself with picking up the clothes strewn around the room after a week's worth of vacation. I actually consider packing but then quickly decide against it, figuring I won't need any of my fancy clothes as a deer witch. Ruby and the boys were always wearing the same clothes and are perpetually barefoot. That was convenient considering I had a tough time finding comfortable shoes and was happiest running around barefoot anyway.

I drop the clothes I am holding and fall face first on the bed like a sack of potatoes. *This is going to be a long night.*

I try to imagine how this will all play out. Jack and I simply won't return from vacation. It happens all the time—like that honeymoon couple we saw on the news that disappeared from a cruise ship. On second thought, I think the husband returned, and she didn't. In fact, it turned out that he murdered her.

Okay, that wasn't a great example.

We are both just going to disappear as if we drowned. Let them think I got swept out in the strong undertow and Jack swam out to save me. Yeah, Jack would like the idea of going down as a hero. I wonder if we should stage something on the beach like leaving a beach bag with some personal effects. How come I didn't ask any of these questions during our little Q&A this afternoon? Oh yeah, it might have been that bottomless glass of sangria they were serving. I rub my head, feeling another headache coming on, and promptly pop two aspirin, afraid the headache might follow me into the transformation. *Could a deer witch even get a headache?*

Now that I'm thinking straight, well, straighter than back on the beach, I feel compelled to leave some kind of written note.

How about a last will and testament?

I don't recognize the voice and chalk it up to my own inner pessimist, although she sounds especially bitchy today.

Pulling the nightstand drawer I reach for a sheet of stationery tucked into a floral box with an antique buckle. My fingers briefly glaze the metal clasp, but it's just enough to generate a series of visions. Like someone dropped a box of photographs from above, they each float by slowly enough for me to examine. The majority of them are male-female couples toasting their goblets and posing around the bungalow. There are some color photos, others are black and white, and there are even a few canvas paintings, men and women in big dresses and old-fashioned garb posing on the terrace. These are mingled with a few group shots of soldiers on the beach hoisting a flag or proudly displaying other such symbols. Some of the subjects look vaguely familiar, but after a while they all start to look the same. The furniture and wallpaper have been updated, but there is no doubt the view of the ocean is exactly the one I am looking at when the visions subside and I find myself staring through the rain-streaked sliders.

These must be the people who stayed in this bungalow. *How many of them were gene carriers? How many of them had been approached by the deer witches?* From what I could tell it had been a long, long time since Ruby approached someone about joining her coven. I think I sensed something about the roaring twenties when I thought the question at Sebastian back on the beach. Is it pure luck that Jack and I are on the island at this moment in time, or was it fate? Like the sense of destiny Jack spoke of when he proposed the full-moon ritual.

And what about the wedding originally planned for this week? Would one of the guests have been a suitable candidate? Or was it possible that there wouldn't have been a gene carrier on the entire guest list? I still wasn't exactly clear on the ratio of humans to gene carriers. But I somehow have the feeling that gene carriers are becoming more rare. And BloodLiners are practically extinct.

Trying to focus on the task at hand, the eloquent letter I am preparing to write, the one that will explain everything away, I hold the pen to the blank page and stare at the *Cernunnos Island* written in cursive script along the bottom. I'm not sure what to say or how to say it, and after a few false starts I abandon the idea of a letter altogether. I crumple the paper into a tight little ball and toss it across the room, where it lands on a pile of dirty clothes with a soft thump.

I jump up with the idea that a picture is worth a thousand words and search for my cell phone, locating it in the cushions of the living room sofa. I flip through the camera roll and stop to stare at the last photo I took of Jack. Zooming in to examine his face, I can easily recall the similarities to the deer I spent time with on the beach this afternoon. I can feel his personality and his sense of humor, and the eyes—*his eyes are exactly the same.*

Flipping to the next photo I can't help but smile at Jonah posing with the guacamole. *Hmm, he seemed awfully familiar with the camera feature.* Was he the one who came into the bungalow and hid my phone? And why would he do that? Was it some sort of freshman hazing or something much more sinister? For now I restore the deleted photos of Monty, realizing that some people will see a cat and others an old man, but it will help tell the story.

I take a few more photos of the *cervus veneficus book*, pictures of PoG, legends of the Elders, and information on gene carriers and BloodLiners. Somewhat of a cryptic message, but the pieces are all there. Anyone who was interested could potentially pull it all together. I set the photos to rotate in a slideshow before powering the phone down.

Returning to the bedroom in search of potential shipping materials I settle on Jack's handkerchief as padding and shoelaces from his sneaker for string. I wrap the phone in the handkerchief and drop it into a pink shoebox, after dumping out a pair of strappy shoes that kill my feet. Looking around the room I spot Jack's little notebook on the nightstand and add it to the care package. Using the shoelace to secure the box I slap on the prepaid postage label, the one I printed at work in case we wanted to ship home souvenirs. I place the pink package on the bed, thinking. After going through my mental Rolodex I finally decide to address the package to the only person who might be able to understand all this.

Valentina.

It is just past eight o'clock and the rain continues to fall, but I remain hopeful that it will let up for my big night. In the meantime I decide to take Sebastian's advice and wear something pretty. *At least I could busy myself with getting all dolled up.*

I know immediately what to wear and pull the long lavender dress from the closet, the one I have been saving for a special occasion. Holding it close to my body, I decide that it doesn't get more special than this. Carefully arranging the dress on the big bed I dig out the lavender bra and panties and toss them next to the dress along with the rest of the ensemble, several long strands of crystal beads, and chandelier earrings. But I decide against the beaded bag, wondering awkwardly how I would even carry a cocktail clutch as a deer.

I stand under the hot shower for a long time, scrubbing my skin with foaming coconut soap and combing green-tea conditioner thorough my hair. I let the conditioner sit for fifteen minutes (just like the bottle instructs) and use the extra time to shave my legs, careful not to knick the curves around the knees and ankles.

From what I can tell deer witches are like other shapeshifters, and transforming into a deer witch would basically freeze my appearance. Let's be honest—*it would suck to live eternity with hairy legs.* It reminds me of the stories of the little vampire girl from the Anne Rice books, the one who never grew up. Because she made the transformation as a child she would always remain a child. She'd try to cut off her long curly hair, but it would just grow right back.

I think about Jack's five o'clock shadow, or should I say six days without shaving, and wonder if he will have the growth when he shifts back to human form. Seeing as it was in that sexy place of somewhere between clean-shaven and a goatee, I kind of hope so.

After the shower I dress carefully, putting on each piece of the outfit from the bed, and spin in the mirror, oddly content with my reflection.

Then I stop and listen for a moment. The tin roof has gone silent, and I am thrilled to realize that it has stopped raining.

Snapping open the curtains and sliding back the doors I step grandly onto the balcony and let the cool salty breeze lift the edges of my dress, the sheer purple material flickering in the moonlight. The waves quietly empty themselves onto the shore, and the water beyond is calm and smooth; no more white caps like earlier this evening. The tide seems to reflect my inner stillness, which is much calmer now than I can ever remember. The full moon hangs like a giant glowing orb in a sky sprinkled with stars, and I don't need to look at the clock.

It is time.

I slip several pairs of shoes on and off before deciding to remain barefoot and clamp on a silver anklet, the one Jack gave me for our five-year anniversary. As I ceremoniously walk through each room of the bungalow I take only the pink shoebox tied with the shoelace and the key to the boat. As I close my eyes I feel the comfort of Jack, his presence, his smell. I could swear he was standing right behind me, and I close my eyes and lean back into him before catching myself from falling to the floor.

Quietly closing the door of the bungalow for the last time I hurry across the deck and stop short at the bottom of the steps. Long branches of flowers are blocking my path, a fragrant bush of tiny lavender flowers that perfectly match my dress. I'd never noticed the flower bush before. *Had it bloomed in the last few hours during the rainstorm?* The tiny droplets of water nestled between the petals seem to answer my silent question. It was like the gift of a corsage on the way to the prom. Carefully picking several of the small flowers I randomly stick them in my hair, happy that I have decided to wear it down in loose curls. I wonder how the fresh flowers will fare in the transformation. Will they too be frozen in time, forever alive and vibrant as they are today? Tucking the shoebox under my arm I continue down the path and find myself humming an unfamiliar melody.

A quick stop at the landing dock, and it takes several minutes to locate the mail-drop box, the one I thought I saw that first day. Searching in the dark I become spooked by random shadows but finally make out the shape of two metal boxes near the edge of the dock. After closer inspection I see that one turns out to be a bait-and-tackle box. *Yuck!* And the other is the mail-drop box. *Bingo!*

148

The pickup time is scrawled on the lid in red magic marker and says "once a week," and then someone has added "give or take." I open the lid with a creak and place the package addressed to Valentina in the empty container. There are no other envelopes in the bin, and I take that as a good sign. It would have been discouraging to see an old pile of mail just sitting there waiting for pickup. With my final task complete I turn on my heel and head for the boat named *Ruby*.

The boat is waiting for me, rocking gently in its usual slip, so I jump in and untie the ropes, wishing I had paid more attention to the process when Jack was still here. Able to get her started, I ease out of the slip, managing not to hit the dock or any of the other boats.

Chugging slowly through the dark water I steer away from Cernunnos Island. With my terrible sense of direction I worry about locating the grotto on my own, but the moon seems to be hanging directly over my target, and soon I spot the familiar peaks just up ahead. Pressing down on the throttle I pick up speed and steer the boat toward the grotto.

If only Jack could see me now, standing confidently behind the wheel of the boat with the wind lifting my hair into long spirals behind me. Never have I felt so alive. *And free.* This is the most exciting thing I've ever done in my whole life, and I am buzzing with excitement.

But as soon as I float under the arches my stomach clenches. I always seem to panic at the last second like at our wedding. I wasn't nervous at all until I heard the first strands of "Here comes the bride." Then I was like, "Wait. I'm not ready. I have to pee!"

Touching my hair to ensure that the flowers are still in place, I give myself a little pep talk. *You can do this, Gwen.* Jack said the transformation didn't hurt; it just feels *strange.* That's the word I think he was trying to communicate: *strange.* I am such a baby about pain. I try to focus on the final result, a strong, immortal, supernatural creature that can shift into the shape of a deer. Yes, this is a once-in-a-lifetime opportunity, and I am not going to let my fear get in the way.

With some concentration I navigate under the icicle-shaped rocks and, in no mood to wrestle with the anchor, I decide to beach the small boat, driving right up onto a mound of sand. Turning off the engine, I jump over the side, my feet hitting the ground with a thump, the only sound in the silent grotto. I immediately regret the jump and place both hands on my lower back with a twinge of pain.

Searching the sea cave I see Jack's nose peek out from behind a wall of coral. When he sees me, his whole face appears, and he comes running over and makes excited circles around my legs, getting caught up in the material of my lavender dress. I try to pat the top of his head, but he is moving too fast for me to make contact. He is as happy to see me as a puppy who has been left alone for a long weekend.

There is a bubbling in the water to my left, and I turn to watch long antlers pierce the dark water as the deer heads of Sebastian and Jonah rise from beneath the depths. Ruby's black doe face appears, and her full lips pull back in a smile as she breaks the surface.

Hey, why are they all in their deer form this time? I feel awkward to be the only human in the grotto, and two lightning bugs flash near me as if to show their support. Okay, let's get this show on the road. I take a brave step toward the water, but Jack nudges me back.

This way. He points his chin upward.

I'm confused. I thought I would need to swim out with the others and slide down the underwater tunnel again. He shakes his head and points up again. When I still don't move, he circles back and pushes me toward the rocks with the tips of his small horns. At first I have concerns about climbing the rocks in my bare feet and I suddenly long for my sneakers or even my trusty gold sandals.

Cautiously, I place my bare foot on one of the lower rocks and pull myself up. To my surprise the stones are smooth, and they have little nooks and ridges like a rock-climbing wall. I take the first step up and then the next. Jack leads the way, hopping from one stone to the next and even lending his back for support on a few occasions.

Okay seriously, where the hell are we going? I direct the question at Jack, but he seems to defer it to the trio floating in the water below.

It's Ruby who answers. *The energy of the full moon is waning, and we want to give your transformation a little boost.*

A running start, if you will, Jonah adds.

"Fantastic," I grumble.

Whenever I stop Jack points with his wet nose, indicating that we should continue moving upward. I stop to rest, place both hands on my knees, and try to catch my breath, as it comes in hard spurts now. Sucking in the cool night air, I take the opportunity to look up at the moon, seeking inspiration.

My face becomes basked in the moonlight, and it spills onto the rocks in a purplish glow, lighting my way. I continue to look up as we climb, and the higher we go the brighter the moon seems to be. And warmer. I never thought of the moon as warm, but tonight it is radiating a comforting warmth.

When we finally reach the top of the grotto my body is hot and sticky with the exertion. Beads of sweat have popped up around my face, and I can feel more sweat pooling in my lower back. Afraid I spoiled my dress with a ring of perspiration around my neck like in *Rocky,* I try to pull myself together by smoothing my hair and straightening my beads. Everything seems to be intact, *sweaty but intact.*

Stop fidgeting. You look beautiful.

I pop a hand on my hip, blowing a wet curl from my forehead. "You know just what to say to a girl."

But then I realize that he is just trying to distract me from the top of the bluff, which turns out to be a flat platform angled downward toward the sea. It reminds me of the time we got last minute tickets to a Yankee playoff game and had nose-bleed seats that were so high and steep that I had to sit on my butt and climb the steps like a crab. Jack is standing at the very edge waiting for me to join him, and I am tempted to drop down and start crab crawling. With the back of my hand I wipe the sweat from my face and try to keep the vertigo at bay, stepping forward with what I imagine is a brave face.

And then I make the mistake of looking down. *Holy shit, we are nearly five stories high.* A wave of dizziness nearly drops me to my knees, but I take a deep breath and am able to recover quickly. The water below is crystal clear, and I can easily locate the blue coral ring glowing like a giant eye beneath the surface.

That's when I realize that they are expecting me to jump.

I continue to survey the water, cursing myself for not having the guts to go through with this last night from the safety of my underwater bubble. Three sets of sapphire blue eyes peer up at me, and I can feel Jack's hope mixed with a shadow of doubt. *This seems a bit excessive to be an accelerator.* And I have a sneaking suspicion that they might be punishing me a little for not going through with it the first time. With a deep sigh of resignation I inch my painted toenails forward and prepare to face my fear once and for all.

Piece of cake, Jonah prompts.

When I hear his voice I am reminded of the drawing in the big purple book, but I don't feel nearly as confident as the curly red-haired boy looked and can't seem to conjure up the courage to move my feet. After a few moments of stillness, I turn my back to the water, thinking it might be easier to let myself fall backward.

A fine idea. Sebastian this time.

The wind picks up all around me and lifts my hair wildly around my face. As I extend my arms out to the side, the material on my purple dress flaps like a flag in the wind. I squeeze my eyes shut and sense an urgent whispering, but I can't be sure if it's urging me to jump or not to jump.

"Okay, here goes," I whisper, and I mean it.

But I remain fixed in place, unable to conjure up the courage to let myself fall.

The wind is blowing stronger now and knocks me off balance like the stop-and-go of a subway ride. I have to bend my knees to stabilize myself. If I don't jump soon, the strong winds will just sweep me off this bluff and I imagine that it would be better to be prepared for the fall. With one more glance up at the moon hovering right above my head, so close I feel like I can reach out and touch it, I take a deep breath, tilt back, and finally let go.

After a strange moment of silence I plunge straight down like a piano snapped from a crane. Somehow I thought it would happen in slow motion, but here I am falling fast, twirling and tumbling, and my teeth clamp together with a crunch.

My dress whips over my head like Marilyn Monroe standing over the subway grate and makes me thankful I wore my pretty underwear. Frantically pushing the layers of material out of the way I try to get a look at the water below, which is approaching at an alarming rate. *Where the hell is that blue coral ring now?*

To the left. To the left. Jack's voice this time.

Kicking my legs blindly to the left I land with an ungraceful splash and drop straight down through the blue-lit water. Similar to last time I find myself in an enclosed water slide, but I am slightly more prepared this time and hold my body straight, sliding feet first down the narrow shaft. A giant explosion rings from above, which I imagine is Jack entering the water.

Through the clear walls of the underwater tunnel I spot Ruby and the twins, their deer legs pumping like racehorses kicking through a muddy track. I frantically search for Jack but can't find him in the chaos of sand and bubbles. The tube quickly narrows, and as I spin through the last turn, I realize that I am bypassing the bubble completely and heading straight for the blue coral ring. They weren't giving me any more chances to chicken out this time. So I squeeze my eyes shut and prepare for the unknown.

Jack was right; it doesn't hurt.

All my muscles feel like taffy being stretched on the boardwalk at the Jersey shore, sort of like that borderline sensation between pain and pleasure that often happens during a deep-tissue massage. The intense pulling runs down my arms and legs and continues through my torso as I feel muscles I never knew I had lengthen and reshape. It almost tickles when thick brown hair travels down my body and quickly covers all four limbs. I involuntary clench my fingers and toes as they curl into hooves. With a tingle that starts at the base of my neck and runs along my spine a tail pops from the tip of my coccyx bone; to my surprise I find I can wiggle it with minimal effort.

My mouth snaps open as the bones in my face crack with small pops like a teenage boy cracking his knuckles. I feel my chin pulled into a point like strong invisible hands shaping wet clay. Sweeping strokes across my forehead widen the front of my skull, and thick hair creeps across my face and neck. I feel my ears grow straight up like short perky pigtails, and the enhanced hearing immediately kicks in. *I find I can actually hear the colors around me.* The blues from the coral ring are emitting a low *Om* sound, the red coral pulses with the beat of a steel drum, and the yellows—well, they sound like violins.

The coral ring glows like a watery crown above me, and I realize that I'm floating in the deep salty water feeling super buoyant and weightless like an astronaut. I am tingling all over and feel fantastic like the burst of electricity you get after really good sex. I stretch my legs and discover my newfound strength as if I am test-driving a car with a turbo engine.

Examining the others with my enhanced vision is like switching to high-definition television for the very first time. The features of Ruby and the twins become sharply defined like characters in a pop-up book, and they glow like soft nightlights. I can easily recognize the unique features present in each and sense the human expressions almost transposed onto their deer faces. I wonder if my face communicates the huge sense of relief I am feeling—relief that it is over, that it didn't hurt, and that it truly feels so liberating. I still feel like me, but an enlightened version of me.

Just then Jack's voice chimes in, clear and precise. Not like the disjointed way we used to communicate when I was human and he was a deer. Now his voice sounds like music as he laughs and welcomes me to the other side. Swimming toward him I move quickly, and not accustomed to my newfound strength, I crash into him, knocking him backward into a school of fish that scatter like shooting stars. I start to laugh or more accurately to blow bubbles. I think about heading for the surface to get some air, but Jack grabs my leg to stop me.

Old habits die hard.

Yeah, old habits like breathing.

Remember when you got Lasik surgery and the doctor clamped your eye open so you wouldn't blink yet you still felt like you were blinking?

Right. So now I can actually breathe under water but I still feel the need to breathe?

Exactly, comes the collective answer.

Oh wow, you guys heard that?

Yes, comes the quartet of voices again.

Wait? You guys can hear all my thoughts now?

Just the thoughts you are projecting at us. Jack's voice this time. *You will get used to it. Right now we can hear all of your thoughts dancing around in chaos. Everything is so new. You are just trying to take it all in. C'mon. Follow me.*

I try to quiet my thoughts and paddle through the water with Jack by my side.

Yes, this feels right, I project at Jack.

Told you so, he whispers back.

We circle the enchanted waters of the grotto while I continue to adjust to the new world around me. My body feels brand new, and my mind feels lighter too. I find it much easier to focus on one thing at a time, something I was never able to do as a neurotic human. Right now the only thing I need to concentrate on is the water around me filled with marine plants, many of them wave in my direction inviting me to come closer.

But I stick close to Jack and the others, frequently copying their movements in the water. I quickly learn that with just a few strokes of my long deer legs I can move fifty feet at a clip. All I have to do is tilt my head forward and I can somersault several times, covering a great distance. *Weeee!* Jack was right, we should have done this years ago.

After a while we rise through the water, break the surface, and climb out onto the sandy beach of the grotto. On land I am happy to find that I am just as limber and strong as I was in the water. All four limbs extend into the sand like strong tree trunks, my imaginary roots digging deep into the sand. I crane my neck and try to examine my new shape but can only see the bottoms of my deer legs and little else. *I am dying to look in a mirror.* By the time I articulate the desire Ruby scratches a circle in the sand, quickly fills it with water, and then blows on it, freezing it solid. I take a step toward the hand-made mirror and bend my long neck forward, gazing at myself for the first time in the icy glass.

It takes me a moment for me to comprehend the reflection before me. Tilting my head this way and that I examine the pointed face, which still sort of looks like me. I feel oddly connected to the deer looking back at me. The eyes are the same shape and color as my human form, and that tiny beauty mark under my left eye is still visible. My coat is a rich chocolate brown with tiny white spots indicating that I am a newborn deer witch. They tell me the spots will slowly fade and eventually disappear along with all the other changes expected in the first year.

Curious about what happens next I look up at Ruby and the twins. The air around them becomes blurry and charged as they jump up onto their hind legs and morph back into human form.

"Wonderful!" Ruby claps her hands. Her face is more alive and animated than I'd ever seen her.

"I didn't think she had the balls," Sebastian teases, and when I think a few choice phrases at him his face ripples with laughter.

"Pay up." Jonah holds out his hand, and Sebastian grudgingly hands him three gold coins, dropping them into his palm one at a time.

It would be a mistake to bet against me, I think at him, feeling sassy in my new skin.

"There is much to do." Ruby claps again. "First things first."

A long, slender finger appears from the sleeve of her white robe, and she holds it up and wiggles it in the air like someone testing the direction of the wind.

Her eyes narrow. "Now, let's see what kind of air witch you really are."

"Jeez, let her get used to the core powers before throwing the elemental stuff at her." Jonah tries to defend me while flipping the coins high in the air and catching them behind his back.

Ruby glares at him, her back stiffens, and I think she might actually hiss at him.

"We have been waiting a long time for a strong air witch to join the coven."

She bends and leans in close to me, so close I can see her pupils dilate. Then she circles me while holding her hands just above my fur. I can feel the hairs stand on end and respond to her energy. Since she is practically touching me I try to tune in again, curious to see how my unusual abilities have fared in the transformation. But I can't pick up anything and think she may have activated some kind of protective shield around herself.

"What about . . ." Sebastian starts, and Ruby turns her anger on him now.

"Do not say their names out loud in my presence." She turns her face and calls out toward a cluster of rocks. "I know you two are hiding back there."

The sound of hooves softly scurrying in the sand indicate that the deer in hiding have moved on.

Ruby continues in a low whisper. "If any of these air witches were truly strong enough we would have succeeded by now." She leans close to my face. "No, this is exactly the kind of air witch we have been waiting for. Someone like *Guinevere*." When she says my name she extends the N sound.

Not sure what to do and unable to shrug I just blink at her.

Close your eyes and try to imagine the air around you, she slips into my head with a commanding presence.

Obediently I close my eyes, and to my relief find I can sense the air around me.

Try to organize the air into a tangible shape like a giant fisherman's net.

I can sense the thin strands of clear thread, and they shimmy like a giant beaded curtain all around me. With a little concentration I find I can easily clump together strands of air into a long braided rope. I throw the imaginary rope at Ruby and can tell she is pleased.

"Good girl. Now take that rope and swirl it around like a lasso."

The iridescent rope swings in my mind's eye, long and thick like the one dangling from the ceiling of my high school gymnasium. I whip the air-rope around the walls of the grotto, kicking up a sudden gust of wind that whips Ruby's white hood right off her head.

My eyes fly open. *Did I do that?*

"Yes, yes you did!" Ruby claps her hands, excited again, and spins on her heel. She begins to effortlessly climb the rocks of the grotto, leaping across the ravines, her long white robe billowing out behind her like a cape.

We all understand that we are expected to follow, and I move with an ease and grace I never thought possible of myself. It was certainly much different than my first hike up the grotto earlier this evening when I was still human. I reach the top of the bluff in a matter of seconds, and this time there's no flop sweat. *I wonder if a deer witch could sweat at all.* I can't imagine Ruby breaking a sweat, as that would be like perspiration appearing on a mannequin.

At the top of the grotto Monty and Cleo are waiting for us. When I see them I feel a certain awe for the elderly couple and a need to show some sign of respect, but in my deer form the best I can do is bow my head. The two of them are draped in long white robes, and when they see us they lower the hoods, exposing pearl-white hair that glows in the moonlight. Cleo's white braid is coiled high on her head like the iridescent air-rope I just summoned, and Monty's long white hair flows freely over his shoulders. Their mismatched eyes of amber and blue examine me with interest.

I can feel their overwhelming sense of pride and anticipation; it's as if they are meeting their grandchild for the very first time. They each take turns touching the top of my head, right between the ears, and I feel a spark of energy like being touched by a magic wand; their ancient energy spreads through my limbs like rows of cascading dominos.

Monty and Cleo walk me through a series of exercises in an effort to evaluate my developing skills. They teach me how to locate various birds and berries from miles away using only sound, smell, and a sixth sense. After the core skills they move on to elemental powers where they focus primarily on air.

Monty shows me how to create winds and lift things through the air while trying to maintain control over their movement. We start by dropping small rocks and then larger ones off the edge of the grotto, and I concentrate on slowing their descent. I find it useful to imagine a little parachute attached to the rock and visualize the swaying, drifting motion of a skydiver coming in for a landing. I am able to balance the object on the surface of the water before letting it drop down below. It becomes more difficult to control the rock once it pierces the surface and I look to the Elders for clarification.

"The further away the object, the harder it is to control," Monty explains patiently.

"And the salt water adds to the complexity." Cleo leans over the side to watch the object sink. "Combining your efforts with a water witch would help here."

The only water witch I know is Ruby, and she is currently draped on the rocks like a lizard basking in the sunlight—in this case moonlight—making no sign of moving. I continue on my own, trying to visualize little hammocks of thread for the rocks as they float through the water. After a while I start to wonder why they want me to control objects falling from the sky anyway.

"First the falling." Monty lifts his palms. "Then the rising."

Wait, what?

When I shift my focus for just a second the porous stone I was working with drops with a loud splash, and I give Monty an apologetic look. No doubt I am getting better at controlling objects as they move through space, but I am getting tired now and want to stop. I can feel each set of exercises zap my energy and have a strong desire to lie down and rest.

But there is one final test Monty wants to try.

The sky is beginning to lighten now, the moon is fading, and the proverbial early birds are singing their first songs of the day. Jack is lying in the sand near Cleo, and she is stroking his back and speaking to him in a low voice.

I try to listen in. *Just relax; it will come when you need it.* He must be complaining about not being able to transform back to human form.

Monty snaps his fingers to get my attention. "Let's try a slightly larger object this time."

A larger rock? I think at him, bleary-eyed.

"Not a rock. Think bigger. Like a deer."

You mean Jack?

"No, I mean you!" He points a wrinkled finger in my direction.

Fine. If this is the last thing I have to do before I can sleep, then I will gladly jump off the side of the cliff and try to control my descent toward the water. After hours of working with rocks I think, *What the hell?*

Stepping up to the edge I remember the panic I felt earlier this evening, but the human fear is distant and faded like an old memory. In fact many of my human insecurities are like something I read about or saw in a movie but nothing I could latch onto in my current form. With each passing minute in my new deer body I feel my confidence skyrocket, and with that thought I boldly hop off the bluff.

Like a hot air balloon I slowly float through the air and concentrate on slowing my descent just like I did with the objects. But it is substantially easier to control my own body. I find that I can easily manipulate gravity and even manage to move horizontally through the air like I am flying. The feeling is exhilarating, and I stretch out and extend all four deer legs like riding on a magic carpet. It takes me several thrilling minutes to free-fall before I land with a soft splash.

When I look up at the faces hanging over the cliff I see their eyes wide with surprise. I examine them with my enhanced vision and zoom in on their stunned expressions. *I thought what I did was expected, but maybe not.* They seem pretty impressed, astonished even.

With a few strong stokes I am back on the beach and leaping my way back up to the top of the grotto. But when I get there, everyone is dispersing. Monty and Cleo drop to all fours, shift to their cat shape, and disappear down the other side of the grotto. Sebastian and Jonah do synchronized cannonballs off the cliff, and Ruby stands at the edge with her back to the water, regarding us thoughtfully.

"Why don't you two get some rest?"

She bends her body into a perfect back dive and transforms in midair, beginning the dive in human form and arching into the water as a beautiful black deer.

As she disappears under the waves, she projects back at us, *Tomorrow you meet the others.*

DAY VIII:

Meet the Others

The next day I wake with the sun warming my face and my eyes open to Jack's long deer legs tangled with mine in the sand. Stretching to admire the long silky fur covering my new limbs, I feel more rested than with my old method of taking a sleeping pill along with a shot of Nyquil. The deer witches certainly were right about sleeping deeply after the first transformation. Always a troubled sleeper, I am looking forward to this new lifestyle, especially if I'm going to sleep this soundly.

Not wanting to disturb Jack, who snores softly, I scan the grotto and search for the boat named *Ruby*. But it isn't on the beach where I left it. *The boat, like my previous self, has vanished.* And I have absolutely no regrets. In fact I wish we had done this years ago. It feels like moving on to the next level, a natural progression and the only sane alternative to growing old. Now all my senses are tuned in to the most complex energy, and the tiny pinprick hole that was pierced into my collective unconscious after the near-death experience has been torn wide open since I became a changeling.

Excited to start the day, I pop up on all fours and look expectantly at the sleeping Jack. When he doesn't move I try to shift back to human form, thinking that it might be fun to surprise him. Closing my eyes, I visualize standing on two human legs as I tip back onto my hind legs. But I just lose my balance, teeter backward, and roll several times in the sand.

163

I nudge Jack with the top of my head. My long ears flip forward, and again I am reminded of two floppy pigtails like the ones I used to wear when I was a kid. Though my bushy pigtails were always uneven, one sticking out slightly higher than the other, and it drove my adopted mother batty as she would endlessly try to tug them into submission. If only she could see me now, she would probably snap a tick collar around my neck and start picking grains of sand from my fur.

Morning, sleepyhead, I think at Jack.

What time is it?

I'm not wearing my watch. I wave one of my front legs. *Can't work the clasp.*

I sense the start of a smile as he hitches his left leg over his head and tries to block the stream of sunlight spilling across his deer face.

Check the position of the sun, he mumbles.

At first I think he's kidding but then make an effort to judge the distance of the sun from the water and try to figure out just how I'm supposed to use this information to determine the time. But I can't determine a damn thing. *Was this something that was supposed to be inherent to a deer witch?*

Jack finally rolls awake and checks the tide, telling me it's around five o'clock.

In the morning? I ask, wondering about the a.m. and p.m. buttons on his method.

No, listen to the bird activity. This is afternoon.

Wow, my father used to say anyone who sleeps past noon is a bum. Or a hippie. I guess he should add deer witch to the list. Jack reasons that we didn't go to bed until five in the morning and that the twelve-hour resting period is pretty much mandatory; whether you like it or not, your body is going to rest. Even though this is Jack's second day he has still slept the twelve hours along with me.

I flap my ears (or should I say my uneven pigtails) back for dramatic effect and project at him, *I'm starving.*

Me too. Let's head back to the island. There's nothing much to eat here in the grotto, unless we want to fish.

I scrunch up my nose at the idea of fishing.

Although I do enjoy sleeping here.

Where do Ruby and the twins sleep? And the Elders?

Oh, I'm not sure they sleep at all anymore.

How will we find them?

They will send for us. Let's get going.

In one impulsive movement Jack skips across the sand and dives into the water. I am right behind him, still astonished by how quickly my body can react to commands. In the moment it takes my brain to send a signal, like *stand up*, I am already on all fours and running through the sand. Leaping into the water I practice holding myself airborne and try to control the air around me just like Monty taught me last night, or more accurately, early this morning. Like hitting freeze-frame on the television I am able to hold myself suspended in midair for a few seconds before skimming the water like a bird searching for food.

Show off. Jack gives me a look.

Just utilizing my new skills.

We glide across the surface until Jack sends me a signal to drop below. Not to be outdone by my show of elemental power, he generates tiny flames with his hoofs and shoots them in the water in front of us, lighting our path like a fire-powered flashlight.

Nice touch, fire witch.

Sebastian showed me the other night. Jack grins. *It also warms the water.*

Not only is it easier to swim underwater, with the underwater breathing and all, but it's so beautiful I can hardly stand it. In our former lives we used to scuba dive, and the heavy tanks would produce bubbles that would scare away most of the cool fish. As deer witch we could control our underwater breathing and even eliminate the bubbles altogether if we wanted to get up close to a reclusive sea creature. They seem comfortable around us now, as if they assume that we are one of them. *And I guess, in a way, we sort of are.*

Floating in my peripheral vision is a fish decorated like mosaic tile, and I turn, reminded of the small fortune we spent on glass tiles for our kitchen remodel in our downtown apartment. It is amazing how much our lives have changed in a little over a week and how detached I already feel from my former life. At first I wondered how I would respond to memories of my previous self and thought I might feel sorrow or a sense of loss. But as it turns out I seem to reflect on the events of my former life with fondness and love but with no longing to go back. Only forward. There is something about the deer witch mentality that fills me with abundant excitement about what lies ahead.

Jack is following a giant frogfish into an underwater cave when a sudden coldness bursts between my shoulder blades. Almost paralyzed with an inexplicable fear I force myself to turn in the water and find an octopus, spotted with blue rings. He is creeping toward the underwater cave where Jack disappeared with the frogfish. I have never seen an octopus in real life, *only in movies*, but I find myself consumed with a numbing fear as I watch it slither through the water, his tentacles bending like a giant fist and then pushing and expanding like the ruffled edge of a salsa dancer's dress.

The octopus circles the opening of the cave, peeking in and waiting. I send a message of danger and anticipate Jack's appearance. Just when I am about to go in after him he torpedoes from the cave like he was shot out of a canon and joins me on a hasty retreat up. The octopus pursues us fast and hard. I can hear him pumping through the water behind us, and when I look back he seems close enough to throw a slithery tentacle around one of our deer legs. I am about to signal Jack to send some of those fiery finger bombs back toward our pursuer when the octopus stops short like a dog hitting the barrier of his invisible fence. He makes a few quick circles in place, the circular equivalent of pacing, and then returns to the depths where he came from.

When we break the surface we silently exchange thoughts on the instinctual fear we both felt in the presence of the blue-ringed octopus. I tell Jack the story about the octopus that chased Ruby after PoG sank for the last time. We think that maybe this creature is a natural enemy of the deer witch, or maybe one of the shadow creatures has taken the shape of the octopus to scope us out, the newest additions to the coven. In any event, we put it on the list of things to ask the others about.

Safe on land we sprint across the beach, and our fur dries quickly in the sun and salt air. Our hooves gently pound footprints into the sand as we cross the empty beach and turn left through the sand dunes, heading toward the lush gardens that create an inner ring to the island's beaches.

With physical distance from the octopus I feel emotional distance as well. The mind-numbing fear that consumed me is now replaced with an overwhelming sense of hunger. It seems that all my emotions were enhanced by the transformation; the pleasant ones, like happiness and excitement, along with the not-so-pleasant ones like fear and right now a powerful hunger.

As soon as I spot a plant or flower that is glowing with a colorful aura or wiggling unusually in the breeze, I know it's okay to eat. And thanks to my training last night I learned that some of the island's most delicious berries are covered with a soft fuzzy skin, just like a sweet Georgia peach. Finding a berry bush that glows an iridescent purple, I pop one in my mouth, where it explodes with a mixture of flavors that closely resemble mango and papaya. Jack leads the way to a hidden strawberry patch, and like kids in a candy store we jump through the low leafy bushes, poking our long pointed faces under the plants. There is an audible "pop" whenever we pull a strawberry that is perfectly ripe and ready to be eaten. These particular berries stand out like glowing red rubies and swing teasingly as if on a diagonal spring.

I am enjoying the berries as the purple-winged dragonflies buzz around us, as they did when we first arrived on the island, but this time I can hear a distinct rhythm to their wings like the repeated chorus of an addictive song. I find my deer lips perfectly capable of humming, and when I share this with Jack he joins in, adding harmony. It reminds me of all the times we'd sing together in the car on the way to a client. Only now we are humming, half out loud and half telepathically, while searching for magical berries on a tropical island.

As we explore the gardens as changelings we discover that the tips of flowers and the edges of fruit trees appear like wet paint, and when I brush up against them I almost expect them to leave a smudge on my fur. It feels like we are traveling through a painting, *an enchanted painting*, where parts are still unfinished.

Jack motions toward a great blue heron, and I crane my long neck to see. It appears overhead and with its six-foot wingspan casts a long shadow over us before landing with a quiet splash. The bird's eyes are positioned so he can see behind him, and I wonder if he can tell that we are deer witches. As if to confirm my suspicion, the bird nods in our direction and then continues his search for dinner in the shallow water around his legs, very much like a flamingo. The edges of his feathers are glowing white like Christmas tree lights, and I feel a sense of reverence like when I'm around the Elders.

I look around for Jack and find him shaking the thin trunk of a palm tree in pursuit of two glowing coconuts that are hanging loosely apart from the others. They give the impression of loners, nonconformists, *just like me and Jack.* After a few forceful shakes, one of the independent

167

coconuts comes raining down and we kick it against a rock to crack its thick shell. After three tries the hairy fruit splits open, and we press our foreheads together, like we are on a date in a fifties soda shop as we lean in to lap the sweet milk from the half shell.

For dessert we go to the Zen garden to feast on rose bushes where the pink petals are definitely the sweetest, *just as Sebastian had predicted.*

We have been feeding for about an hour when the sky turns pink, *as pink as the rose petals,* and the clouds transition to dark blue in preparation for the sunset. The sunset seems to be the featured event, not to be missed, like movie time at the Playboy mansion. Stopping to gaze up at the sky with my new vision I pick up subtle colors and textures dancing across the sky like I'm seeing the sunset for the very first time.

Without peeling his eyes from the colorful display, Jack says, *Are you up for a sunset run?*

Hmm, shouldn't we check the notebook for today's itinerary?

Smartass, he teases, and I smile inwardly.

As the sun and moon perform a shift change in the sky we race across the sand, weaving in and out of the paths worn deep into this crescent-shaped island. The first seven days we had only covered a small fraction of the island, but now in our deer form we are running fast, and the scenery is speeding by as if we are driving down I-95. I glance back and see Jack closing in on me. Looks like the competitiveness we shared in our former life is going to follow us into this one. Up ahead there is a pile of rocks, so I leap high into the air to avoid it. Still hammering out the details of my new strength, I accidently leap too high, and by the time I land Jack passes me, a flash of triumph on his deer face. Increasing my pace I try to chase him down, but he keeps speeding up. He is trying awfully hard to prove himself, and I wonder if the whole "gene carrier vs. BloodLiner thing" is going to bug him.

As the sun slips into the water we both settle into a comfortable side-by-side prance, and the lightning bugs begin to blink around our legs. It's then that we receive a message from Ruby in the form of a low internal tone, a telepathic beep that both Jack and I sense at the same moment. We lock eyes and listen hard for instructions. All six senses are on high alert. We make out faint strains of music and laughter drifting from the far corner of the island, so without a word we turn and head in that direction.

With the tips of his horns Jack pushes a low-hanging branch and lets me pass to the beach, where my eyes adjust to the sight of a dozen deer witches in human form milling around a bonfire that burns bright near the sea. I quickly scan the faces of the bohemian creatures on the beach. There are definite similarities. They all have those intense sapphire blue eyes, they are all barefoot, and most of them are playing an acoustic instrument. The quiet melodies dance through the night air like smoke rising from an incense stick.

My eyes immediately search for Ruby, and I find her seated comfortably on a white velvet couch strumming her blue guitar. There are two girls in the sand at her feet, and the excess material of their white dresses poofs out around them like two vanilla cupcakes. The three of them are focused on Sebastian, who is animated in a story, gesturing wildly with his martini glass and oblivious to the fact that the clear liquid is sloshing over the side with every point he tries to make. The couch is positioned slightly forward in front of the others, and the setup reminds me of the velvet ropes positioned outside a trendy club.

"And I shant hear anything to the contrary." Sebastian finishes with a purposeful sip.

When Ruby spots us, she stands and opens her arms in a welcoming gesture, but not before leaning her guitar carefully against the couch. I wish, not for the first time, that I could muster up the strength to transform back to human form. It's as if my tiny deer body and smattering of white spots are a dead giveaway to how young and inexperienced I am. *But then again I guess everybody starts out this way.*

I concentrate on turning off my internal monologue, or at least trying to keep it politically correct, and send Jack a message to keep our mental banter to a minimum. There is an audible click of his telepathic walkie-talkie as he shuts down. The silence is shocking at first, *and a bit lonely*, but then I become aware of the new exciting energies buzzing around me now.

The unusual melodies swirl across the beach, and I can feel the energies percolating as we wait for Ruby to begin the introductions. I assume that she will take us around to meet everyone like the first day of a new job and I am buzzing with anticipation.

Trying to tune into the mental chatter of the group, I find that everyone seems to be protecting their private conversations. All I can make out is a low rumble like a car traveling over a gravel road. I haven't had much time to test my previous gift, but here is where I think my ability has fared with the transformation. It seems that deer witches are able to block their thoughts from me even if I am touching them. Yet it seems that they can rummage through my head and push thoughts at me like a pull-push communication method. The trick is that they can both *push* and *pull* whereas I can just *push*.

And sometimes I don't even mean to push when they are able to intercept a private thought. Like the time I found my mind wandering (and then lingering), on what it might be like to have sex as a deer witch. *I assume it would be intensified like everything else.* I remember how it got very quiet and then there was a mental throat clearing as Sebastian informed me that I was on speakerphone. My deer face turned bright red, and I quickly learned how to protect my personal thoughts, though it exerted a lot of energy to keep the walls up for extended periods. I imagine this skill, like all the others, will improve over time.

Ruby motions toward the two giant cupcakes at her feet. They look familiar, but I can't quite place them until Jack pops into my head with the squelch of an overhead announcement system.

It's the wedding musicians!

I do a double take and catch a slow smile from the dark-haired girl who played a cello the other day but tonight seems content with a compact violin made of wood so dark it is almost black. The other girl is tapping a leather tambourine, and when Ruby places her hand on the tambourine player's shoulder the spot where they touch glows a brilliant blue.

"Let me present Lady Emma Ellington, a water witch governed by Pisces."

Oh wow, one of the Ellington sisters. I struggle to remember their story from the big purple book and seem to recall that they were the first to join the coven. And if Emma is a water witch like Ruby that would explain the blue glowing. Sebastian smiles over his drink as if to confirm my suspicion on both counts, the famous sisters and the water-water connection.

Emma stands and floats in our direction. "So happy to see you again."

The long skirt of her dress swings like a bell, and the light trail of footprints she leaves in the sand behind her are edged with water. Her long dark hair is sprinkled with thin random braids and fresh colorful flowers. When she reaches us she sweeps the crinoline of her dress along my back and playfully taps the tambourine against Jack's hind legs. *I instantly like her.*

No sunglasses tonight, her brilliant blue eyes are nestled in her heart-shaped face and turned up to the sky. "This is truly a magical blue moon. The planets are in perfect alignment." Clapping the tambourine once over her head she says, "Come meet my sisters."

She introduces Lucy, the dark-haired girl with the scar pulling on her lower lip. Lucy examines Jack with cagey blue eyes and drops the dark violin to her lap, holding it like a ukulele and plucking the strings with conviction. Then she purses her lips like she is about to blow us a kiss but instead produces a puff of smoke that floats directly into Jack's face and makes him cough in surprise.

"Be nice, Lucia," Emma scolds appearing at her side. I realize that you can't always see the deer witch move from point a to point b. They can just appear in a new location at will if they want to. Emma strokes her sister's long hair and says, "You must excuse my little sister. You see, Lucy's elemental power is fire, and she is governed by Aries, the warrior. That's why she's always fixing for a fight."

Ah, Lucy is a fire witch. That's probably why she is sizing up Jack and getting in his face with a puff of smoke. *Must be a fire witch thing.* I try to tune in to Lucy's thoughts and find that she is blocking me out with a protective shield that has the strength and smell of old black leather.

Just beyond the bonfire is a stand-up piano and although the wood is worn and shows signs of damage, the music emanating from the old instrument is clear and distinct like ragtime. The song pulls my attention, haunting and familiar.

Emma tilts her tambourine to a girl seated on top of the piano like Cher doing the vamp and says, "And this is the oldest of the Ellington sisters, Lady Bridget."

"Hey, I'm not that much older!" the girl protests, playfully kicking her feet, but Emma dances out of the way and continues banging her tambourine on everything and everyone she passes.

We trot over to meet Bridget, who has a crown of flowers surrounding her small head of bouncy blond curls. She plays an instrument across her lap, and the word *dulcimer* pops into my head before I can even formulate the question. I remember her as the third musician in the wedding trio, the one behind the white piano. But tonight I can't see who's playing this piano, painted a variety of colors and patterns like a patchwork quilt, and from my low deer perspective think maybe it's a self-playing variety.

Bridget does the push communication thing and pops inside my head, her voice light and musical but most of all familiar, as if we just picked up on a previous conversation.

Hey there. Love the color of your coat. So I am an air witch too, but my power is gifted by the free spirited Aquarius. It is said that we Aquarians march to our own drummer.

There is a warm amber glow that surrounds Bridget. Unlike Lucy eyeing Jack as an adversary, Bridget seems to enjoy the fact that we both share the same elemental power, and I feel an instant connection to her. *Perhaps air witches are more civilized than fire witches.*

Not necessarily, but most witches are more civilized than my little sister, Lucy.

Just then Bridget's face becomes flushed, and out of nowhere a surge of excitement, which takes me a moment to identify as flirting, bubbles up inside me. I quickly scan the area and spot Sebastian giving Bridget the bedroom eyes over his martini glass. And just as the butterflies start to flutter up in my belly the two of them quickly and expertly cover the microphone, concealing their private exchange. My guess is the equivalent to some serious telepathic sexting.

I find it encouraging that I can feel Bridget's emotions and figure it's the air witch connection. Or maybe she is just really laid back and letting her guard down around me.

She recovers with a giggle. "He is such a tease, but I do love the boy. And I love the ocean, the animals, the stars, the sun, and the fact that I can do this."

Placing the dulcimer down, she slips off the piano like a pat of butter melting off a baked potato and drops to all fours. Whipping her blond curls back and forth, she is in mid-shake when her face morphs into the long pointed face of a deer. Random flowers from her floral crown are still tangled near her head, and Sebastian fastidiously plucks them from her fur while she bats her large deer eyes, still surrounded by long lashes, at him. He pops one long flower in his mouth and clenches it between his teeth and then grabs Emma in a tango pose, pressing his cheek to hers and dancing her across the sand. Laughter fills my head, a combination of my own laughter and that of the other deer witches around us.

I am relieved that Jack and I aren't the only ones in our deer form anymore and think that maybe Bridget has picked up on my unspoken insecurities. Perhaps this was the reason for her sudden transformation. I am grateful for the gesture but still feel envious about how effortlessly she made the change. She reminds me that she has been a deer witch for centuries whereas I have only been one for less than twenty-four hours.

Patience is a virtue, Gwen. And air witch aren't known for their patience.

An oversized multicolored butterfly lands on Bridget's back as she morphs into human form. As she stands before us, in her period dress and forever fresh ring of flowers, the butterfly perches comfortably on her shoulder. I can't help but wish I had my camera when she turns her face in profile and blows him an exaggerated kiss.

My ears/pigtails perk up at the sound of approaching hooves pounding across the sand. It's coming from the far side of the beach, beyond the rocks, and I stretch my neck to see the source, *from the sound of it one big ass deer.* To my surprise an ivory-colored horse comes into view, and everyone on the beach stops to stare in the direction of the stallion. The music even shifts to keep time with the rhythmic beat of the horse's galloping hooves.

As the rider comes into focus I see that he is wearing a large black hat with white feathers sticking high in the air. He swings his legs to one side and leaps off the tall horse, letting the animal continue in a full gallop down the beach. As the horse disappears beyond the rocks, the long white tail seems to be waving good-bye to its companion.

"Quite an entrance," Sebastian mumbles into his martini.

Bridget whispers, "Gabriel is just showing off."

"His name means archangel, but don't let that fool you," Lucy says before ducking into the flames of the bonfire. "There is nothing angelic about Gabriel."

The rider removes his leather gloves and struts over to us, clicking his heels and bowing deeply from the waist while Sebastian rolls his eyes.

Gabriel is dark-skinned, devilishly handsome and dressed like a pirate complete with black swashbuckler pants, a long velvet jacket trimmed with gold, and a gleaming black shirt unbuttoned down to his belly button like a Bee-Gee. While I am trying to remember what I read about Gabriel, he pulls a long silver sword from his sheath and expertly stabs the olive from Sebastian's unsuspecting martini. I catch a glint of mischief in his eyes as he slides the olive from his sword and drops it into his mouth to the clear annoyance of Sebastian.

Gabriel is a magical creature governed by the deep and powerful Scorpio. He is a formidable water witch, among other things.

Bridget keeps the internal introductions going and explains that the tension between Gabriel and Sebastian is very common between a fire witch and a water witch.

"Sometimes the extreme opposite energy manifests as an alpha-dog competitiveness." She gestures toward Sebastian. "Other times it shows itself as unbridled passion." She tosses her blond hair toward Lucy, who has emerged from the bonfire and is approaching Gabriel with slow purposeful strides. "Case in point, ex-lovers who still insist on tormenting each other."

"Lucy, knock it off." She hisses at her sister. "We have company!"

Lucy ignores her and slinks behind Gabriel like an African lion stalking her prey. Gabriel turns with his whole body to watch her pass, and the energy around them is pulsing, palpable. When he reaches out to touch her face I look for the fire-water connection, and sure enough the blue glows brilliantly from his hand and illuminates her cheek with a reddish hue. The blue-red glow follows his fingers as he gently pushes a piece of hair behind her ear. Lucy closes her eyes and leans into Gabriel's touch and then suddenly slaps him hard across the face and propels herself to the far side of the beach.

"Lucia, *por favor!*" he says in surprise.

Ah yes, now I remember reading about Lucy and Gabriel having a torrid affair. *I guess the honeymoon is over.*

Gabriel shakes off the slap and turns his attention back to us, rubbing his chin and smoothing down his ink-black beard. "So, you two are the newest additions to the coven?" He raises one perfectly sculpted eyebrow and waits for confirmation.

"Yes, this is Gwen and Jack," Bridget confirms.

"Ahhhhh yes, Lady Guinevere. We have been waiting for you." He removes his hat and drops it on the sand, revealing a long curtain of shiny black hair. He speaks with a thick accent, and Bridget silently tells me that Gabriel speaks many languages, including Spanish, Portuguese, Italian, French, and Papiamentu (a language of the Caribbean islands). He bends on one knee and places his left hand over my face while muttering a series of foreign phrases quickly and quietly. Several oversized drops of water appear from the palm of his hand and land on my head, rolling down my forehead like a priest who just flicked holy water into his congregation.

Hey! I project at him, trying to duck out of the way.

Gabriel laughs. "This one's got spunk!"

He leans in to retrieve a drop that's rolled its way down my pointed deer face like a fast-traveling teardrop. He lifts the molecule to his mouth and tastes it, nodding slowly. Not sure what kind of test this is, I figure I must have passed, because a slow smile spreads across his face.

Then he turns his attention to Jack, examining his deer horns like a set of kitchen knives, placing his left palm over each tip. After a few minutes he calls for Ruby, who appears at his side instantly. They speak softly in what sounds like Spanish, but even with my basic knowledge of Española, I can't pick up anything except for one word: Jack. They seem to be saying Jack's name a lot, but it sounds more like "Jock" when Gabriel says it. I look over at Jack/Jock to see if he registers the multiple occurrences of his name. But his face is blank, and his internal walkie-talkie is still clicked off.

Like a well-trained hostess, Bridget leads us away from the discussion with a smile similar to the one Ruby flashed yesterday when trying to hide the burned pot roast. We settle in near the bonfire, and Bridget tucks the material of her dress around her legs and leans forward like a schoolteacher about to commence story time.

At this point the party is in full swing and the music shifts in mood and genre with unspoken communication between the musicians scattered across the beach. I watch Jonah pass, half-walking and half-dancing, around the stone pit with a joint tucked behind his ear. Emma has flipped her tambourine upside down and is using it as a tray to carry drinks to the others gathered around the fire. I realize that we haven't quite met everyone yet, but all the strong energies are a little overwhelming, and I'm grateful for the break in the meet-and-greets.

Bridget begins speaking in that light musical voice that manages to carry high above the background noise. "Before you arrived we had twelve members in our coven with equal distribution of elemental fire, earth, air, and water."

I bob my pointed head and try to tally up the deer witches I'd met so far by elemental power. Let's see, for fire we had Sebastian and Lucy. The element of water was represented by Ruby, Emma, and Gabriel. Bridget was an air witch, and I'm not sure about earth. *Oh yeah, Jonah is an earth witch.*

She looks pleased with my retention level and continues, "Some covens harbor only one type of elemental power; for example, during the Great War there were many covens made up entirely of fire. Some say that is probably what led to all the violence, and most sages now agree that the most powerful covens are created from the diversity of elements. For example, this bonfire is a perfect combination of fire and air; one could not truly exist without the other."

Emma slides in next to Bridget and offers her the last cocktail from her tray/tambourine before continuing the debrief. "See, a typical coven usually includes twelve or thirteen members with no relation closer than the sixth degree." She pauses for a quick sip of the re-gifted drink. "But deer witches are different. Our covens are often made up of members who are very closely related, like in the case of me and my sisters." She throws her arm around Bridget and snags another sip.

Lucy appears on the other side of Bridget and continues the oral storytelling in her low husky voice. "Tell them about the changeling birthmark."

All three Ellington sisters simultaneously flip over their thin arms to expose a marking on the inside of their left wrist. What I mistook for a tattoo was apparently some kind of birthmark that accompanies the transformation. With their other hand they continue to pass the last cocktail, sharing the drink between the three of them now.

Jack and I lean in to examine their almost, but not quite, matching birthmarks. These are the same markings I remember seeing on Ruby and the others. Now that I have an opportunity to see it up close I examine the circular outline, the size of a half dollar, divided into twelve slices with tiny colorful symbols scattered throughout the pie.

"The symbols on your changeling birthmark represent the planets and their position in the sky at the moment you are born," Emma explains.

As I study the birthmark in the light of the bonfire a random memory from my previous life drifts through my mind and I recall one particular office holiday party when we hired an astrologer to give readings to all our drunken employees. I remember leaving my session with something called a natal chart (that looked very much like these markings), and some rambling I couldn't make heads or tails of; something about my ancestors being mushroom farmers as I recall.

Bridget smiles at my memory and points out two particular symbols from the birthmark; one looks like a half-moon and the other a horseshoe. "The moon dictates the elemental power. See here?" She points to the half-moon. "This shows Aquarius as my moon sign."

Emma places her pale wrist over Bridget's arm and points to the horseshoe. "The placement of your south node determines your home coven."

"Not the coven you voluntarily choose but rather where your bloodline stems from," Lucy clarifies.

"How will I know what my south node says?" I ask, encouraged that I might finally be able to learn something about my family history.

"We must wait for your changeling birthmark to appear."

I feel an insane itching on my left front leg, and the sisters confirm that this is a good sign because this means the birthmark is already developing.

Just then all the instruments drop away and create space for the rhythmic tapping of a small drum, pulling my attention to a man seated on the other side of the fire pit. It's like an unexpected acoustic set in the middle of a jam-band show. I find myself drawn to the drummer and amble over like a puppy at an animal shelter spotting his new owner.

Jack is still asking questions about the symbols on the birthmarks while I step around the bonfire and stand in front of a man with three small drums clamped between his strong thighs. He wears an old military shirt with the sleeves cut off to reveal muscular arms covered with intricate black markings like ancient tribal tattoos. He is built, *as Valentina would say*, like a brick shit-house, and you definitely didn't want to run into this guy in a dark alley. He has strong, classic features like a statue or painting of Jesus even; there's something biblical in his intensity. His upper lip is dimpled almost like a cleft palate, and his dark goatee has grown around the strange scar. His nose is flattened as if it has been broken, probably more than once, and when he lifts his eyes to meet my gaze, I find myself squirming under his scrutiny, just like when I studied the drawing of Cernunnos in the big purple book.

Jonah settles down next to the intense man, clapping him around the shoulder and passing him the joint, which he dismisses with a curt shake of his head.

"This here is a decorated military soldier. Nobody knows his real name, and if he told you he'd have to kill you." Jonah smiles, but the soldier does not. "Everyone just calls him Bean."

Around Bean's thick neck hang old military dog tags, some rectangular, some oblong, all made from different kinds of metal. I zoom in on the tags with my enhanced vision and see that they all contain one word: Bean.

Told you so. He slips into my head with a gravely baritone voice that I can feel, as well as hear, like the low rumble of approaching thunder.

When I try to remember what I read about Bean, I can't remember much and recall skipping over the section on the Great War, which probably featured him in the starring role. But still I feel a connection to this man similar to the pipeline I feel with Bridget, and I assume that he must be an air witch too.

"No, ma'am." He curls his lips into a reptilian smile and reveals slightly crooked teeth. "I'm a fire witch. Governed by the mighty Sagittarius."

Jonah explains that Bean lived on the island during Ottoman rule and later after the Great War when it became a military protectorate. When the coven was in dire need of elemental fire Ruby approached Bean and persuaded him to join the coven. Over the years Bean has fought in many wars and continues to serve even as a deer witch, his sapphire blue eyes slightly dulled from the many battles he has seen. He is the ultimate mercenary and only participates in causes he believes in, still contributing to recon missions and special military operations for various governmental organizations.

Bean stands to his full height, drops the drums to the sand, and stares down at me with a mixture of confusion and interest. I blink up at him, waiting. We stand like that for a few moments, studying each other in the light of the bonfire before I notice someone waving from the rocks. She is using both arms straight up in the air, impossible to ignore.

Jonah turns and seems grateful for the distraction. "Come on, let me introduce you to Willow and the boy wonder."

We leave Bean behind and pick up Jack on the way to meet the two witches seated on the rocks near the water, away from the others. The woman has smooth dark skin, strong high cheekbones, and large soulful eyes. Her long dark hair is pulled into a thick braid and hangs over her left shoulder. I recognize Willow immediately and remember her having a strong connection to the earth. In fact I believe that she is the one responsible for planting all the gorgeous flora around the island, and I remind myself to thank her for that.

"You're welcome." She smiles. "Earth witches, especially Capricorns, are happiest with their fingers in the dirt." She speaks in a clear, confident voice. She lifts her arms to adjust her white lace shawl for a split second I see Willow as a giant white owl, although I thought Capricorn was connected to the goat.

She nods and smiles with affection at the boy on the rocks who is scribbling into his notepad, she says, "This is my son, Choovio."

I remember the drawings of young Choovio as he napped under a rose-sunflower, and although he still has the appearance of a young boy of eight or nine, his essence is moody and rebellious like a teenager. His long dark hair covers his face like a veil, and he peeks up briefly to reveal dark skin and sharp cheekbones just like his mother. He nods his chin impatiently in our direction before burying his nose back into the notebook. He is quickly filling the pages with symbols written from right to left like Arabic writings. When Willow touches his arm, he shrugs away, but not before I spot the green glow symbolizing the earth-to-earth connection.

"Choovio's elemental power is earth, governed by Virgo, the perfectionist." She lowers her voice. "Virgos tend to be super critical of themselves and everyone around them."

Jonah chuckles. "Look, who's talking, you stubborn goat."

I knew it, a goat. She straightens her back and speaks passionately, as if she were standing at a political podium. "I'll have you know that stubbornness is the shadow side of persistence, and obsessiveness is the shadow side of detail-oriented. But determination is what is evident in both me and my son."

As a case in point, Willow proudly describes the complex formula Choovio has been working on for years now. It was said to determine the exact location of PoG under the sea. Based on his most recent findings he believes that he can narrow down the searchable radius to one thousand paces from the sunken island. He still needs to work out some of the details, but early findings suggest that the target area could be more than two miles under the sea. That's more than two thousand feet, the territory of sunken ships from the seventh century.

"That's my old stomping ground." Gabriel suddenly appears behind Choovio and reaches over his shoulder, grabbing for the notebook.

Choovio snatches it back, his small artistic hands moving faster than my eye can comprehend. "Knock it off." He speaks in a high voice like a young boy who hasn't gone through puberty yet.

He clutches the notebook close to his chest and yanks up the bottom of his pants to step through water and get to a rock further down the beach, even further away from the others. I try to tune in to his nervous energy and feel the responsibility of the world on this kid's shoulders. He continues to scribble the strange letters while raking his free hand anxiously through his dark hair.

Willow shrugs. "Give him a few hundred more years and he might grow out of this loner phase."

Out of nowhere Jonah drops to all fours, and the air around him becomes charged as he shifts into his deer form. *Who wants to surf!*

Willow shakes her braid, Choovio ignores him, but Bridget skips across the sand singing, "Me, me, me!" as she shifts into her deer form.

Jonah and Bridget stand before us as deer-like mirrors of what Jack and I hope to grow into. It looks like it's just going to be the four of us for surfing, and as I am wondering how this is going to work Bridget signals for us to watch her. She dives directly into an approaching wave and quickly and gracefully lets herself be lifted to the top of the white foam. She holds her position at the top and rides the wave all the way back to shore, *literally surfing without the board.* When she lands on the beach she leaps around excitedly, alternating between her front and back legs.

Your turn, she thinks at me.

I stare down the next wave. *Way too big.* I turn to Bridget, and she nods her head encouragingly. She must have sent me a goose of courage, because the next thing I know I am toppling through the water and reaching for the white foam. She made it look so easy, but right now I'm swimming in quicksand, and the harder I try to swim to the top, the further I get pushed down. It's a good thing I can breathe under water or I would have drowned by now. The wave gives you only so much time to succeed before it spits you out onto the beach. When this does happen I topple several times and crash right into Jonah, who absorbs the impact of my tiny deer body without even flinching.

This is your wave. He pushes me back into the water.

I decide to take his word for it and leap headfirst into the oncoming surf. This time I try to relax and let myself be lifted into the white foam. As I find my balance on top of the wave it's exhilarating, *like finally mastering tree pose in yoga class.*

The smell of salt water sprays around me in a gentle mist, and I can see for miles over the beach using my enhanced vision to penetrate through the darkness. The wave starts to atrophy as I approach the shore, and I prepare myself as if getting off an escalator, taking several quick little steps and then plopping down on the sand, panting and relieved.

Watching Jack and the others continue to ride the waves I am content with my surfing excursion. *Best to leave on a high note.*

In the light of the bonfire, I scan the activity on the beach and see clusters of deer witches milling around. From this angle I can see the small stool behind the standup piano, but instead of the self-playing mechanism I had suspected earlier, I see a man wearing a hat hunched over the piano and a woman standing behind him singing a torchy ballad. They both have their backs to me, and I pop up on all fours and curiously make my way over to them, figuring that these are the only two deer witches I haven't met yet.

Playing the final note with a long trill with his second and third finger, the piano player swivels on his stool, and I see that it's Roscoe!

Wait a minute. What is Roscoe doing here with all these deer witches? Is it possible that he is a deer witch too? I think back to the times when we met at the bar and remember that his eyes were always covered with sunglasses, hiding the intense sapphire blue that would have given away his true identity.

As I am still digesting the fact that Roscoe is a deer witch I am about to get another surprise. I examine the singer standing next to Roscoe. Her back is toward me, and she is humming in a rich, deep voice that reminds me of Nina Simone.

"I may sound like Nina, but they call me *Billie*, as in Billie Holiday." She turns, and I see that it's the movie star lady from the rope bridge. She looks directly at me, her eyes void of any sunglasses, and the distinctive blue shines bright in the light of the bonfire.

I wonder if my deer facial expressions can register shock and confusion. I had suspected she was a deer witch but never guessed that she was part of this coven.

Billie extends a black lace glove, ignoring the fact that I can't actually shake hands in my deer form. Part of me is tempted to raise my front leg like a trained monkey, but I resist the urge.

Roscoe tips his fedora. "Bootlegger, at your service." I remember the time we had the metal-to-metal connection and I picked up images of an old speakeasy. With this new information, that vision makes perfect sense now.

Billie swats his shoulder. "Oh baby, you haven't been a bootlegger for quite some time."

"You know what they say, once a bootlegger ..." Roscoe slips a silver flask from his jacket and takes a long swallow.

On top of the piano is a bottle of amber liquid and several empty glasses. Billie fills one, twisting the glass in the sand in front of me. She fills another and holds it out to Roscoe, but he waves her away, apparently content with his flask.

She keeps the drink for herself and raises it in an exaggerated toast. "To Guinevere!" Then she empties the glass in one swallow.

Did she really expect me to start lapping up my drink like a dog drinking from a bowl? She examines me as if she could sense my growing uneasiness, and a slow smile spreads across her face as she looks me over.

I decide to return the favor.

Billie is a pretty girl, the kind of girl who knows how to make the most of what she's got. Tonight she looks like a 1920s fashion magazine with her fringed dress and crushed velvet hat decorated with thin piping and beaded embellishments.

"1925 to be exact." Billie reads my mind again and smiles in her unsettling way. "Roscoe and I came to the island to celebrate New Year's Eve, and that's when we ran into this crew of misfit toys." She gestures with her glass toward the others on the beach and then refills her glass again.

What are your elemental powers? I ask, looking from Billie to Roscoe.

"Air and air." Billie's eyes flash with authority. "I'm a Gemini like you." She pauses for a sip of her drink. "And Roscoe's moon sign is Libra. That makes us double air." Strange, but I did not feel the air connection to these two that I felt for Bridget. Her energy is much lighter than the thick energies surrounding Billie and Roscoe.

"By the way, Libra is the only sign of the zodiac not represented by an animal." Roscoe interjects with a sip, "Fun fact."

Billie ignores him, draining her drink again. She bends to pick up my untouched drink, swallows it in one gulp, and then looks at me, sober as a judge. She takes a step in my direction, and I can tell that she enjoys the fact that she is towering above me in my baby deer form.

"Well I assume you can count. So you realize there are now fourteen of us instead of twelve or even thirteen."

"That means one of us has got to go," Roscoe adds while I try to figure out if they are kidding or not.

"Pink dolphins! Pink dolphins!" shouts Choovio, and everyone turns to where he stands on the rocks, pointing with disbelief.

We scan the water for a moment and sure enough see two pink dolphins arch high into the air, spiraling, and then landing with a soft splash.

All around me the others are quickly transforming into their deer form, and the air is charged with energy like remnants of fireworks. Ruby is first to shift, quickly followed by Bean and Gabriel. Billie and Roscoe morph in unison, and Emma and Lucy join Bridget, who is already in her deer form. The last to transform is young Choovio, who is frantically trying to show Willow the last few pages of his notebook. But she is busy consulting with Monty and Cleo, who have appeared on the beach in their cat form, concern in their eyes.

Soon the beach is crowded with twelve strong deer, two white cats, and me and Jack, the newborns. The mental chatter is loud and chaotic as everyone seems to be talking at once.

Cleo explains the significance of the pink dolphins. *The pink dolphins never stray far from PoG. When one appears it means we are close to the site of the rising.*

Willow stares down at Choovio's notebook and examines the strange writings before speaking to him in a low voice. *You must share this information . . .*

Choovio starts and stops a few times and then telepathically clears his throat. *I believe . . . it appears . . . this island is actually a small piece of the ancient PoG.*

Silence.

He pushes on. *My findings show that Cernunnos Island represents one end.* He points with his deer chin. *The grottos there, they represent the other end.*

Disbelief spreads throughout the group, and some, like Billie and Roscoe, strongly nay-say the idea. But Sebastian's eyes grow wide with understanding, and he shares an analogy. *Like a giant semicolon from the sky, Cernunnos Island is the coma and the grotto is the period.*

Precisely. Willow nods her dark head. *PoG lies dormant in the miles and miles of space in between.*

DAY IX:

A Witch's Circle

Darkness falls over the beach, and around the dying bonfire there is an urgency to formulate a plan before daybreak. Ruby silences the whole group with a high-pitched squeal in her deer voice, the equivalent of a two-fingered whistle, and everyone snaps to attention. I step closer to Jack as we look up and await Ruby's instructions. She is on a high rock looming above the rest of us like a military captain addressing the troops.

Let me get this straight. Am I to understand that we are actually standing on a tiny piece of PoG right now?

Willow speaks for her son, who seems too nervous now to back up his own claim. *Yes, that is what Choovio is trying to tell us.* Even now in deer form Choovio is fidgeting, looking down and kicking the sand with his hoof. Since I've met them all in their human form it is easy to pick up their distinct mannerisms as deer.

So all this time I have been searching for PoG . . . I was actually standing on it!

Choovio nods his pointed head slowly. *There's more. From what I can tell, there is a hollow tree stump.* His voice is small. *And it's marked with a silver ring.*

Ruby freezes. *There are no hollow trees stumps here. All the trees on this island are tall, healthy, and strong.* She fires back.

187

Billie and Roscoe muscle their way into the internal debate. *You're not making any sense here, kid. If the trees were hollow they wouldn't have any rings.* Roscoe rolls his deer eyes.

Willow opens her mouth and shuts it again before Bean says what no one else wants to say. *We need to cut the trees in order to examine the stump.*

With the words "cut the trees" I detect a noticeable flinch in all three of the earth witches, Jonah, Willow, and Choovio.

That's why my son was hesitant to share his theory. It seems we must first destroy the trees for a chance to bring PoG back to life.

Ruby narrows her eyes. *Let's say I agree to cut the trees and we find the stump marked with this ring of silver. Then what?*

Willow lifts her deer face defined with high cheekbones and large soulful eyes. *Well, the message is somewhat cryptic. The first sign is the pink dolphins; that much is clear. The second sign is not so simple. From what we can tell the tree with the ring is symbolic in some way. Does that imagery mean anything to you?*

Ruby just stares and says nothing, but a flicker of a memory begins to curl over the group before she shakes her head no.

Willow presses on. *At first Choovio thought it was the word* king *but then decided it was* ring. *In any event, once we find the marker we must walk one thousand paces to the east, and the third and final sign will be the rising of PoG.*

This is ridiculous, Roscoe grunts. *According to his cockamamie code breaker we could just as soon be looking for a king up a tree.* He takes a step toward the young deer with the unconventional ideas.

Hold on now. Bean steps in between them. *Let's at least consider what the boy is trying to say.*

Bridget sweeps into the center of the circle and extends her long neck to address Ruby, who is still looming above, regarding us like lab mice. *Perhaps we could isolate a few of the trees and only cut those down.*

After more discussion, and some lively negotiation, we finally break up into groups. Jack and I team up with Bean, Willow, and Gabriel, and the five of us set out to search for potential hollow tree stumps.

Together we examine a group of trees, tag a few candidates, and then circle back to do the chopping. Willow prepares the tree for destruction, speaking to it in a low whisper and stroking the side of her face against the dangling leaves. Then Gabriel uses his sword or Bean taps into his elemental fire to sever the trunk. I had seen Sebastian generate a flame from the palm of his hand, but Bean shoots fire from his eye sockets, hot and controlled like a glassblower's torch, until the tree cracks and collapses to the ground with a colossal boom. Distant booms ring out from across the dark island as the other deer witches perpetuate the inspection, *and in turn destruction,* of the trees.

Peeking inside one stump after another we are unable to locate any indication of silver, in the shape of a ring or otherwise, and with each failed attempt we grow less optimistic. By keeping mental tabs on the others we learn that they are not having much luck either, and the destruction count on trees is growing steadily. The moon is still shining brightly in the sky, but the clock is ticking, and the false sense of hope the group once had of raising PoG tonight is slowly fading.

Madera! Shouts Gabriel inside my head while Willow translates it to *Timber* and the tree crashes to the ground with an angry smack.

We all eagerly stare down the stump, our five deer faces spaced out around the circular edge like the petals of a strange flower. *This one immediately seems different.* First of all, it really *is* hollow, as though a tunnel had been carved into the bark. The inside is old, but well preserved, and all the way down both sides of the bark tunnel are silver—and gold-braided threads that immediately draw our attention.

Bean pops his front legs on the stump and leans in. *There! Right there!*

What is it?

I strain to follow his gaze down the metallic threads as they intertwine all the way down the stump, but I'm unable to tell what he is so excited about. By the time I look up, Bean is standing there in human form, powerful tattooed arms perched on either side of the stump and long dog tags dangling over the hollow opening.

Gabriel joins Bean in human form and mirrors his position, and they immediately begin arguing about who is going to take the hero's journey down the stump. In deer form they are concerned about their antlers in the narrow shaft, and there is a mini debate over Gabriel's longer horns vs. Bean's thicker ones. Now in their human form they continue the pissing contest about who is better equipped to handle the job. I suppose this is just an example of Bean's fire and Gabriel's water manifesting into intense competition.

The air around Willow turns fuzzy as her long deer ears pull back into one long braid. She easily slips into human form and tries to talk some sense into the boys. "Both of you are too big to fit down the shaft in either deer or human form."

"Hmm, how tall are you, my dear Willow?" Gabriel strokes his dark beard thoughtfully.

"You're not claustrophobic, are you?" Bean makes a move toward her, but she stops him with one firm glare.

"Way too much testosterone in the air." She sighs. "What I was going to suggest was that perhaps Jack or Gwen, still in their baby deer form, could fit down the stump?"

She turns to me, and I am about to defer to Jack when I find him nodding his small pointed head in my direction too.

Why me?

I have these to worry about.

Jack sways his tiny antlers in the air, and I think, *"What is it with these deer witches and their horns?"*

Oh please! Those little stubs aren't going to be a factor. I smile at Willow and silently agree with her assessment of the testosterone index being rather high today.

Hey, I'll have you know I felt another little growth spurt in all the excitement. He looks toward his horns and goes cross-eyed like someone trying to spot his own nose on his face. *Plus I am one day older than you, so technically you are the youngest and in turn, the smallest.*

Fine. I'll do it.

A wave of relief flows through the group as I hesitantly move forward to peek down the stump. It's like a telescope facing into the earth instead of up at the sky, and I can't see the bottom, just blackness. *Great, what have I gotten myself into this time?* Hopping up with more confidence than I feel, I position my legs around the stump and lock eyes with Willow, who gives me an encouraging nod. Slowly inching down, first with my back legs, I creep along the inside wall, easing myself down like the Grinch sneaking down the chimney on Christmas Eve.

Long threads of gold and silver circle down the inside of the trunk, but there is nothing that stands out to me as significant. I keep projecting images back to the group like an underwater camera transmitting video back to a control center, and they keep encouraging me to go deeper.

I try to zoom in on what lies beneath, but it seems the night vision is taking a bit longer to develop. *I can't see a damn thing down here.*

"Do you hear the sea?" Gabriel, the water witch, asks.

I listen hard for a moment and look down. Blackness. Maybe it's moving. *Could be water,* I send back.

Continuing to crawl down the stump like a giant spider I try to keep my deer torso horizontal and let my legs do most of the work, but I'm getting dirty and tired, and at one point I manage to get my legs all twisted up in a knot. Pitching forward, I try to readjust my position but find myself slowly tipping until I am upside down.

Terrific.

And that's when I see the silver ring.

It does not encircle the tree trunk as I had imagined but instead is a thick band of silver like a wedding band, and there is a C etched into the metal sparkling with the white-hot intensity of a million tiny diamonds.

"Si! Bonita!" Gabriel booms from high above.

"Affirmative," comes Bean's gravelly voice. "Execute a retrieval when able."

Stretching my small deer body to full capacity I reach for the glittering ring but fall short. *About three feet short.* Hooking my back legs into the bark I try to swing my body and scrape at the sides of the earth's wall. I use my front hooves in an effort to dislodge the ring. But it doesn't even budge. It has been here for so long that the inside roots have grown around it, and it is part of the tree now, spidery bark fingers holding it firmly in place.

Stopping to rest I hear slow lazy waves and realize that the hollow stump extends clear through the earth like a pipeline out to the sea. Even if I were able to knock the ring loose with my clunky hoof I was afraid of losing it to the water below.

A strong desire for fingers burns through my limbs, and I close my eyes, visualizing the transformation and almost willing it to happen. *People are depending on me and without my hands I don't have a shot in hell.* Since becoming a changeling I've wanted to shift back to human form on various occasions, but never like this. Just then a tingling sensation shoots down my left leg and my hoof splits into five pieces and long tan fingers spring forward and clutch wildly for the ring. The developing birthmark on the inside of my left wrist appears, faint, as

191

if drawn with white ink, and I am curious about it wanting very much to study it in great detail, *but there's no time for that now.* Two human legs, longer and thicker than my deer legs, are extending straight up the stump, and my torso (particularly my boobs) fills the cavity, restricting my breath and making me regret the impulsive desire to shift. The bark of the tree now feels like the band they squeeze around your arm when checking your blood pressure, and I'm ready for the nice nurse to release the air ball right about now.

I struggle to move but realize that I am stuck pretty good, crammed into the tree stump and hanging upside down like a bat. Although my body is wedged into place I thankfully find that I can move my arms. *Okay, that's good news.* So I reach with my left hand and start working the silver ring from its resting place. But it's like easing a dry, cracked cork out of a stubborn wine bottle. The tips of my fingers are burning by the time the tree finally relinquishes its treasure, and I blow it free from dirt and reveal an ancient Celtic cross surrounding the letter C. Careful not to drop it into the ocean below I want to slide it on for safekeeping but find it too big for most of my fingers, so I end up sliding it onto my thumb and close my fingers around it in a protective fist.

Okay, one problem solved and a new problem created.

"I have the ring, but I'm stuck!" I shout back and can feel the surprise that I am speaking rather than using telepathy.

"Are you near the bottom?" Bean asks.

"Yes, I can hear the water beneath me now."

"Okay. Stand by."

There is muffled whispering, and I push my hair off my face and wait. When I try to tune in to Jack there is nothing but static. After a long minute of my hanging upside down, Bean calls down, all business now.

"We are in agreement; your own element of air is going to be the best way to blow yourself free."

Willow now. "But when you are released from the tree, you must take care to swim straight to the bottom. Remember, this chosen stump is the marker. Use the roots on your descent and wait for us there."

"Once at the bottom we must travel one thousand paces to the east." Gabriel adds.

Bean's baritone voice warms my chest like a port wine. "We will be able to track you and will bring the others."

192

"See you down there, chica," Gabriel calls, and I can't help but smile, remembering how Valentina used to call me that.

I close my eyes and focus on the air around me like a lion tamer assessing the potential of a new animal. Gathering up the long threads of air circulating near my upturned feet I shape it into a huge ball of yarn before aiming the air ball down on my stuck torso. But the tiny gust of wind just blows the edge of my dress like a dud firecracker. I try three more times before finally generating enough wind energy to dislodge my trapped body from the stump.

There is cheering from above as I free myself and dive headfirst into the water. Underwater, I quickly search for the roots of the tree, remembering Willow's instructions. My hand connects with a thick ropey root, and I wrap my arms and legs around it like I'm sliding down the bannister of a grand staircase. And one grand staircase it turns out to be, almost two miles under the sea.

On my descent I'm happy to see that I'm wearing the same lavender dress from the night of the transformation, the sheer material floating around me as I alternate between the bannister pose and sitting upright like on the ultimate's fireman's pole.

Able to open my eyes under water without feeling the burn of salt water, I watch the sea creatures join me on my journey down, a frogfish, a seahorse, and a giant lobster. Passing sea urchins and eels and navigating through underwater marine plants I continue spiraling down through the sea, dangling on the long spidery roots of the hollow tree stump.

Eventually the ocean floor comes into view with its uneven mounds of sand and wide fan-like plants swaying in the underwater current and reminding me of chocolate lace cookies from that awesome Italian bakery in Brooklyn. Clusters of marine plants appear like an underwater forest. Down here the fish seem larger, and swarms of colorful jellyfish the size of small dogs swim through the maze of coral and vegetation. Some fish appear see-through, with their skeletal system glowing like strands of tiny white lights; others appear in bursts of orange and gold.

When the root finally comes to an end there is a twenty-foot drop to the bottom, and I disengage myself and point my toes, mindful to float straight down. When my bare feet land on the sandy ocean bottom I look up to check my marker, happy to see the tip of the root dangling directly above my head.

Mission accomplished.

That's when I see the others swimming toward me in their human form, traveling fast and compact like dolphins. They are blowing tiny bubbles that trail behind them like the wall of water at a sushi restaurant, the one that always makes me feel like I have to pee.

Gabriel, Willow, and Bean are out front, Ruby and the twins are traveling together, and Choovio is surrounded by the Ellington sisters, and off to the side I spot Billie and Roscoe like outsiders even on the swim to the bottom.

Searching the water for Jack I am hopeful that he was able to transform back to his human form, *maybe in all the excitement.* But I see him paddling through the water still in his small spotted deer body. He seems to be struggling to keep up with Monty and Cleo in their cat form as they are torpedoing through the water like furry white bullets.

As the coven gets closer I try to tune in to the dynamics of the group, but the strongest energy is coming from Billie and is dark and murky. I figure that she is probably annoyed about two things. First, that I was the one to find the silver ring and second, that I was able to transform back to my human form so quickly. I smooth down my dress and chalk up the rapid transformation to the strong emotions I had while trapped in the stump and remember Cleo telling me that when I really needed to change, I would.

One by one the members of the coven land on the ocean floor in their human form. Ruby hovers in front of me and gently nudges me to the side so she can place her feet directly in my wet footprints, like on the Hollywood walk of fame. She turns to the east and motions for us to follow as she begins walking underwater. I can hear a collective counting as we travel one thousand paces under the sea, marching together like a small, *but powerful*, army.

. . . 996, 997, 998, 999, 1000.

Ruby stops and turns, motioning for Choovio. He sheepishly floats forward, pushing his hands deep into his front pockets, and lets his long black hair fall over his face. Even though the hollow tree stump and the silver ring panned out, he still hasn't gained any conviction in his theory.

Is this not the place? She stretches her arms wide, and the material of her long white robe drags lazily through the water.

Looking around I must agree. There are oversized coral balls and tufts of seaweed but nothing to signify this as the site of the rising. I sort of assumed we would see pieces of the underwater city intact. In fact I thought maybe the tips of the white castle might be peeking out of the sand, but this area is deserted and doesn't look much different from the thousand paces we just trekked across.

Choovio looks around for a landmark and drops to his knees, rubbing his hands along the sandy bottom and trying to confirm the coordinates. *I guess it's possible that PoG has been dormant for so long that everything has been pushed deep under the ocean floor like a penny left to sink in a pool of quicksand.*

The Ellington sisters hold up the hem of their crinoline dresses, point their toes, and push the sand from left to right, but they reveal nothing but more sand underneath.

Ruby looks from Sebastian to Jonah, and they each shrug as if to say, *What have we got to lose.*

Bean taps his wrist, where a human might wear a watch, indicating that we are running out of time.

With a resigned sigh, Ruby clasps hands with Jonah and signals for Sebastian to do the same. Then she extends a white porcelain hand toward me. They are standing in a u-formation, and I realize that they want me to complete the symmetry.

Guinevere.

Yes?

Come.

So I take my place in the witch's circle and face Jonah, his eyes so blue that they are almost transparent in the seawater. When my hands make contact with Ruby and Sebastian I feel a jolt of energy like being plugged into an electric socket.

Jonah shuffles his feet moving to the left. *Your back should face the north and mine to the south.*

Ruby and Sebastian complete the circle with fire and water at east and west, respectively.

Without a word the others arrange themselves around our inner circle to create a second ring of elements. Bridget stands behind me to double the power of air and connects with Gabriel, who stands behind Ruby to enhance the water energy, Bean intensifies Sebastian's fire, and Willow takes her place at Jonah's back to support the element of earth.

The third outer ring is formed with Emma for water and Lucy for fire, and Choovio stands behind his mother to complete the layer of earth energy.

The last spot in our three-ringed circle is reserved for air and could technically be filled by either Billie or Roscoe. Everyone holds their collective breath waiting for Ruby to make the call. The bootlegger and his girlfriend both try their best to act like they don't care, looking around as if they had somewhere else to be.

I am secretly hoping she picks Roscoe as I didn't want Billie's negative energy affecting the circle. But after a moment of contemplation Ruby nods at Billie, who shimmies into the circle with a satisfied smile, making the fringe of her dress dance in the water like strands of wet spaghetti.

Sit this one out, Roscoe.

Roscoe drops to his hands and knees. For a moment I think he might throw a temper tantrum, but instead he shifts back to deer form and trots over to the Elders, ignoring Jack. They are spread out on a long piece of colorful coral that strangely resembles a park bench.

With everyone in position now, all eyes are on Ruby, as if she were the conductor of a philharmonic orchestra, and we all hold our instruments poised and waiting for her signal to begin. She drops her head back, and we all copy her pose to watch a beam of moonlight snake its way down, all the way down here to shine into the center of our witch's circle. She begins humming, slow and soft, and the others join in with the quiet chant that I hear inside my head as well as in the water around me, where it resonates like sonic waves.

I am officially feeling the pressure to hold my own in this circle of ancient magic when Bridget tells me to close my eyes and concentrate on the center of my forehead where the third eye would be.

Picture PoG in all its glory and let the imagery burn into your mind.

She sends me an image similar to the painting in the big purple book, and I focus on mentally tracing the lines of the castle walls, the edges of the beaches, and each palm tree and flower. Soon a low rumbling emanates from the center of the circle, and I can't resist taking a peek. The sand in the center is beginning to respond like being struck by a jackhammer under our cosmic digging.

The water around me becomes thick with sand, and there is a whooshing sound like a geyser erupting. Sebastian swings our arms forward and back. I feel a radiating heat, and then a burst of fire spits from our joined hands. He does this several times, blasting fire darts at the large gaping hole.

Brightly colored flowers bubble up from the ocean floor, and butterflies emerge and fly upward, making Willow smile so wide I can see her white teeth from behind Jonah's red curls. Several blood-red starfish appear from the opening, followed by larger objects, gold and silver goblets, a giant vase, and then small statues of granite and marble. Suddenly a baby palm tree bursts through the sand under my feet and I find myself awkwardly straddling it as I am lifted straight up like a ride at Universal Studios. With little effort Ruby and Sebastian yank me off the tree and back down to my core position in the circle.

Jonah slips into my head, telling me to close my eyes and embrace the energy. He encourages me to direct the air upward and keep the momentum going.

It's easier if you keep your eyes closed.

Sure, but that palm tree almost gave me my Christmas goose early.

He spits out a laugh, apparently unfamiliar with this phrase, one Valentina was fond of using year-round. He tells me to concentrate, explains that we are reaching a pivotal point where everything could just fall right back into place.

I slam my eyes shut and try to feed off the energy of the other deer witches in the circle. I can feel their magic from all around and especially emanating from behind me. The triple dose of elemental air coming from Bridget and Billie is intense and seems to only make me more powerful. That's when I realize that nobody is strong enough to do this alone and that it is the combined effort that is the key. The elements of fire, earth, air, and water must all be in perfect harmony to lift PoG to its rightful place in the sea.

Mentally pulling a strand of thread from an internal spool I let it rise through my chest and dance out the top of my head, directing all available air upward. Things continue to escalate as the earth rumbles and shifts under our bare feet. Soon we are rising through the water, and the three rings of our circle become stretched to capacity. Eventually our hands are forced to break loose.

I watch the others sprawl awkwardly on random objects, riding them up and down through the water like being on a strange merry-go-round. Bridget and Emma are seated together, cupped in the wings of a giant swan statue, and Bean is standing on the shoulders of a sculpture that resembles Neptune, the keeper of the sea.

That's when I feel a slithery rope wrap itself around my wrist and work its way toward my fingers, most notably the thumb protecting the silver ring. I force myself to look down and find the tentacles of a blue-ringed octopus snaking its way around my arm like a vein, his rubbery flesh against my skin. I am paralyzed with fear and open my mouth to scream, but only bubbles appear and remind me of a faraway dream. I suck in salty water and feel myself start to choke, so I clamp my mouth shut.

Wait, what's happening? Why can't I breathe under water anymore?

It seems the contact with the octopus is sucking my supernatural power, and I feel myself getting light-headed as he turns me mortal down here, *all the way down here*, miles under the sea. The others are too distracted by the rising objects to take notice of what's happening to me.

Help, help! Why can't anyone sense my fear?

I reach out to the others and sense loud excited chatter as they all speak over each other like a big Italian family around the dinner table. They are probably misreading my signals for excitement as I struggle to be heard over the mayhem.

What appears to be a bust of Ruby rises past me, and I try to latch onto it before a quick forceful tug yanks me back down to the bottom. The small octopus is stronger than I could have imagined. He slithers along the sandy floor, dragging me behind him, his large lazy eye watching me with interest. I struggle to free myself from my octopus-handcuffs as he reshapes his flexible body against the rocks to disguise himself from onlookers above. I am able to take a few breaths like sucking on an oxygen tank that is depleting and know I don't have much time before I drown down here. It's ironic that I was planning to let people believe I drowned on vacation and here it is about to actually happen. *Though nobody could have predicted these circumstances.*

A giant fountain bursts through the ocean floor, and I unsuccessfully try to hitch a leg onto the stone ledge. I am frustrated that I am being held captive by this tiny octopus, the same type (maybe the same one) that instilled so much fear when Jack and I ran into it this morning.

Ridiculous amounts of sand are being unearthed and are kicking up a dust bowl suitable for a Woody Guthrie song. The water is so clouded at this point that it is impossible to see an inch in front of my face. With my free hand I flail wildly in the water around me, hoping to latch onto one of the rising objects but feeling doubtful that I will be able to hold my breath for very much longer, certainly not for the long ride up.

Just when I feel myself about to slip into blackness, my fingers touch something furry. I think its Monty and tug on his tail, which I realize you are not supposed to do to a cat—*but this was an emergency.* The water around me ripples, and I just barely make out Monty and Cleo shifting into human form. They calmly and matter-of-factly take hold of my captor, one on either side, and I feel the octopus reluctantly relinquish his grip on me. As soon as he releases me, my supernatural powers are restored and I'm able to breathe comfortably under the water again. As I reestablish my breathing I watch the Elders stretch the octopus like silly putty until he breaks apart and greenish liquid oozes from his bulbous center.

Ewhhh! I guess that's one way to kill an octopus. *Good to know.*

I give Monty and Cleo a quick underwater hug, and the three of us race toward the top like Olympic swimmers after the gun goes off. We duck around objects as they rise around us—large stone columns, covered bridges, and fully intact meadows. All the pieces of the island are fitting together like a giant jigsaw puzzle, the bits and pieces all rising separately and coming together at the surface. I am reaching for the underbelly of the fast moving PoG and am directly underneath a large patch of land now, but the surge is making it impossible to reach the top; like the suction of a sinking ship the intensity keeps sucking us back down.

I force myself to keep swimming upward and dodge flying debris in my journey to the top.

Suddenly the island comes to an abrupt stop like a boat on a lift being locked into position. Cleo and I follow Monty as he swims the length of the island, motioning toward a kidney-shaped watering hole sliced into the earth as if by a giant cookie cutter. It occurs to me that Monty would know his way around this island, and I follow him as he swims up through the opening. We emerge on the other side under a waterfall that starts to circulate and flow with seawater. Stumbling onto dry land, I slowly look around and take in my new surroundings with awe.

The sun is just beginning to rise over Playground of the Gods for the first time in centuries.

It's breathtaking.

Jonah calls to us from the top of the waterfall, raising his voice above the chorus of birds, and performs a perfect swan dive into the water below. I look around for Jack but don't see him, so I try to reach out mentally but can't sense him anywhere near.

I follow Monty, Cleo, and Jonah across the island in an effort to locate the others, my eyes and mind frantically searching for Jack. We spot Bridget and Emma splashing in a fountain, and when they see us Bridget leaps over the edge and Emma spits out an arc of water and poses like a mermaid until Bridget drags her from the water, both of them wet and giggling. Once on dry land they point to an elaborate castle made entirely of white brick, its long cylinder columns towering high above the trees.

"The castle." Bridget breathes. "I remember hearing stories about the castle when I was a little girl."

"Oh the castle stories were my favorite." Emma links arms with Bridget, and they practically skip up the curvy cobblestone streets toward the enchanted castle.

As we travel across the ancient city square I copy Bridget, who is sweeping her arms over monuments and blowing seaweed and sand from the dusty artifacts.

It is satisfying and fulfilling to relieve the heavy statues from centuries of grit and grim built up from their time under the sea. "I got this one." I call to Bridget.

"Missed a spot," she teases, re-cleaning a statue I already swept.

With the second round of cleaning, even more detail becomes visible in the statue's face, and it comes alive with fine lines and shadows around the mouth and nose. There is something proud, even noble, in the profile, and the pupils are carved into the stone in a way that makes it look like the eyes are following us as we pass.

We continue to restore all the dusty relics to their former glory, and I revel in the intricate carvings and elaborate designs uncovered from long ago. Emma follows close behind, filling the fountains and birdbaths with fresh water, and Jonah restores all the flower boxes with fresh blooms and revitalizes the creeping ivy climbing the stone walls in unusual patterns of greenery.

While cleaning one particular statue by simply blowing in its direction, I am surprised to find Gabriel standing on the other side of a massive winged horse. He is stroking the stone face with affection and looks like he is about to mount the carved animal and ride it through the village square. When he sees us he jumps down off the pedestal and joins the parade, but not before looking back to appreciate my handiwork. He places his hat to his chest in a gesture of respect, and I wonder what his connection is to this animal.

The looming outline of the castle is getting closer now, and Bridget and Emma dance in and out of the shadows cast on the cobblestone path. Preceding the kingdom is an ornately carved arch, and we pass under it now, close enough to touch the heavy white brick. My fingers tingle with warm sensations as I stroke the stone, and I slowly feel my little radio frequency spark to life as a deer witch.

Bridget and I run our hands over the smooth stone, partnering up to blow it free from sand and seaweed, and together we return the ancient castle to its pristine glory. While tilting our heads to the sky and blowing the walls clean, we uncover sophisticated murals painted on many of the walls facing the east. Staring in wonder I wish I had my camera to capture these spellbinding depictions of angels and dragons.

The drawbridge is down, and we cross over the thick wooden door opening like a plank across a moat. Emma extends her arms wide, and the deep ditch around the castle quickly fills with fresh bubbling water. Jonah shakes a loose fist over the moat until several alligator heads bubble to the surface. Then with a flick of his wrist he adds a few frogs who blink several times as if they are not sure how they got here.

Join the club, little buddy.

Once inside the large round foyer we hear a familiar humming echo through the entranceway and find Sebastian draped comfortably in the center of a chandelier. His long legs dangle over the side, and he is swinging in the empty room, humming to himself. When he sees us he jumps down and points two fingers up at the light fixture to ignite each empty candleholder with a warm, golden flame. Then he snaps his fingers at the tall fireplace against the far wall and a healthy fire bursts alive in the hearth, blowing back his long blond hair and drying it to perfection. I warm my hands near the fire, feeling the warmth restore my depleted elemental powers. Generating all that air to help clean up PoG has zapped my energy supply, similar to the blue-ringed octopus experience, *but much less deadly,* and I find that this Sebastian-made fire is a perfect way to refill my magical tank. Rubbing my hands together I feel them tingle from the newly infused energy.

"What took you so long?" Sebastian crosses his arms and taps his foot, feigning a mock impatience.

"Some of us did not take the express train." Gabriel motions toward the chandelier that must have lifted Sebastian directly into the castle.

"I had the best seat in the house. The white bricks arranged themselves around me as if being constructed by invisible hands."

He moves down a long foyer, and we follow to find Ruby quietly running her dark red fingernails over the white walls and rattling through the hallways, in and out of the empty rooms. We trail behind her as she steps through thick burgundy curtains, down a velvet staircase, and into a grand ballroom surrounded by mirrors and graced with dozens of crystal chandeliers. We all stand there dumbfounded in a grand ballroom so immense and elegant that it must have hosted the most extravagant parties in its heyday.

Suddenly the ballroom comes to life around us. The chandeliers burn alive with bright candles, and laughter and conversation reverberate through the empty room. The massive space echoes like an old empty stadium, and ghost-like images of women dressed in satin ball gowns and men in tights and vests swirl into existence like we are standing in the middle of the king's court.

Chamber music fills the room, and the women flip open their hand-painted fans, covering their mouths and batting their eyelashes in an effort to entice their dance partners. Monty pulls Cleo close and swings her around the ghostly couples, the material of their robes piercing through the enchanted party guests as they pass. Bridget and Emma link arms, dance each other around in a circle, and then click their heels and clap three times over their left shoulder. They continue the sequence, copying the ghosts on the dance floor.

A knight almost bumps me as he awkwardly dances past, and when I raise my hand to steady him, my fingers pass right through his metal vest. That's when I realize that this is not real but a collective memory like a home movie transmitted by the group, specifically Ruby, though we could be tapping into the stories retained by Bridget and Emma. I watch Gabriel approach a young redhead while Ruby makes a beeline for a tall man with long dark hair who stands off by himself. The mysterious man leans casually against a stone column, arms crossed, and his face flickers with amusement as she approaches. He holds her gaze with his intense blue eyes and encourages her deeper into the shadows.

They disappear behind a mirrored pillar, and that's when I spot Jack in the glass.

"Jack!"

Spinning on my heel, I am afraid he might float away like one of the other ghosts. But there he is standing on the far side of the dance floor in his human form. He stands among the formal party guests in his black wetsuit with the electric blue stripes. I laugh out loud when I see him, laughing with relief and happiness and amusement that he will spend all of eternity in a wet suit. I run to him, jumping into his arms, and he swirls me around the dance floor, reminding me of our wedding dance onboard the *Skyline Princess*.

"We pulled it off!" His eyes are green and excited.

"Which part?"

"What do you mean?"

"Are you excited that we both became changelings? Gained the strength to transform back to human? Or raised this island from the bottom of the sea?"

"All of the above." He pulls me close, and we join the other phantoms twirling around the dance floor.

While we dance he silently tells me how he was able to shift back to human form in all the excitement of raising PoG, and I am thrilled to find that our lines of communication have been fully restored. He tells me he spoke to the Elders about the wetsuit situation, and although it appears that the clothes you are wearing when you first become a changeling is what you are stuck with whenever you shift, the good news is that you have the option to change clothes once in human form.

It's just that the silly wetsuit will show up every time I transform back and forth.

I throw my head back in a laugh as he examines my outfit, my favorite lavender dress, which hugs my curves and hangs almost to the floor.

You are going to be so overdressed every time you shift, he teases.

Ha! Not many places your wetsuit is going to be welcome.

He insists that he is happy with his choice, especially about the dive knife strapped to his ankle, and only regrets not wearing his fins.

Bridget and Emma pass, and I wonder why they were all wearing white dresses when they became changelings. I guess I could imagine them getting dressed up for the full-moon ritual and they were on vacation, so perhaps the fancy white dresses made sense.

Wait a minute—why were Sebastian and Jonah wearing jeans?

They are not changelings, silly. They were born this way and can wear whatever they want. Besides, Cleo says they are appearing to us in a way we can comprehend. I look up into Jack's face and find it clear and smooth, free of any blemishes. His eyes glimmer with green speckles, his five-o'clock shadow is still sprinkled with grey, and his face is tanned and happy. We continue dancing with the imaginary guests, and he ends the dance with a deep dip, extending me backward with a kiss.

Ruby appears from the shadows and takes swift strides in my direction. All the guests (real and imagined) part like the Red Sea and allow her to pass. She extends her hand, palm upward, and at first I mistake it for an invitation to dance. But then I realize that she is asking for the silver ring. *Right, I had almost forgotten.* Easing it off my thumb, I drop it into the palm of her waiting outstretched hand.

She looks like she is about to cry as she examines the ring, turning it over and over in her palm before looping it onto a long thin chain hanging from her neck. It is then that I understand that this ring belonged to Cernunnos. It was the ring he used to secure her braid that night in the tree. Not only was it a marker for the site of the rising; it was also proof that Cernunnos was in fact real and validates the twin's magical bloodline. She protectively drops the ring into the neckline of her white robes and hides it from view. Then she touches her stomach where it must have landed, closes her eyes, and sighs as if she just swallowed a piece of cannoli cake.

When Ruby opens her eyes again the party abruptly ends like a bartender snapping on the fluorescent lights after last call. The crowded dance floor is reduced to three couples: Bridget with Emma, Monty with Cleo, and Jack and me. Gabriel has one hand planted on the wall behind the redheaded ghost as he leans in for a kiss, but she disappears with the others and he is left kissing the cold stone. Lucy appears from behind the next column and lights a torch directly above Gabriel's head, setting one white feather aflame.

"Lucia, she's not even real!" He pulls the still burning feather from his hat and throws it to the floor, stamping it out.

As we leave the castle and travel back through the village we find Billie lighting her long cigarette from a lamppost. She smirks at us as we pass. Roscoe is strolling over the cobblestones and sipping from his flask, his jacket casually thrown over his shoulder, and he too is enjoying a smoke and a smirk.

Just when I am wondering who lit the lamppost for them, we find Bean, the fire witch, squatting under a covered bridge and stitching up a gash in his arm like Rambo.

I find myself oddly flooded with concern. "Yikes, what happened?" I ask and try to avoid looking directly at his injury.

"Got blind-sided by some flying debris." He shrugs.

"Don't worry; it has already begun to heal. See?" Bridget points.

I force myself to look down at the skin being pulled together with long, white thread. The gash is deep, but there is no blood, and the area around the stiches is already turning pink near the edges, showing signs of healing.

"Between you and me, he doesn't really need to stitch it at all. Our healing powers would meld the skin back together, but Bean is a creature of habit." Bridget tells me and then goes on to silently explain that it is difficult to injure a deer witch and even more difficult to kill them.

"Difficult yes, but certainly not impossible," Emma chimes in.

"The one sure way to kill a deer witch is decapitation." Bean continues the morbid topic out loud. "Forget about burning a witch at the stake. Deer witches, especially fire witches, could easily come back from that."

A cold smile spreads across Lucy's face. "And it only pisses off the fire witch."

"Those killed at the guillotine are the only ones who face the true death." Gabriel removes his hat, placing it over his heart, the other hand perched on the hilt of his sword. He looks very much like one of the statues from the village square, and he remains still as a statue for several long moments.

We continue through the meadows and into the woods to find Willow and Choovio basking in the plentiful nature of PoG. The two earth witches are running through the trees, restoring them back to their natural beauty, and I am amazed to see that many are already in full bloom. Willow is filling baskets of apples, oranges, and grapefruits while Choovio collects olives and figs being offered from the low-hanging branches. It is as if the trees are handing us the fruit with their outstretched branches, and everything looks ripe and ready to be eaten.

We all help carry the food down to the beach; it seems that deer witches always gravitate toward the beach. Bean is already there getting the bonfire started, the gash in his arm completely healed now. The group comes alive with chatter, everyone sharing stories of narrowly averted disasters, and some of us relive the inauguration ball at the castle.

There are muffled discussions of Cernunnos. Some are disappointed that he has not shown himself yet, and others say he is probably waiting for nightfall to make his appearance. So far I have only seen drawings of Cernunnos. But since the transformation I can feel the collective unconsciousness of the other deer witches in the coven, and there is an awe and respect that cannot be communicated via a book or through a series of drawings.

Ruby's memories contain the most distinct details, and she depicts Cernunnos as a tall muscular man who smells like the wind on a late fall day when the air is turning cold, and the scent of snow-covered pine trees clings to him. Ruby conveys the protectiveness of his embrace and how he would encompass her in a bear hug, wrapping his long arms around her and rocking her to sleep. Yes, in a very short time I already share the reverence the others feel for Cernunnos.

And I also feel the adoration for this place that Ruby calls home.

Admiring PoG from the beach I realize that it is the best way to appreciate the island, as it appears to go up in tiers like a wedding cake. First the sandy white beaches like buttercream icing blending into a ring of meadows and forests that provide the rich floral colors and then the city with its magnificent castle made entirely of white brick. Above the city are snow-covered mountains, and beyond that are the grottos peeking out from the furthest point.

Zooming in on the twin peaks with my enhanced vision, *which is getting sharper by the minute*, I detect two figures scampering over the pointed rocks. Based on the trail of smoke following the female figure I have a sneaking suspicion who it might be. Looking around the beach and doing a quick inventory I confirm that it must be Billie and Roscoe, again separating themselves from the others. But I was glad to see that we hadn't lost anyone on our mission and wonder if there will be some kind of roll call later.

Bridget and Emma prepare steaming pots of herbal tea and arrange platters of fresh fruit while Lucy warms a pile of rocks and then builds a small oven with the hot stones, one that produces delicacies like apple turnovers, almond scones, and fig preserves. As we enjoy breakfast on the beach a dozen swimming cats come looking for the Elders. Wiping crumbs from his beard and smoothing down his mustache, Monty crouches into his cat form and trots off into the forest, perhaps for some kind of situation recap. Cleo holds up a finger to indicate that she will join them momentarily as she refills her mug with a steaming flowery tea.

Jack and I are holding hands and walking along the water's edge when I tell him about my harrowing experience with the octopus and how Monty and Cleo came to my rescue.

"Guess there was a reason we felt fear around the octopus yesterday."

"Yeah, like some kind of built-in warning. We should probably learn to pay more attention to those instincts."

Like a zap from a hand buzzer Jonah sends a shot of excitement through the group, and Jack and I turn to the smiling redhead. I assume he is going to suggest another round of surfing, but instead he points to the snow-covered mountains, the smile slowly stretching across his face.

"I remember sledding on mountains like that when I was a kid."

"Righto." Sebastian sits in the sand, spreading fig preserves on his apple turnover. "I remember riding on the shell of a giant turtle when I was a boy, but I'm not going to suggest we do that."

"Come on. Who's up for some sledding?" Jonah rubs his hands together, and his enthusiasm is infectious. "Last one to the top has to build the sleds."

Jack and I look at each other, and I shrug. "Nothing feels better than a run after a big meal, right?"

The majority of the coven is feeling game, and they gather around Jonah with excited anticipation. We decide to maintain our human form, and I find that on two legs I can run with the speed and power of an ostrich. Superior reflexes enable me to duck around trees in the forest and hurdle over monuments in the village square. From above we must look like a flock of birds holding our shape and position throughout the journey. I follow Jonah as he leads us across the island and up the tiers of the giant cake.

When we reach the mountaintop, I am happy to find that I am *not* the last one. Some accuse Choovio of being last, but others say it was Gabriel, who protests loudly.

"Non. E impossive!"

"Oh great, he's mixing languages again." Sebastian rolls his eyes. "That's how you can tell he's agitated."

In the end we all build the sleds together. We pull long arms of branches from the low-hanging pine trees, shake off the excess snow, and work together to construct two sturdy sleds. Then we split up into teams like we were organizing a neighborhood game of kickball. Jonah jumps on one sled and motions for his buddy Bean. *Good choice.* Bean seems to be the kind of guy you want on your side. Sebastian claims the other sled and crooks his finger toward Bridget. Jonah rounds out his group with Gabriel, Choovio, and Jack while Sebastian picks the remaining Ellington sisters and me. I find it interesting that Sebastian surrounds himself with an all-girl team, but with Bridget, Emma, and Lucy I am feeling hopeful about our odds.

Stamping my bare feet in the snow I realize that I'm not cold as a deer witch. I can feel the cool air on my body, and it certainly feels different than being on the beach. But I'm not in danger of frostbite or anything. It is quite nice to be able to adapt to the weather like this, never needing a winter coat or even a sweater.

"Another little perk." Emma drops back in the snow and flaps her arms and legs to make a perfect snow angel.

When both sleds are loaded and positioned at the highest peak, Sebastian holds a bejeweled finger in the air and indicates that we should wait. After a moment he looks at me as if I should do something about the wind. I obediently close my eyes and try to concentrate on the air around me, commanding it to be still.

And suddenly it is.

In the silence that follows Jonah lets out a "Yeehaw!" before easing his sled down the side of the icy mountain. Sebastian tips our sled forward, and we pause for a brief moment before shooting straight down. *The view is amazing, but the speed is terrifying.* I sprawl flat on my ass like a bug, clutching the edges of the sled in a panic. Bridget lets out a squeal and pulls me back up to a sitting position.

"Keep your head down!" she shouts, a long blond curl whipping across her face.

Ah, much better.

To the left, left, now right.

We call out cues in our mind, and once I try to tap into Jack probing for information on his team's strategy. But he realizes what I'm doing and promptly starts humming "Fur Elise" in a loud sing-song voice in an attempt to conceal his thoughts.

You guys are dead meat, I think over at his sled.

Oh, it's on, Jack thinks back at me.

I note the magnified competiveness again and wonder how much is ingrained in the deer witch and how much Jack and I brought from our human life. Sebastian's all-girl team ends up winning the first race, and Jonah challenges us to two out of three. Racing up the hill in my bare feet I skip through the snow, clutching the bottom of my long lavender dress and feeling excited, happy, and free. I've never sledded like this in my previous life, *always too afraid of breaking something,* but here I am mastering the black diamond course on my very first try.

We take slightly different paths down the mountain each time. Sebastian's team keeps winning, and Jonah is getting more and more annoyed, though he tries to cover it with a shrug and a smile. Soon the brothers are challenging each other to five out of seven.

On our sixth run we are slightly behind, and Lucy seems to think it's because Jonah's sled got a jump start at the starting gate. She is still accusing him of cheating as Jonah and his team drops down the next ravine and out of sight. Suddenly we spot Ruby in the snow, almost transparent in her white hooded robe. A coating of snowflakes is caught in her long black hair, and her blue eyes glow like lanterns. We try to hit the brakes to avoid hitting her, but by the time we arrive in the spot where she stood she is already gone. Bridget points at her as she runs toward a row of pine trees that hang heavy with snow.

The sled forgotten, we follow Ruby as she makes her way through the trees and toward a hidden cavern of ice and snow.

The sun is streaming through the tall pines, and a bright red fox appears out of nowhere, sniffing around the bottom of Ruby's robes. Monty and Cleo leap from the branch of a low-hanging pine and startle the fox, whose red ears shoot straight up on alert. The fox and the cats roll around like children before running together into the entrance of the snow cave.

We all ceremoniously follow the animals into the long corridor of ice. Ruby is walking in a trance, almost doing the step-together-touch of a bride, and she is fidgeting with the long chain around her neck, the one that supports the silver ring. Sebastian is walking directly behind Ruby, and I link arms with the Ellington sisters as we follow close behind.

My bare feet keep slipping on the slick ice, and I'm half walking, *mostly sliding*, down the icy hallway while Bridget and Emma keep hoisting me up by the elbows and placing me back on my feet.

Sebastian stares at the back of Ruby's head as she lifts the hood of her robe, and it is impossible to read any expression through the thick white material. But the mood in the snow cave is ominous. Staring at the ground and trying my hardest not to fall, I see the group suddenly stop short, jerking me to a halt.

I lift my head to see a tall figure standing before us framed in an archway of dripping icicles, long and sharp like a row of dinosaur teeth. From the longest icicle drips a large droplet of water, which lands on one of the two giant antlers that spiral up from the figure's head. He wears a dark hooded robe, his face is partially hidden in shadow, and he is holding an archer's bow.

It's him. He's returned!

Ruby drops to the ground in a full curtsy, collapsing in a heap and lowering her forehead to the ice. The rest of us, unsure what to do, mimic her pose, and Sebastian drops to one knee, head bent.

The figure does not speak or move. After a few minutes I lift my eyes to see what's happening.

Ruby has risen from her curtsy and is slowly making her way toward the horned creature.

DAY X:

No Show

R uby stares up at the dark figure and lowers the hood of her white robe. She says his name softly, reverently. "Cernunnos."

Still the man does not speak or move.

She motions toward Sebastian, and the man turns slightly to examine one of his prodigal sons. Sebastian lifts his porcelain face, smudges of black eyeliner around the wide curious eyes, and with an unexpected grunt he punches two horns right through the top of his head. The tall antlers climb through his blond hair and almost scrape the ceiling of the ice cave. Now Sebastian resembles his magical father as they both maintain their human form with the addition of deer horns.

Jonah comes clamoring into the icy scene, running through the snow cave at full speed and wearing his antlers like a headband through his thick red curls. I imagine that he received word from his brother that Cernunnos had returned, but they must be communicating via some private channel because I haven't picked up any of the conversation. The airwaves are eerily quiet like the calm before the storm.

As usual, Jonah's excitement is bubbling to a rapid boil, and in a grand gesture he drops to his knees and slides past us, arms open wide like Elvis greeting his fans. I imagine that the plan is to slow his approach and stop just in front of his father's robes. In fact he looked very much like an attention-seeking toddler, shouting, "Look-at me-look-at-me-look-at-me!"

But he has too much momentum, or perhaps the horns are affecting his equilibrium, or maybe the floor is just too damn slippery, but Jonah goes ass-over-teakettle and slams right into Cernunnos. But instead of knocking him back with the impact, Jonah passes right through his long dark robes like a hologram.

Ruby does a double take and hesitantly reaches out to touch the face of Cernunnos. But her hand slips into his dark hood, and she pulls back with surprise. Similar to the figures in the ballroom, whispery like ghosts, Cernunnos is appearing to us as some kind of apparition.

Ruby shakes her head slowly, and comprehension covers her face as she examines her lost love. *He is not really there but is just a figment of her willful imagination.* All the memories over the centuries had painted a vivid imprint of Cernunnos, and that is why she was able to project him so clearly. As she understands this, the horned creature begins to fade and slowly disappear.

Ruby rushes toward the vanishing figure, arms outstretched and grasping at the wisps of smoke that still hangs in the frigid air. The archer's bow, the material of his robes, and finally the shaggy dark hair and long deer horns diminish into thin air like a photograph curling in a fire.

We stay that way for a long time, Ruby and the twins speechless around a puff of smoke while I sit with the Ellington sisters, motionless in a curtsy on the icy floor.

The others eventually come thundering into the snow cave, and I *feel* them before I see them, trying to pick through our heads and determine what's caused the strange energy in the icy air.

Everyone keeps their distance from Ruby and the twins as the three of them have a private conversation, their facial expressions registering a back-and-forth dialogue. An eyebrow arches in surprise or a quick inhale of breath stifles a sob. Although no words are audible, I am blown away by the waves of disappointment and sadness emanating from the trio.

When Ruby finally turns to us, her eyes are brimmed with tears and her voice is thick with sadness.

"It is not to be," she says simply.

One tear gets caught in her spidery lashes and instantly turns to ice. Tiny dots of ice-tears cling to her face as she collapses to the ground, shifting to deer on the way down. Landing on the icy floor, her four legs sprawl out around her like a turtle. The ice-tears continue to fall down her angular deer face and drip off the pointed chin as she gradually drags herself up to a standing position.

Bridget silently explains that strong emotions are easier to deal with in animal form. *The human mind can be a powerful and cruel thing when it is filled with sadness.*

The twins allow their deer bodies to fill out around the antlers to complete their transformation. Ruby and the boys break into a full gallop down the icy cylinder and send a rumbling through the snow cave, causing the energy, *and in turn the temperature*, to shift. As the heavy-hearted pounding of their hooves echoes off the icy walls, the inside of the cave begins to sweat and tiny beads of water appear at every seam. The row of icicles that once surrounded the archway for Cernunnos are melting fast, droplets of water pouring off the tiny spears until they weaken and snap, striking the ground like coins hitting the bottom of a tin can.

The edge of my dress floats in a puddle of cold water, one that is steadily growing.

"We should get out of here." Emma scoops up a handful of water and lets it run through her fingers, trying to understand the full extent of its meaning. After a moment, a look of worry creeps across her heart-shaped face.

We run quickly through the ice cave and silently consider shifting back to deer. But part of me is afraid of losing my human form forever. What if I shift and am unable to transform back again?

"Ridiculous." Bridget dodges a falling icicle. "After the first transformation, you know how it feels and can easily do it again and again."

"Like water skiing or riding a bike," Emma adds.

"Or having sex." Lucy smiles.

Thanks, girls. This is all very helpful.

It's difficult to determine where the thawing snow cave ends and the melting mountaintop begins, because the icy water extends over large patches of exposed green grass. As we continue down the watery mountain and through the city, I am alarmed to see fountains and statues in the main square surrounded by growing puddles. And the majestic white castle appears to be shrinking in the distance.

Wait a minute. Are we sinking again?

Sparks of panic shoot through the coven, and down on the beach we find Ruby standing at the edge of the shore carelessly taunting the tidal wave before her. A large swell of spraying seawater is rising, and the giant wall of water pounds down on the sand, reclaiming the island piece by piece.

Bridget shouts over the wind, water streaking her face, "Ruby is the oldest and most powerful witch in the coven, so her emotions greatly influence the rest of the group."

This would explain the overwhelming waves of sorrow I feel as the sky turns dark and releases a heavy, *hail-like*, rain. Ruby's emotions are so strong that she is unintentionally causing a tsunami, one that will surely sink Playground of the Gods back to its former resting place under the sea.

Gabriel calls to Ruby, trying to be heard over the waves, but she ignores him. He is pleading with her to control her emotions before they consume her and she inadvertently destroys PoG.

He grabs Emma by the hands and yells something in her face. She nods several times and closes her eyes. It looks like the two of them are trying to pool their elemental power of water in an effort to counterbalance the uproar of Ruby's emotional waves.

Good idea.

But even their combined powers are nothing compared to Ruby's ancient strength. Gabriel orders the rest of us to make a circle around the two water witches, and together we try to stop the inevitable. We tap into our individual powers of fire, earth, and air to try to balance out the extreme energy of Ruby's water. Trying to save the island from sinking once more, I slam my eyes shut and try to redirect the strong winds around me in an effort to keep everything lifted.

But there is no denying it; I can feel everything slowly slipping away.

Rain and seawater thrash down on the sandy beach and waves thunder high above our heads, but we maintain our circle and continue to try.

Just like the first time, I visualize PoG in all its glory. But in my mind's eye all I see is angry water rushing across the island, first claiming the meadows and forests and then, with the intensity of a freight train, crashing down through the city square, demolishing walls and structures and everything in its path.

The statue of the winged horse, the one Gabriel adored this morning, is smashed into hundreds of pieces. The fountain that held Bridget and Emma in a mermaid pose crumbles, and the remains rain down on the cobblestone streets in a stream of broken stone and dirty water. The cobblestone streets themselves are being lifted like someone has tugged on a row of riverbed tiles, the small stones snapping apart in midair.

Instead of the island sinking fully intact, this method of destruction is completely demolishing the island, probably keeping it from ever being fully recovered again. I wonder if Ruby understands the consequences of her uncontrolled emotions.

The big white castle on the hill crumbles with a series of thundering crashes that are hard to distinguish from the rolling thunder in the distance, courtesy of Ruby's storm. Heavy chunks of stone come crashing through the city, demolishing the meadows and continuing down to the beach where the fragments disappear into the sea.

Fruit trees in full bloom that served our breakfast just this morning are sucked back into the earth along with all the other trees of the forest. Birds shriek from high above and scatter, flying high into the clouds and trying to flee the destruction.

There is a low rupture from below like the earth letting out a belch, and spider cracks appear across the island, multiplying in the sand, through the grass, and across the melting snow. PoG splits into hundreds of bits and pieces, and they all lumber back into the sea with a resigned splash.

Then everything goes silent and I reluctantly open my eyes to see what's left. The circle of energy that we created has managed to spare the beach beneath us, which survived along with the crescent-shaped mound previously known as Cernunnos Island.

But that is it.

Everything else is gone, and instead of tiered levels of a wedding cake all I can see now are miles of ocean and the tips of the grotto off in the distance. They are visible now as a separate entity, and we are left standing on the beach gawking at the large gaping hole in between where the majestic island of PoG stood just moments ago.

Already it feels like one of those surreal dreams, and part of me is expecting to wake up, although I'm not quite sure which part I would be waking up from.

The island rising? The island sinking? Or everything in between?

Maybe I will wake up in New York City with my alarm clock blaring and will just roll out of bed, hop on the subway, and head to work, telling everybody of my fantastical dreams.

But I doubt it.

And I'm not even sure I want it.

The last few days have been emotionally and physically grueling, but I'm pretty sure I want to face whatever happens next as a changeling. Besides, I was never really human anyway. I am a BloodLiner, and this is my destiny.

Or so they say.

I frown, unable to stop myself from feeling like a failure somehow, like a soldier returning from battle, all bloody and bruised from a lost war. Wasn't I supposed to be the key to the rising of PoG? I guess technically I did manage to help raise the island, even if it was only for a short period of time, but still I feel as if I have let Ruby and the rest of the coven down.

Emma is slumped in the sand looking defeated, and Gabriel pats her head in an effort to comfort her. When I look around I find that Ruby and the twins are gone. And so are Billie and Roscoe.

Bridget slowly breaks from the circle, walking toward the waves. She closes her eyes and reaches into the air, palms facing out.

I can feel Sebastian's pain. The three of them need to be alone. But they are okay. At least they will be in time.

What's left of the shell-shocked coven ambles around the beach somewhat in a daze and then slowly disperses to take inventory of what's left of the island. The Ellington sisters clump together, picking debris out of each other's hair, Willow and Choovio head for the trees, and Bean and Gabriel walk off in opposite directions, Bean breaking into a run as he disappears down the beach. Jack and I slip away together, eager for some alone time.

We are able to identify portions of the original sandy path, the one we walked upon when we first arrived, and amazingly most of it is still intact. The flowers bordering the path have taken a beating, but even now many of them are trying to heal and bloom in spite of their recent trauma.

"Hey, let's see if our bungalow is still standing." Jack puts his arm around me, and I let myself lean into the rubbery material of his wetsuit.

"I would love to flop down on that big bed and take a nap right about now."

Surprising myself that I still had the human instinct to nap, I quickly realize that I am still a newborn and in dire need of sleep. In my deer form I am perfectly content to curl up on the beach, but in my human shape I want a big comfy bed.

The path is riddled with debris and fallen trees, and Jack easily clears the way as I grow more tired and feel like the Energizer Bunny running out of batteries. Jack complains that he feels the same, but I argue, *with what has quickly become my old stand-by,* "Yeah, but I'm a whole day younger than you!"

We wander around in circles, disagreeing about where to look for the bungalow. But after a while we realize that the reason we can't find the bungalow is because it has completely vanished. Either the whole structure was lifted up into the eye of the storm or the piece of land that supported the bungalow has snapped off into the sea.

Either way, it's gone.

I think the reason we continue the search for so long is because this realization holds a certain kind of finality, one I feel in the pit of my stomach. There truly is no going back now (as if there ever was), and I realize that I'll never be able to look up anything in the big purple book again; that too was lost to the sea.

We continue our search and find what's left of the spa, flattened as if it has been bulldozed. However, the chandelier that hung over the massage tables is nestled in a nearby patch of grass like it had been thrown from a car wreck. Already flowers have grown around the wrought-iron vines and birds are drinking from the candleholders, now filled with fresh rainwater. Looking around, I'm certain the earth witches have been here.

As we wind our way around the crescent-shaped island it seems to be about the same shape and size but much more compact and desolate. The only structure that still appears to be standing is the white restaurant with the wraparound porch.

The roof of the restaurant is partially blown off, but we decide to climb the crumbling steps and see if there is anything salvageable inside. The door is cracked and crooked, hanging on one hinge, and all the windows have been blown out. But I am still hoping for that nap and think we might be able to push together tables and make a big bed out of chair cushions and tablecloths.

In the shadowed dining room Roscoe is shaking a martini mixer behind the bar and Billie swivels on her stool to face us. The whole scene is a big déjà vu from our first night when we didn't know that Billie and Roscoe were a couple, *much less a couple of deer witches.* All around them is destruction, but here they are having cocktail hour.

"Where have you two been?" I step hesitantly into the collapsing room.

"We've been right here, doll face."

"Why weren't you on the beach helping the others?"

"Personally I don't give a rat's ass if this island sinks or not. That's Ruby's obsession." Billie lights a cigarette. "And speaking of Ruby, I hear she's MIA."

"Yes, she is taking time away to recover from the loss."

"Her loss." She snorts. "The only thing she lost is her credibility."

"What do you mean?"

"I'm sure she gave you the whole song and dance about wanting to reunite with her lost love. Blah, blah, blah."

I nod. "And introduce the twins to their magical father."

"What she should have said is that she wanted a paternity test. You see, the other covens have been sniffing around, demanding proof that her born-out-of-wedlock children are truly the rightful heirs to the throne."

"I don't understand."

"Ruby's coven has been in power for centuries now, and the twins were victorious in the Great War . . ."

"But times they are a changing." Roscoe sings, sampling the martini mix and adding more liquor.

"I still don't understand."

"They used us." Jack says quietly from behind me.

"Exactly." Roscoe looks around for a glass but can't find one that hasn't been shattered, so he sticks a straw directly into the martini shaker. "Sure they needed to raise the island, but don't kid yourself—it wasn't for a family reunion. It was to prove that Cernunnos is real. After all, many still believe that he has always just been a figment of Ruby's imagination. And those bastard sons of hers could have anyone's blood pumping through their veins. When the other covens find out that PoG was risen and Cernunnos did not appear, well, she will need to answer to the Magister."

"You see, my dear Guinevere, she is not recovering from her loss. She is going into hiding. And while she's gone, her little pet students are, how would you say . . ." She trails off.

"Unprotected," Roscoe finishes.

With the speed of a deer witch Billie leaps off her stool and grabs a fistful of my hair, yanking my head back. I can smell her musky perfume, and it hits the back of my throat and stings my eyes.

Jack moves toward us, and I can tell that he is thinking about using the dive knife. But I silently try to talk him out of it. Right now there is just a little hair pulling, but the appearance of the knife might escalate the violence. That's when Roscoe hops over the bar and ups the ante by pressing a gun to Jack's ribs.

"Okay, let's all just relax here." Jack pats the air.

Roscoe growls, "You two just waltz in here and think you're going to take over."

"It's not like that. *They* approached *us*," I say between clenched teeth.

"Yeah, yeah, they approached *us* too," Billie snorts. "Back in the twenties when we were the new recruits with all the potential. Not enough air, that's what they thought. We were gene carriers with elemental air, a true power couple, the missing piece to the rising of PoG. We were like pinch hitters, the ones hired to help the Yankees win the World Series. During the twentieth-century alignment of the planets we tried to raise PoG but failed, and Ruby was like Steinbrenner on acid, fit to be tied. So we laid low and waited for another opportunity to prove ourselves. But then you two came along and spoiled everything."

"Air and fire." Roscoe pushes the gun deeper into Jack's side. "That makes the elements uneven again."

While Billie is delivering her speech I can feel her energy so clearly because we are in such close proximity, with the hair pulling and all. With the strong connection I am able to load up a reel-to-reel tape of Billie's human life and access an old grainy home movie, *one that is detailed and intimate.*

I see Billie as a young girl with the same kewpie-doll face peeking over a thin scratchy blanket and hoping her father will not come to her bed that night.

Then the young girl and her father traveling on a large ship. She bounces her small suitcase down a narrow flight of stairs with a sign that reads "Third-Class Passengers." Her wide eyes become transfixed, and I realize that even as a human, she was sensitive and had the power of sight. Her spirit guides tell her to hide deep inside a lifeboat on the fourth night of the voyage, and she does just as she is told.

When the chaos breaks out, the first-class passengers are top priority, but Billie is already sitting in one of the lifeboats, and in all the commotion everyone assumes she belongs there. Billie's father is among the fifteen hundred people who died that night, but Billie reaches land safely.

The ship was of course the *Titanic,* and I absorb her history as if watching an old film reel of the event. I slowly realize that the vision I had that first night when I touched the doorknob was from Billie.

"Hey, get out of my head, you freak!"

Billie wrenches away from me, and I use the opportunity to shove her into Roscoe. But my plan backfires and the gun goes off with a deafening explosion.

Jack slumps to the ground while Billie and Roscoe scamper for the door. By the time I get to Jack, he is bleeding badly. I apply pressure to the wound, trying to remember what Bridget told me about the healing powers of a deer witch. If Bean was able to heal that gash in his arm, then why does Jack's injury look so serious?

Pressing my hands over the bullet hole and willing it to close, I wonder if I can use my element of air to somehow stop the bleeding. But I can't figure out exactly how that would work. Jack's blood continues to seep through my fingers, and I feel myself screaming but can't hear a sound. His eyes are half closed, and he looks like he is about to pass out.

Come on, Jack. We didn't come this far to have it end like this.

Bean's massive frame appears in the door, and with one tattooed arm he is holding Roscoe by the scruff of his neck like a cat. Roscoe's legs are dangling, and he is insisting that this is all just one big misunderstanding. Bean tries to scrutinize the scene and looks at me for an explanation.

"They were trying to kill us!"

"Is this true?" Bean looks at Roscoe as judge, jury, and executioner.

"Noo, nooo," he stammers. "The gun just went off. Besides, you can't kill a deer witch with a bullet; you know that. We were just trying to scare them."

"Jack is bleeding badly, and it's not stopping," I shout.

"He is still young. His powers to heal are not fully developed yet."

"Please, we've got to get help!"

Bean places Roscoe on his feet. "Fetch the earth witches and tell them to prepare a tincture for a gunshot wound."

Roscoe just stands there frozen and unblinking until Bean gives him a shove toward the steps.

Jack is passed out in a pool of his own blood, and Bean sprints over to him, ripping a tablecloth from one of the tables. I remember planning to use those linens to create a big bed for Jack and me to nap in, and now here we are creating a tourniquet to try to stop him from bleeding to death.

Both Willow and Choovio appear with Lucy, who ignites a small fire. The earth witches boil herbs in an old metal pot, and Willow examines the wound, shaking her head and grimacing. Lucy leans in, and when she sees the extent of Jack's injuries she curses and spits on the ground.

Choovio rips through the bandages, which are already soaked with blood, and widens the hole torn into Jack's wetsuit by the bullet to expose the injured flesh. With two small fingers he dips into the bloody wound and scoops out the bullet, tossing it into the pot of boiling herbs. Jack does not even flinch, and I am thankful he is not awake for any of this.

Willow and Choovio apply the steaming remedy to Jack's injury, each of them reaching into the metal pot and rubbing the potion in and around the wound. Willow insists that Jack must ingest the rest of the tonic, but since he is still unconscious they need to prop him up and tilt the steaming pot to his lips, urging it down his throat. Some of the yellowish-green liquid drips down his chin, and Choovio catches it and rubs it on the wound so as not to waste a single drop. When the contents are gone, the earth witches place their hands over Jack's abdomen and begin chanting several phrases over and over with a hypnotic intensity.

I stand back and observe the healing ritual, still in shock and waiting for Jack to respond. The bleeding has slowed to an oozing trickle but won't stop completely. Still I anticipate the flicker of an eyelid and stare at his closed eyes, willing them to move.

But he just lies there as if in a deep sleep.

"The herbs have been absorbed," Willow says with one hand on her heart and one hand on her stomach. "Now we wait."

I turn and run, and as I run, I develop a strong desire for vengeance. Out of the restaurant and down the beach. *I want—no, I need—to find Billie.* I sense that she and Roscoe are fleeing the island. A few hours ago I would have been thrilled with their departure, but now I want revenge.

Shifting into a deer, I remember what Bridget told me about being better equipped to handle strong emotions in animal form. The feelings of rage are still intense as a deer, but I can't imagine trying to handle them as a human.

Running clear across the beach I dive into the water and swim for the grottos, as all indicators are pointing there. My need for sleep is dueling with my desire for revenge, but the rage is all-consuming and fueling me forward. Traveling quickly under the water I arrive in the grotto, crawl up onto the sand, and stare down the long coral hallways, listening.

You cowards! Show yourselves!

Silence.

You think you can shoot my husband and get away with it?

Billie steps from one of the coral hallways, a puff of cigarette smoke preceding her, and makes herself known. I see Roscoe hovering behind her in the shadows, and although I somehow feel brave enough to take them both on I tell myself that I should probably deal with them one at a time.

"Think carefully here, Guinevere. Just what exactly do you plan to do?"

I'm going to make you pay for what you did to Jack.

"And just how are you going to do that?"

First admit that you were trying to kill us.

She rolls her eyes and shrugs impatiently. "We just wanted to get rid of you. Whether you got scared and left or we actually managed to kill you, it really made no difference."

Suddenly she drops to her knees and morphs into a deer, a still-burning cigarette rolling in the sand near her hooves. Then before

I can react she charges toward me, propping up on her hind legs and waving her front legs in the air like a boxer. Instinctively I mimic her pose and find myself about to embark on my first-ever fistfight. But we don't have fists; we have hooves, which turn out to be much more vicious, and we start knocking them together, taking dangerous swipes at each other.

Confrontation, especially physical confrontation, is something I avoided like the plague in my previous life, but it seems that my fighting instinct is alive and well as a deer witch. I survey my opponent, who is older and more powerful than me, and quickly learn that she is a dirty fighter to boot.

She weaves and ducks around me, diving onto her front legs and kicking her hind legs like a donkey. When she lands the kick squarely in my chest I topple several times. I try the kicking thing and find myself much stronger with my hind legs, so we continue to circle each other, kicking and swatting at each other.

Ouch. I take another kick to the gut.

Billie's deer face is tight with concentration, and my pony kicks and baby swats are having little effect on her. That's when Billie slams me to the ground and pins me under the weight of her body. *Uh oh.* Kicking and squirming I try to free myself, and as we roll around in the sand we both spontaneously morph back into our human form. Billie in her fringe dress and I in my lavender favorite are scratching, kicking, and hair pulling like in a good old-fashioned girl fight.

Just then Gabriel emerges from another hallway and places his hands on his hips. "Attempted murder of another deer witch is *tradimento*."

"Treason," Bean translates, shouting down from the top of the grotto. "Punishable by death."

Two does emerge from the water, an almond-colored deer I have grown to know as Bridget and one with darker colored fur recognizable as Lucy. They leap onto the beach and stand protectively around me like Ellington bookends. I glance around the grotto at the four deer witches who had come to support me and smile at them with great appreciation.

Bean and Gabriel are closing in on Billie, and she jumps up to a standing position and taps her foot impatiently in the sand. "You clowns can't condemn me to death; you've both killed a deer witch or two in your pathetic immortal lives."

"Murder or attempted murder of another deer witch is only acceptable under conduct of war," Bean says as if reading from an official declaration. "And the covens are currently in a state of peace."

"Oh please. The peace is about to end, and you know it." She tugs at a piece of fringe that must have come loose in the fight. "It's only a matter of time before the other covens come looking for Ruby. Or have you forgotten that I have the power of sight?"

"Before you shot Jack you could have voluntarily left the coven, but now you must pay for your crime." Gabriel pulls his sword from its sheath and takes a purposeful step toward her.

Holy hell, is he going to behead her right here?

She charges toward me and lifts both arms straight over her head, and I brace myself for another blow. But instead I watch in amazement as she lifts herself into the air, flying upward, and lands on the high rocks above. She bounces off the tips of the grotto and lifts into the air a few times like a windsurfer coming in for a landing.

"Ah, I thought she might try something like this!"

Gabriel yells for Bridget as he morphs into a black winged horse, one strikingly similar to the sculpture from PoG's village square. I clutch my side where I'm sure I've cracked a rib and gaze up at the magnificent animal that is Gabriel as he gallops past me with giant feathery wings. I watch him leap into the sky and continue to climb through the clouds, drifting over the rocks in search of the escaping air witch.

Billie is flying in her human form with speed and agility, and I am in awe of the fact that she has developed her ability enough to actually fly! I wondered if that skill will develop for me in the first year or if it takes years to unleash such power.

With centuries of experience under her belt, Bridget leaps into the air and continues to pump her legs as if she is still running on land. Black winged horse and almond-colored deer gallop through the moving clouds and vanish from sight in pursuit of Billie. The last thing I see of Billie is the fringe of her dress flapping in the blue sky as she disappears into a fire-eating dragon cloud.

The fire witches, Bean and Lucy, focus their attention on Roscoe, tossing a thin metallic net over him so he won't fly away like Billie. Since Jack is a fire witch too they must feel the need to avenge their elemental brother, because they both look ready for combat. Lucy has exercised her option to change clothes and traded her cumbersome white crinoline dress for a black tank top and shorts with weapons strapped to her body like the video game adventurer Laura Croft. Bean's skullcap is pulled down low over his eyes, and black war paint is smeared on his cheeks.

They both look like they mean business.

Roscoe shifts from one foot to the other trying to talk his way out of it. "Look, guys, this is all one big misunderstanding. You can't hold me accountable for Billie's crazy antics."

"I believe you were the one who pulled the trigger."

Lucy takes small steps around the pleading Roscoe, and a circle of flames sparks up from her footprints. She reaches under the net to snatch the fedora, and her movements are so swift that I never even see the net move; she just stands there with Roscoe's hat perched crookedly on her head.

"But the gun was her idea!" His eyes grow wide as the flames leap and grow around him.

"You should pick your partners more carefully." Bean steps through the ring of fire and moves toward Roscoe, who is in full bargaining mode now.

"Come on, Bean, my man, we can work this out."

The fire leaps high above Roscoe's netted frame, and through the thick haze of smoke I see Bean reach for him and make a swiping motion at his neck. He does it so casually and so swiftly that it takes me a moment to realize that he has taken Roscoe's head clear off. Unable to see a weapon I wonder if he used his elemental power of fire to sear his head from his body.

Bean stands in a rising mist of smoke clutching Roscoe's head by the hair like Perseus presenting the head of Medusa to the Kraken. The whole powerful scene is illuminated on the grotto wall behind him like a frightening mural. He tosses the head into the water, where it lands with a morbid splash, and I squeeze my eyes shut, not wanting to see what Bean does with the torso. But before I turn away I see him pat down what's left of Roscoe, finding and pocketing the silver flask.

What was that about? Maybe some kind of souvenir of the kill like a prisoner getting a tattoo of a teardrop for every man he's killed. I imagine that Bean's face might be covered with tattooed tears if he subscribed to that belief. *Lucy's too.*

The black winged horse appears on the beach galloping toward us and morphing into Gabriel as he gets closer. The fringy black mane of the horse blends into long black human hair as he slows to a stop. Quickly surveying the scene he pauses at the ring of fire that has burned a crop circle in the sand and looks to Bean, who nods his head in confirmation.

There is no sign of head or body anywhere. The only thing that remains of Roscoe is the fedora perched on Lucy's head and the stolen flask that Bean has already hidden away somewhere.

Bean wipes his hands on his pants, and I try not to focus on the color of the stain. "What's the status on Billie?"

Anticipating his answer, I turn my head toward Gabriel and wince with the effort. My healing powers are still new like Jack's, and although the initial pain is beginning to subside, I have a long way to go to recover from some of those deer kicks. Rubbing a bruise on my left buttocks I anxiously await the news of Billie's demise as if that might help me heal. *In the very least it should make me feel better.*

But Gabriel shakes his head regretfully. "Alas, she is still at large."

"Come again?" Bean spits out.

"She has the elemental power of air and flew away like an oiseau." He flaps his hands like a bird.

"Bridget has the power of air too!"

"Yes, and Bridget is still pursuing her." He takes off his glove and rubs his hand, grimacing. "However, I lost sight of them both over the scattered islands of the Maldives."

Struggling to stand, I am disappointed that Billie might be getting away. But I am truly touched by the efforts of the others to avenge the attack on me and Jack. Not sure what to say, I simply say, "Thank you." *And I mean it.*

Hopping back on my hind legs I morph back into human form and step on my left ankle, flinching and remembering how much it hurt every time I landed a kick on Billie. She was so strong and solid it was like sparring with a marble statue. So I jump into the saltwater, feeling cocooned in the comfort of the sea, and slowly swim back to the beach, flipping over and doing a back stroke, thinking of Jack and anxious to check on his recovery.

They have moved him to the beach, and I am thrilled to find him sitting up and taking slow sips from a steaming mug of herbs. Running to him, I fall on the sand, covering his face with kisses. Willow assures me that he is recovering nicely but that he still has a long way to go.

I thank her and hug her, but when I turn toward Choovio he looks embarrassed, so I shake his hand instead and tell him how grateful I am for his help.

Snuggling up next to Jack, I am being careful of the wound that has finally stopped bleeding.

"You two are very lucky." Willow arranges the warm blanket around us and hands me a cup of herbs, she says to help with my bruising.

I drift in and out of sleep, long overdue for my nap, and silently tell them what happened in the grotto, careful to leave out the goriest details. When I tell Jack that Roscoe is dead and Billie is being pursued he squeezes my hand in appreciation.

Choovio kneels in the sand to take Jack's pulse, but instead of the usual place on the wrist, he checks three places along his arm, including the armpit. Jack is dozing, but already color is returning to his cheeks, and the hole in his wetsuit is slowly mending like the flesh and muscle underneath.

The small boy chews on a pencil riddled with bite marks and inspects the developing birthmark on the inside of Jack's left wrist. I flip over my own wrist with curiosity and examine my own personal blueprint of planets. The white lines are becoming more distinct and have turned pale pink like a scab healing. It is easy to make out shapes and patterns, although they tell me that the lines will turn black and the planets will appear in full color after the first year.

Choovio appears next to me and takes hold of my arm to help decipher the faint markings of the birthmark. The young boy I have known for only a short time has the mind of an old genius but is trapped in the body of an eight-year-old. His eyes hold years of experiences and emotions, but he is painfully shy and plagued with anxiety. I am able to confirm all this from our connection when he holds my arm and describes in detail the meaning of the symbols branded into my skin.

Pointing with his small dark fingers he confirms that my sun and moon are both in the sign of Gemini and that my elemental gift is air just as they had predicted. He also tells me that I have powerful strains of earth in my chart and explains that air and earth are neutralizers for the more intense energies of fire and water.

Long strands of hair tickle my skin as he leans in to examine the placement of my outer planets, and I ask about my home coven.

"Can you tell me anything about my true heritage?"

He examines the symbols more closely. "Hmm."

"What is it?"

"There's something about this aspect on your south node . . ."

He lets my arm drop and sweeps through a notebook, running his fingers over the pages as if speed-reading.

"Hmm," Choovio says again.

Okay this can't be good. It's like stumping your doctor with a strange mole.

He calls over Willow for a second opinion, and the two of them have a silent exchange; *now I know something is up.*

"Come on, you guys are starting to scare me. What is it?"

When they whisper to Gabriel his face grows serious and he pulls Willow and Choovio aside, speaking in a mismatch of languages.

I remember that this is a sign of his agitation and am trying hard to eavesdrop when I see Bean approach, kneel down next to Jack, and place the silver flask on his sleeping chest. I was right about it being some kind of keepsake—but not for him; rather for the person he is seeking to avenge. As Bean places his hands in the sand and begins to rise, Willow grabs his forearm and sucks in her breath.

"The coven of the dark moon." She lowers her eyes.

Bean pulls away as if reminded of something he would rather forget. Willow repeats the phrase, and I begin to understand. The marking everyone is so stumped about is a symbol I share with Bean.

"What does it mean?"

Willow meets my eyes and confesses. "It appears that you and Bean share the same bloodline, the strain traceable back to a particular coven."

"Bean and I are related?"

I remember that inexplicable pull when we first met at the bonfire and wonder if the strange connection was due to a similar blood pumping through our veins.

It's Gabriel who answers. "In a way, yes. Think of Bean as a great-sibling, and every girl should be so lucky as to have an older brother like Bean to look out for her."

But what did that really mean? And why did Willow look so fearful when she said, "coven of the dark moon"?

Bean grows quiet and folds his tattooed arms across his heaving chest, hiding the one marking he doesn't want anyone to see. I try to read his mind but find two names running through his head in a continuous loop.

Nathanial and *Aurora.*

Just then there is a loud whirring of propellers overhead, and we all look up, unaccustomed to the sound. I can't remember a plane flying overhead the whole time we've been here.

"What the hell?" Bean coughs, and Willow shakes her head at the trail of pollution streaming from the small seaplane.

I quickly count off days on my fingers and realize that this is day ten, the last day of our vacation. "This must be the pilot here to pick us up."

Bean springs into action, grabbing Jack by the armpits and dragging him into the sand dunes, out of sight. Choovio crawls behind them, erasing the drag marks in the sand with his small hands. The two earth witches stay with Jack while Gabriel disappears into the water and Bean and I set out to deal with the pilot.

I quickly try to remember which way the landing dock would be, wondering if it is still accessible or even above water. We morph into deer as we run, tracking the plane overhead. It lands with a soft splash beyond a row of trees, and we hop into the bushes and move along the waterline trying to get a better view. Poking through a patch of greenery we step into a small clearing.

From our hiding place we can see the landing dock slanting down as it dips into the water with clumps of seaweed clinging to the planks. Although it is pretty beat-up, it still looks functional.

We watch the pilot awkwardly hop down onto the sinking platform and step into the sunlight with his aviator glasses. He takes off his hat, scratches his head, and looks around. It's the same pilot who dropped us off. I remember his build, thin but not skinny, his upper body strong like someone who enjoys physical exercise.

"Hello?" he calls out.

Bean stiffens beside me. Then, like an animal spotting another animal, he backs up slowly, concealing himself deep into the brush, bending his legs, and dropping his deer body into a deep crouch. One firm look from him convinces me to follow his lead. I feel him raise a shield of protection around both of us, and I understand that we are *going dark*, as in radio silence.

As I push back into my crouch I accidently snap a branch underfoot, and the pilot turns and stares into the bushes. *Shit.* I freeze.

"Hello?" he calls again. "Anyone there?"

We stay perfectly still, and finally the pilot pulls out his cell phone and curses when he can't get a signal. I watch with amusement as he shakes the phone and holds it out in all different directions as far away from his body as he can manage.

Silly man. You can't get a signal out here.

He checks his watch again and paces, waiting for Jack and me to come running down the dock with our luggage, looking tanned and rested from our vacation. Hands on his hips he looks up at the sky and then slowly scans the surrounding area. Taking tentative steps down the dock he slowly moves about the island as if trying to assess the damage of a recent storm. Bean and I follow but stay far enough back so we won't be detected. But I am starting to wonder why Bean is so afraid of being seen as we would just appear as a couple of deer, *innocent enough.*

From our hiding place in the sand dunes we can see the pilot searching the restaurant and watch him through the broken windows as he picks through the rubble. He stops and bends, brushing his hand against the floor and then rubbing something between his fingers before bringing it up to his nose.

Bean and I realize it at the same moment. *He has just found traces of Jack's blood.*

Still I think this might work in our favor. Let him think that Jack and I were killed in some tropical storm that swept across the remote island and maybe hit landfall near here. That would explain our disappearance *and* the damage to the island. Why was Bean so freaked out by this guy? *Was he always this uptight around humans?*

After fifteen more minutes of poking around and taking pictures of the damage, the pilot tucks his cell phone into his shirt pocket and heads back to the plane. He starts the engine but not before doing one more obligatory scan of the dock, and I feel his gaze settle on the mail-drop box. The metal container is still clinging to the dock but dips into the water, and the pilot has to get his feet wet to reach it. He stretches his long limbs and reaches in to retrieve a pink box tied with a shoelace.

The package for Valentina!

I had almost forgotten about the care package I had prepared on the eve of my transformation. The package looks well preserved, perhaps from the protection of the metal box, and the pilot shakes it close to his ear and reads the address written on the outside.

He throws the package in the backseat of the plane and then stops and cocks his head. Turning toward the clearing the pilot takes a purposeful step in our direction and lowers his aviator glasses, peering deep into the bushes.

And I gasp when I see his eyes, the unmistakable sapphire blue.

ACKNOWLEDGMENTS

Cover artwork by Weeda Hamdan—www.weedahamdan.com
Photo credit by Carl Malaney
Hair and makeup by Inson Neglio at the SoHo Salon in Brookfield—
www.sohosalonbrookfield.com

Thank you to the amazing and talented women of the Irene Sherlock writing group and to all my early readers for their inspiration, encouragement and candid feedback.

And a special thanks to my real life "Jack" for indulging me and my imagination.

CPSIA information can be obtained at www.ICGtesting.com
Printed in the USA
BVOW030859081212

307517BV00003B/11/P